BOOK 1 OF THE ME...

A ROSE OF STEEL

KATHERINE MACDONALD

Cover design by: Rebecca F. Kenney (RFK Designs)

Chapter headings and graphics: Elisha Bugg (InkWolf Designs)

Contents

1

THE CLOCKWORK CITY

Even two years after moving to the city of Petragrad, Asami was still not used to the quality of the air, how it seemed grainy with smoke. In the early hours of the morning when she rose for work and the artificial sun was still rising over the dome, when the skies were grey and shuddering, she felt like she could reach out and mould the smoke like putty in her hands.

Her homeland of Toulouse was little different from the other mechanical kingdoms, but Petragrad pulsed with smog and a strange, dense energy, even in the middle ring where she resided, far away from the outer industrial districts that manufactured the fabricated coal the city needed in order to function.

It was not precisely unpleasant, and yet neither had she grown used to it. Whenever her parents asked how she was finding her new home, she found herself able to say, "I don't dislike it", "it's larger than Toulouse", "the Imperial Palace is magnificent" and "the public gardens are delightful."

Petragrad, like all the other cities, was a sprawling mass of gears and clockwork, a jungle of steel and bronze, the snarling of cogs as normal to her as the sound of birdsong must once have been to others long, long ago.

Sometimes she liked to go to the menagerie in the public gardens and listen to them tweet. Most were artificial, of course, but it had a handful of real birds, fat, brightly-feathered things with plumage like sunset and starfire. Their song was no different from their man-made cousins, but she liked to imagine what a flock of them must have sounded in the wild, without the clackity undercurrent of wheels and gears.

It was difficult to imagine, and her mind usually engaged with other business.

"I enjoy the work," she'd tell her parents, and this always seemed to satisfy them in their replies. Asami always went wherever the work was, and Petragrad's scientific facilities were second to none. She had been overwhelmed when she first arrived, as the imperial scientists were allowed access to the limited, older forms of technology: computers, books made of wires, complicated machinery beyond her wildest imagination.

And yet she had adapted far more quickly to that than the rest of the roving metropolis.

Toulouse was busy, but it wasn't *this* busy. It was one of the smaller mechanical kingdoms, not as sparse as Navarra or built-up as Firenze, but there were fields and wide open spaces, natural trees. Nothing natural existed in Petragrad outside of the park or the grounds of the Imperial Palace, and sometimes she felt like a bean in a can, shoved onto a tram on her morning commute, closer to absolute strangers than she'd been to any one of her friends in weeks.

Not that she had many friends outside of work, or... or any, really. When did one find the time? There were a couple of neighbours she was on friendly terms with. Mrs Sokolov from apartment twenty-seven had even made her a cake for her twenty-fourth birthday. They'd eaten two slices of the dense, dry sponge, and then Mrs Sokolov had given her the rest to disperse among her friends.

She'd taken it to work. Where else?

The tram came to an abrupt stop outside of Central Station, the colossal village of platforms sprawling the gap between the middle and upper sectors. The middle ring was by far the largest, a bustling hive of shops and stalls, concert halls, theatres, and public parks. The upper was little more than a handful of gleaming streets fringing the radiant shadow of the Imperial Palace. Asami was obliged to walk a little further before reaching the gates to the lifts which would take her up to the palace grounds. As usual, the palace guards patrolled the entrance in their navy uniforms, sabres and pistols at their sides. Although she recognised their faces, she did not know any of their names, and they checked her just as thoroughly as they had done every other day since she arrived.

Before long, she was escorted to the lift, along with a few other staff members—day maids, gardeners, a few soldiers or guards returning from leave, and another scientist she didn't know, distinguishable by her white coat. It was a coat Asami herself wore with pride, over her white ruffled blouse and pleated pinstripe skirt, although little but her ankle boots and thick ribbed stockings were visible outside of her carefully buttoned jacket.

The lift rose above the artificial cloud, the rest of the city reduced to nothing but a handful of spires that stood out like sculptures in a sea of pink candyfloss.

The Imperial Palace appeared before her, a shimmering vestibule of white and gold, glowing in the dawn light. It was as smooth and contoured as the city was rough and garish, a diamond in the gravel. Perfectly manicured lawns stretched out behind the glistening gates, complete with statues, hedges, fountains. Several white peacocks strutted over the grass, golden bells round their necks twinkling against the steady thrum of gears and clockwork. When the lift descended, for one brief moment all stood still and silent.

It was Asami's favourite moment of the day, the quiet few seconds before another cart arrived, before work began. Everything stood suspended, and she was thrown back to another, simpler time, a time when gardens were everywhere, when food was plentiful, when sunlight was real. A time spoken about like it was the fanciful creation of a children's story, rather than a history faintly-preserved.

She sighed, looking up at the great domed roof of the city. There was nothing about the sky that suggested it was artificial at all, nothing about the glow of the sun that suggested it was manufactured. And yet it was, in every city in every corner of the ravaged world, and had been for centuries.

Like all children, she'd grown up on tales of the lands

outside the cities, a vicious, barren wasteland, full of deformed monsters and men that had grown misshapen under the harsh radiation that had almost destroyed the world, too long ago for anyone to fully comprehend what had happened. Asami enjoyed mysteries, but she enjoyed solutions more. It was one of the many reasons she'd decided to become a doctor, a scientist bent on researching ways to help people, to improve the quality of life.

Two years after qualifying as a biochemist, she was not sure she'd done anything of such *yet,* but she was determined to make a difference at some point.

She made her way through the manicured gardens to the research wing attached to the corner of the palace grounds, and slid into her laboratory. As usual, she started the day with a cup of strong tea, checked in with her supervisor, Dr Malcolm, and wrote herself a to-do list for the rest of the day. She checked ongoing experiments, carefully documented any changes, and then settled down to read through the research notes of the late Dr Arcum Mortimer.

Dr Mortimer had been the previous overseer some three years ago. He was, by all accounts, something of a mad genius, his work incredible but his manner erratic. His former employees praised his mind but said they could sometimes barely understand him; it was like grasping at smoke.

Apparently he'd set fire to his own lab accidentally and died trying to go back into the flames to collect his research. He'd left behind several unfinished projects and hundreds of virtually indecipherable files of notes.

Except, as his successor Dr Malcolm had discovered last

week, Asami *could* decipher them. She'd come across one of the files by accident and realised that he'd encoded part of his research with numbers pertaining to an inverted periodic table. It had been easy to read, after that.

Malcolm laughed at the mad simplicity, and asked her to decode the rest.

It was fascinating stuff. Mortimer had been experimenting, at least at a theoretical level, with genetic engineering, the act of chemically altering a body's make-up in the hope of making the recipient stronger, faster, or immune to certain illnesses and defects. The notes had just moved on from the theory side of things to actual experimentation on rat fetuses, with immensely promising results.

Unfortunately, Asami discovered that morning, that was where the notes ran out.

She checked his dates, and then looked up when he'd died. There was a good three months between the two. Where was the rest?

She placed the e-reader down and went to report to Dr Malcolm, rapping sharply on the door to his office.

"I've finished decoding the notes, sir," she said. "Unfortunately, they end rather abruptly. I was wondering if there were any more?"

"What?" Malcolm looked up from his screen, running a hand down his dark, neatly-trimmed beard. He was a smart, well-dressed man, never out of his three-piece, pinstripe suit. Middle-aged. Well-groomed. He had the look of all of her parents' respectable friends combined, with little but his fancy beard to set him apart from any other middle-ring gentleman. "No," he continued. "I'm afraid that's all we have."

"There are three months between—"

"The rest must have been destroyed in the fire."

This seemed unlikely to Asami. She wasn't particularly adept at the technology used at the research wing—knowing just enough to do her job—but she thought that the computers had some way of storing things automatically. All his notes so far had been typed.

"I'll take what you've managed to recover," Malcolm prompted. "Then you may return to your usual work."

"Of course," said Asami, and followed his instructions without complaint. Never mind his abruptness; he was her supervisor. It was not her job to question him.

But she didn't like dropping things. She didn't like not having the solution, the conclusion. It was like someone had ripped away the final few pages of the book and was holding them above her head, just out of reach.

She was half-tempted to replicate the experiment herself, just to see the end of it.

"Something wrong?" asked her colleague, Anya, looking up from her own work. She was about Asami's age, but the similarities ended there. Anya was tall and red-haired, with piercing blue eyes. Asami was small, with brown hair the colour of dark chocolate, and eyes darker still.

"I'm missing the rest of Dr Mortimer's notes," she explained. "Three month's worth. Dr Malcolm says they were lost in the fire."

Anya frowned. "Unlikely."

"I know."

"He was so old school. He would have had paper copies. And he wouldn't have kept them on site."

"I thought he was mad?"

"He was… eccentric," said Anya, with a lot more tact than most others used when describing Dr Mortimer. "But he was fastidious about the work. No way he wouldn't have had back-ups."

"That's what I was thinking."

There was a knock at the door, and both women shot up. Colonel Bestiel, one of the queen's most decorated officers, stood in the doorway.

"Colonel!" they snapped, offering hasty bows and awkward salutes. Asami tried to do both at once and ended up making a mess of both. Military visits were unusual, and Asami was never sure of the proper protocol, even though he'd been around a few times of late.

"How can we—" Anya began.

He held up his hand, offering them both the ghost of a smile, an action that didn't quite suit his worn, weather-beaten face. The colonel was a great, hulking tank of a man, a battleaxe made human. If his bones were made of iron, Asami wouldn't have been surprised. Despite being a military man and his role at the palace largely keeping him at the side of Queen Mira, it wasn't unheard of for him to visit the laboratories, but it was unusual to see him twice in one week.

"Dr Thorne," he said. "How goes your decoding of those notes? I'm on my way to see Dr Malcolm, but I thought I'd check in with you first."

Asami was a little shocked that he knew her name. They'd

only spoken once before, and briefly at that. "I've deciphered everything I have, sir."

"Excellent. Most excellent. I shall speak to Dr Malcolm then."

He left without another word.

"That was odd," said Anya. "Why would Colonel Bestiel be interested in genetic enhancement?"

"My thoughts exactly." Asami scrubbed at her temples, trying to dislodge any whirring thoughts, refocus. Anya turned back to her own project and Asami returned to the rest of the day's tasks.

Yet she couldn't quite lose herself in the work like she usually did, the abrupt end to the project an itch inside her mind. The numbers didn't blot away the world, and she was conscious of things that often passed her by: the scrape of Anya's chair, the ticking of the large clock, the hum of the machines, the scratch of pencil lead.

It was a relief to break for lunch for once. Asami frequently worked through it, too focused to remember, only to rouse at past two and cram a quick bite in. Today, however, there was no such escape from the world. She went to the cafeteria, conversed with her colleagues, and even took a stroll around the gardens to try and clear her head.

She rested beside the monument dedicated to Princess Ivory, the queen's deceased stepdaughter. The statue was still missing an arm. The rumour was the queen's distant cousin, Prince Nero, had broken it off during a tryst, and Asami tried not to think about the physics of that. The arm was awfully high up.

Instead, she tried to relax. The thing was, work *did* relax Asami. Work made sense. Work was a beautiful, challenging kind of easy. Work was where she was happiest.

She would not be happy until she solved the mystery of Dr Mortimer's missing research, or knew she'd exhausted all avenues pertaining to it.

After lunch, she tapped into the old personnel records and looked up his former address. If there was anything to be found on site, she reasoned, someone would have found it.

Unless, said a strange, slippery voice inside her, *unless it's being kept from you.*

She quickly shoved that thought aside, not wanting to give it weight. Why would anyone want to hide anything, when they were all working towards the same goal: human advancement?

There was no next of kin listed for Dr Mortimer, but it was her only starting point. She was not going to do nothing.

According to his records, shortly before his death, the doctor had moved from his comfortable middle-ring apartment to an address in the outer ring. Asami couldn't think of a single reason someone would do that. Only the poor, destitute and factory workers resided in the lower sectors. There was no reason Dr Mortimer would have done that on his salary. Asami couldn't imagine anything tempting her to desert her comfortable quarters. Nothing except—

The job. The work. A problem that needed fixing, that she thought she could solve. She always went where the work was. What if Dr Mortimer was similar?

Asami tugged at the end of her sleeves.

She was going to the outer ring.

2

SECRETS IN THE SMOKE

Despite always having a plan, Asami didn't know what area of science she wanted to specialise in until her final year of university. Her entire life up until that point had been "follow the sums, follow the science"—dedicated to completing the short-term task with the long term goal of just finishing university.

Most people expected her to become a medical doctor. She was intelligent, she cared about people, and she excelled at the medical components of her course.

It was a great surprise to her family when she turned around and told them she wanted to focus on biochemistry instead.

Her father had fretted, her friends and sister had gasped, and her mother had merely nodded sagely and told her to follow her instinct.

"Her *instinct?*" shrieked her little sister. "She can't catch a ball. She can't follow her instinct!"

Asami had glared. "What does my ball-catching skills

have to do with instinct?"

Sakura's response to this had been to hurl the nearest soft object—a balled-up dishcloth—in her face. It smacked her in the nose and fell to the floor before she could even react. "You're supposed to catch it, dummy!" Sakura sighed. "You won't last one day in Petragrad."

"Petragrad?" Her father's voice went as squeaky as a badly-played violin. "Who said anything about Petragrad?"

It was typical of Sakura to realise in an instant that of course that was where Asami was headed. Doing what she had always done.

Following the science.

It was a strange memory to come to her now, as she caught the first lift down to the rest of the city, and yet it pulsed inside her along with a growing feeling of unease giving way to recklessness. Her parents would not have approved of this. She felt like the heroine in one of the gothic horror novels she used to read as a teen, meek and trembling and heading into danger unknown.

At least more than faint curiosity drove her. It was science. The pursuit of knowledge.

And maybe a *little* curiosity.

Asami rode the tram all the way to the outer ring, until the carriage was almost empty and the air thick and smoky. The skies were darkening into an inky, purplish black by the time the tram clattered to a halt. The false stars would be glittering above the upper rings, but their light did not permeate the smog of the outskirts.

She dipped her hands into her satchel and removed a black silk mask and goggles, fitting both around her face. Many lived out here for years, decades even, without succumbing to the ill effects of the smoke, but she wasn't taking any chances.

Stepping off the tram, she was hit by a rush of warm steam, jostled forward into the slow throng of people moving along the streets. The movements of everyone around her seemed slower, like they were trudging through mud. She was conscious of the pristine whiteness of her coat next to the greys and browns of everyone else. Even the few with coloured garments were worn to threads, the brightness leached from the fabric.

Asami had had little reason ever to come to the outer ring. It was all at once noisier and far quieter than any other part of the city. Everything still hummed and clicked and whirred, great chimneys vomited out black smoke, but the people themselves were muted, their voices silent.

Asami walked on, studying the map she'd taken from the archives to navigate her way to Mortimer's old lodgings. The throngs thinned, the alleyways darkened. In one, a woman sat hunched in rags, coughing up her lungs, the noise hard and brittle in a way that crackled against Asami's chest. She wanted to go to her, to offer her what, she wasn't sure, but something. Anything to help.

Before she could, a shadow cut across the woman.

A dread doctor.

A guard from the palace, dressed in a long leather robe, a colour between brown and green, a pair of blackened goggles, and a long, hooked mask, like a beak. It housed a portable filter that made breathing safe even in the harshest of conditions.

The woman looked up, blinking wearily. "Come for me then, have you?" she rasped.

The dread doctor scanned her and merely nodded. She lifted herself up on his arm, walking away with him.

Another victim of the coal sickness.

Despite having adopted the moniker of the Black Death, the coal sickness was not contagious. Caused by breathing in too much of the dangerous fumes, what it was was fatal and bitterly unpleasant. Asami had never been to the hospital the Crown had erected in order to care for the victims, but she'd read all the files, seen the pictures, the evidence. Your lungs filled with dust, poisoning your blood, and you died coughing out your chest.

As it wasn't contagious, many patients tried to conceal it for as long as possible, many families wanting just a little longer with them, but eventually the pain became too great, and the dread doctors were called to collect them. They would spend their final few days being cared for by the Crown, their bodies returned to the outer ring in urns.

Better air filters would have prevented so many from sickening, and wearing masks around the industrial buildings certainly helped. But it was impossible to wear them all the time, the dust had a skill for sneaking in through every crevice, and war with the neighbouring kingdom of Sparta meant that many resources and materials were lacking. They were always intercepting their goods trains, and sometimes, when news of several attacks happened within a few short days of each other, Asami wondered if they weren't rabbits in warrens, with Sparta trying to smoke them out.

You are not here to help victims of the Black Death, she reminded herself, as the woman was loaded into a van. *You are here to find out anything you can about Dr Mortimer. One thing at a time, Asami. One thing.*

With that in mind, she made her way through the blackened streets to the old lodgings of the deceased doctor. She had no idea what she hoped to find there. It had been three years since his death and the place had surely been occupied by other tenants since. It might even be rented out currently. It was possible some things of his remained in storage, though. Or maybe the owner could tell her something about him, a reason he'd decided to move out here.

I am following a trail of breadcrumbs, she thought miserably. *They all ought to have been gobbled up by now.*

But the trail still existed, and needed to be followed to the bitter end.

"No one ever made a difference standing still," her mother used to say.

And Asami had to make a difference.

Eventually, she arrived at the boarding house. It was a narrow, spindly, four-story building, squeezed in between a blacksmith's and what looked like a brothel. It was early, but two people, a man and a woman, stood outside the doors, smoking cigarettes on bronze holders, both in fishnet stockings and corsets, with expertly-rouged faces.

Asami was always a little self-conscious when she saw

other people wearing make-up. She'd never quite got into the habit and she didn't feel she had the time to learn how to do it effectively, or even if she wanted to sacrifice a slice of her time to the routine of applying it. Nevertheless, she admired the skill of others.

"Little far from the palace aren't we, *ma cherie?*" said the man. He was toned to the point of chiselled, lithe, dark-skinned, handsome. He gave her outfit the once over, and Asami wondered if she should have gone back to change. Usually her uniform offered her a modicum of respect, but out here she wondered if it wasn't inviting trouble, or at least flaunting her privilege. Suddenly, she felt self-conscious for more than a lack of make-up.

"I'm here on business," she explained, offering a slight smile. She had no wish to be impolite.

"Well, if you need to unwind after..." said the woman, flashing her a bright grin. "You know where to find us..."

"Um, thank you," said Asami. "I'll bear that in mind."

They gave indifferent shrugs as she turned away from them, rapping on the door. A few minutes later, a thin woman with a gaunt, grey face answered.

"Yes?" she barked.

"My name is Dr Thorne," Asami replied, glad of her coat again, of the credence it would bring. "I work at the palace, I believe one of our doctors, a man by the name of Mortimer, lived at this address for a short time?"

"Aye," said the woman, "I remember him."

"We've been going through his notes recently and realised some files were missing. We wondered if perhaps they'd been left at this address?"

The woman shook her head. "Those horrid dread doctors cleaned out everything the day after he died."

Asami's heart sank. "I see."

Was that the end of it already? The woman seemed to think so. She started to close the door.

"Wait," said Asami, well aware she was now grasping at straws, "is there anyone in his rooms at present?"

"Why?" said the woman shortly. "You looking to rent?"

"No, I just... would it be possible to take a look? See if anything was missed?"

"Had three tenants in since. Doubtful."

"Please," said Asami. "I just need to look."

The woman eyed her skeptically, as if trying to work out what her game was.

"I can, of course," said Asami, digging into her purse, "pay you for your trouble?"

She brought out a gold coin. The landlady's eyes widened, and Asami wondered if she had overpaid. She wasn't used to bribing people.

The woman seized the coin from her fingers and bit into it. "Top floor," she said, when the metal didn't yield. "Room 12. Don't be too long."

Not losing any time, Asami took the key thrust in her direction and made her way up the narrow, winding steps, though the dark hallways of the boarding house. The peeling wallpaper looked like it had once been forest green and printed with violets, but years and the thick, heavy air had sucked away all vibrancy from the pattern.

She reached the top floor, a little out of breath, and took a moment to collect herself before stepping inside the room.

The entire bedsit could have fitted neatly inside her bedroom in the middle ring. It was stripped of all furniture except a shabby bed frame and single chair, and Asami had a hard time imagining where everything else would have fit when it was occupied. A small cooking area was squeezed into the corner, a large copper pot hanging over a blackened fireplace that merged into the dark, dreary walls.

Nothing else remained.

Asami sighed, but tried not to let herself be deterred. If this was a gothic novel, there'd be a secret compartment somewhere in the room, a note stuffed up a chimney. She examined the latter thoroughly before giving up, washing her hands in the sink and wiping them on one of her handkerchiefs. The basin was so stained that the darkened water was almost invisible.

She traced her hands over the room, searching for a stray bit of wallpaper, a loose floorboard, a message someone had missed. There was plenty of peeling wallpaper and loose floorboards, but no messages.

She searched the doorframe, remembering a mystery novel where someone had "stolen" a painting from inside a locked room by sliding the canvas alone in a narrow gap between panels. Nothing again.

Finally, she did what she often did when she encountered a problem she couldn't solve; she lay on her back, and stared at the ceiling.

For some reason she could never quite discern, changing

positions and staring at something blank often helped dislodge the ghost of an idea, gave her a path through her problems, or another one altogether.

She concentrated on her breathing until her thoughts flattened, and her gaze drifted to the tacky faux-chandelier installed on the ceiling. Several of the crystals were missing or broken, and one was a different shape altogether. It was the sort of thing that no one else would notice in a run-down place like this, no one who wasn't thinking.

Asami frowned. If guards were sent to strip Dr Mortimer's room, would they have stopped to check the light? How often did anyone check it? The thing was covered in dust and grease.

She grabbed the chair from the side of the room and pulled it into the centre. It was barely tall enough to aid her, and she cursed her short stature. She ended up taking down half the chandelier tugging the fake crystal free.

Only it wasn't a crystal at all. It was a small glass vial, stuffed with a slip of parchment.

She unrolled it hastily, and smiled. It was a string of letters and numbers. Her brain immediately clicked into gear, decoding them in the same cipher Mortimer had used in his notes.

Co-ordinates. They had to be.

She took out her map and found the point on it—the warehouse district, not too far away. Giddy with anticipation, she rolled the note back and stuffed it into her pocket, hurrying down the stairs, only remembering at the last minute to return the key to the landlady.

She flew out into the street and disappeared, black stone now swallowed up by night. Nothing reached her, the thrum of the city and trudge of the crowds lost to the thrill of the chase. She barely looked anywhere but ahead, taking no note of anything until she reached the street of warehouses and slowed to a halt. Something almost like silence settled around the building, devoid of people, lit only by the faintest of lamps.

Something moved behind her, sending a shiver coursing down her spine. She wheeled around, but saw nothing. Only shadow.

The thrill of adventure deserted her.

She made her way to the warehouse marked with the number on the paper, or at least, the number she hoped it was if she'd cracked it correctly. It was secured with a huge bronze padlock, rusted with age.

No one had been here in a long, long time.

There was no code on the paper, no further numbers that hadn't been exhausted. She flipped it over, as if hoping another set would reveal itself.

Nothing.

She turned back to the padlock.

Four digits. Nine numbers. Ten thousand possibilities. Not enough time before she'd have to return to the middle ring. She didn't want to be out too late in a place like this. Perhaps she could start making a list and start working through them, a hundred or so a visit...

She sighed. It would take weeks. There had to be an easier way.

She thought about trying to convert the word "open" into the periodic table, knowing Dr Mortimer's love for it from decoding his notes, but the right letters didn't exist and it was more a word riddle than a science one. It seemed almost lazy. 0123 was another option, the table being divided into s, p, d and f sections. She tried all combinations of his date of birth, duly memorised, just in case, and any other popular codes that came to mind. She was not surprised when they all came to nothing.

No. It would not be something so easy, but she couldn't believe it was something random, either.

8314, the ideal gas constant? Nothing.

She sighed. He loved the periodic table, but he wouldn't have wanted something easily guessable.

What would most people not know about it?

Its history, sprung a voice deep inside her. *History. History is lost*

Well, not quite lost. But it was true that education generally regarded a lot of history from the time before as superfluous. The results and the findings—like the table itself —had been carried forward, but the origins were largely ignored.

But not by Asami, who wanted to know the beginning and end of everything.

1869. The date Mendelev first published the periodic table.

The door clicked open.

At the side of the door was a fluorescent lamp lit by crystal; unusual in the outer ring, common enough in the palace.

She took it from the hook on the wall and descended down the steps, the groaning of the district shrinking behind her, the stillness hardening. Her breath gathered in her throat.

She counted the steps as she went, feeling comfort in the firmness of the numbers, the action, the same way one might seek comfort in an old childhood toy.

One, two, three, four, five...

She willed herself to move faster, to race down the steps, but she was trembling too much to summon the energy.

Six, seven, eight, nine, ten...

Somewhere in her mesh of thoughts was one telling her to turn back, reminding her of the feeling of being followed. The pulsing shiver that made her think the shadows had eyes.

But she would not stop. She couldn't.

Eleven, twelve, thirteen.

Another door. A heavy handle. A dial for light. A faint, shallow hum as a lab opened up ahead of her.

It was a horrific blend of technology both old and new; wires and glass cylinders, computers and gears. An operating table sat at the centre, the bars at the side bent, a chunk missing as if it had been torn off. Wires pooled to the floor, ripped in two.

Gears and garters, Dr Mortimer, what did you do here?

Tentatively, Asami crept forward. The dust in the room was limited, the space being sealed, but the air still felt stale and thick. She walked towards the desk in the corner, covered in papers and images, and swallowed a gasp.

Photographs, photographs of men and women with

twisted bodies, faces half-melted or covered in welts, giant limbs, horrific malformations...

She ought to have been used to seeing such things in textbooks, but the horror remained the same, accentuated by the eyes of the patients, the pain flaring there.

What had happened to them?

She seized up more of the notes. They were disordered, out of place, but Asami's mind made fast work of fitting them into something readable.

She half wished they wouldn't.

The Crown's experiments hadn't stopped with rats. They'd been so promising that they pushed forward with human testing, not on embryos, but on soldiers.

The results had been disastrous. Many had died, suffering a range of horrific side effects, unbearable pain.

They had found no way of fixing them, and—

A clang sounded out above her. Asami wheeled around, stuffing the notes inside her satchel.

Two dread doctors pooled into the room, accompanied by Dr Malcolm. His silver hair gleamed in the low light as he tilted his glasses towards her.

"Dr Thorne," he said dryly.

Asami wasn't sure whether to be relieved or terrified, but her mouth started babbling before her thoughts could catch up, too confused and too horrified to assess the situation.

"Did you know?" she stammered. "What Dr Mortimer..."

Her voice trailed off with the shake of his head. "Oh, Dr Thorne. For someone so smart, you really can be astonishingly stupid."

Asami tried not to tremble. Realisation hit like a gong. "Dr Mortimer didn't do these experiments alone."

"Dr Mortimer," Malcolm continued, "was against human testing from the start. Said we weren't ready. He was right, of course, but that's neither here nor there. He did what he was told. We all did. And when we were told to put the poor victims out of their misery... he did that too."

Asami sucked in a breath.

"Then he came down here for whatever reason. We suspected he had a lab somewhere, somewhere he was trying to replicate or fix or enhance what we'd done, but we could never find it. You though... you and he are one of the same. I had you followed, hoping you might lead us to his missing research."

Asami shrank towards the desk, fingers scrunching over her satchel.

"The government... the government did this. To its own soldiers."

"In times of war, we do what needs to be done," Malcolm insisted, taking a step forward. "The war with Sparta is not going well. We needed an advantage—"

"You couldn't have waited? Done the proper testing—"

"Desperate times call for desperate measures."

"Did Mortimer really die in a fire?"

Malcolm shrugged. "Above my paygrade, I'm afraid," he said, as if it mattered little. "Come now, Asami. Hand over the research. Let's take it back to the palace and see if we can't make something good come out of this horror."

"Something... good?" She swallowed. "Those people—"

"Will have died for nothing if you don't give me that research."

"This… this isn't right. Those soldiers deserve justice. Their families should know what happened—"

"What good would that do? Come, girl. It's for the science."

It was the 'girl' that did it, the flippant remark that turned horror into anger. "This isn't for science," she hissed.

"For our country, then."

"What kind of country are we protecting?"

Malcolm narrowed his eyes. "I know technically you're not from here—"

"I am from the United Nations, thank you very much, but my loyalty isn't to them. It's to people. People who deserve it —"

"Are you saying you won't give us the papers?"

"I…" Asami's thoughts were scattered in a way she couldn't comprehend, like moths loosed in a room full of lights. Fear and sense suspended amidst the absolute confusion. "Yes. Yes, you can't have them. The public deserve to know—"

"Hmm," said Malcolm. "Pity."

Too late, Asami realised her mistake, realised why he'd brought the dread doctors, realised she was trapped. They were covering the only door.

Malcolm was right about one thing. She really was very stupid for a smart person.

The dread doctors lunged, streaming across the lab. Asami hit the floor at the same time as something else, a round silver ball spitting out smoke.

"Stay down!" roared a hard, gravelly voice.

Asami did as she was told, coughing and blinking through the smog. A pistol went off. Sparks and bullets reverberated on the pipes. Malcom let out a hard cry. There was a roar, a clanging of metal.

The smoke reached her lungs, along with her commingling panic. Her chest heaved, her head surged, and her vision turned spotty and black until it faded from her altogether.

3

A BEAST IN THE
BLACKNESS

Not for the first time, Beau wished he could actually melt into shadow. He'd grown good at concealing himself in the military, learning how to blend in with his surroundings despite his large stature, but physics were physics and sometimes he was simply unavoidable, like when he went to market to haggle and exchange with the genuine merchants in the outer ring,

He didn't like to go often, lest they start remembering him, in case someone started talking about the deformed man in the outer ring, and word got back to the wrong people. He was never sure how dead the palace wanted him, whether or not they'd be satisfied with "dead enough," "as good as dead" or "out of mind, out of sight."

He didn't want to push his luck.

Whenever he had legitimate cause to visit the market, he always went late, cloak drawn up, mask on. It hid most of the damage, and if people caught a glance of his distorted face beneath the hood, they probably mistook it for old burns, scarring caused by some horrific accident. Not uncommon, out here.

Today's market had ended a while back, but he'd yet to return below. It had been a long time since he'd been up to the surface, and he was keen to enjoy what little of it he could. Instead of leaving, he climbed up to a nearby roof, the smog behind him, and chased the pale purple lines of manufactured dusk with his gaze.

There was precious little in the outer ring that could ever be described as beautiful, but for a few moments at this time of day, it was easier to pretend.

This was one of the spots he'd discovered shortly after Mortimer's death, when he was waiting to be discovered, certain the government would follow some trail of breadcrumbs to Mortimer's secret lab. The place where Beau had been brought back to life, or died completely, he wasn't really sure.

He'd waited for them instead, waited for them to come, so he could...

Well, he didn't want to think about that, anymore. That anger had simmered in the years.

And no one had come. For almost three years, he'd stalked this spot, coming by every so often to make sure the padlock was still intact. It was. Rusted over now.

No one had been in that place in a long, long time.

Which was why it surprised him today to see a small figure in white tottering down the dark street, jumping at shadows and glancing around furtively.

Beau peered closer, glad of his enhanced eyesight, one of the few parts of the experimentation that had actually worked as intended.

While her coat marked her out as a scientist, she didn't look like one of Malcolm's lackeys... or at least, if she was, she wasn't happy about it. Beau wasn't sure he'd ever seen anyone look quite so nervous. She embodied every anxious feeling he'd ever had, every childish crush and awkward flirtation pressed into a human face.

What by the Dome was she doing here?

Maybe she was just lost. Perhaps someone had spooked her and she'd come running down here to get away from them. At that thought, he was tempted to drop down and see if she needed assistance, before remembering that his presence was far more likely to terrify her.

He groaned. *When will I learn?*

Beau kept his eyes on the girl as she stopped in front of Mortimer's door, and tried the padlock.

He leaned forward, heart lurching. Had someone finally come for the research? What was he supposed to do about that? He'd had ill-thought plans of revenge years ago, but that didn't involve taking down a tiny, defenceless woman, especially one so clearly terrified.

At the same time, he didn't want the government getting their hands on Mortimer's work. He didn't precisely know what it entailed, but he was fairly sure if they discovered that Mortimer had found a way to stabilise the mutations caused by the serum, they wouldn't much care about the side-effects.

No. He wasn't letting what happened to him—what happened to his entire squad—happen to anyone else.

He scrambled down the side of the building and landed

soundlessly on the ground, sticking to the shadows as he crept after the woman.

He wasn't going to hurt her. He'd scare her, if necessary. Steal the notes. Set fire to the lab. He always kept explosives on him for such emergencies.

Or... or he could talk to her. Explain why she shouldn't report her findings.

Although that was risky. It might be better just to scare her.

The woman entered the lab, oblivious to his presence, and after a moment of staring at her surroundings, made her way to Mortimer's old desk.

Beau tensed, remembering lying on that gurney, barely conscious, pumped full of drugs, wondering if he was going to die and if he wanted to.

He suspected he might have begged for it at one point, but he couldn't remember.

His fingers flexed automatically, reaching for the pocketwatch Ash had given him, feeling the steady tick-tick like a second heartbeat.

"Time is passing, Beau," he'd said. *"This will too. Just hold on a little longer."*

It had become his mantra over the years, saving him more times than he cared to admit.

Ash. The one part of his old life he'd carried over. The one thing that felt just the same.

The flinching feeling of terror looking over his old operating room distracted him from movement above, and he dipped into the shadows of the theatre, dropping behind the equipment. Something rumbled down the steps, too quiet for the average human ear to discern, and his fingers sprung to his pistol.

His eyes went briefly to the woman, staring at the files on Mortimer's desk. He could not see her face, but her entire body looked stiff and tense.

Whatever her reasons for coming here, she had not expected this.

Something clanged on the final step, finally alerting the woman to the presence of others, and she spun around just as two dread doctors ducked into the room, accompanied by a thin, well-groomed man with silver hair and a sour expression.

Beau's stomach dropped, anger rising like bile.

Dr Malcolm.

"Dr Thorne," he said dryly.

Beau's hand closed around his pistol, old thoughts of revenge twisting inside him. But he kept them tempered.

You are not a monster, he told himself.

But Malcolm was.

The woman—Dr Thorne—stammered something back, and Beau knew in that moment that Malcolm hadn't sent her, that she'd acted alone, that she was just as horrified by these experiments as he was.

And she had no idea about the danger she was in.

She kept talking, kept refusing to hand over the research, most of which she'd scrunched into her satchel.

Did this woman have *no* sense of self-preservation? She was quaking as if she did. He couldn't work out if he admired her bravery or abhorred her stupidity.

Just give him the notes! Beau urged, quite forgetting that that was exactly what he was keen to avoid.

Malcolm's patience wavered. "Are you saying you won't give us the papers?"

"I..." The good doctor stumbled again, and Beau found himself once more praying that she'd just see sense and give in. "Yes. Yes, you can't have them. The public deserve to know —"

"Hmm," said Malcolm. "Pity."

The dread doctors lunged, streaming across the lab. Knowing he couldn't hit two targets at once, Beau reached for one of the smoke grenades on his belt and tossed it into the space. Smog erupted.

The doctor hit the floor.

"Stay down!" he roared.

He heard her coughing on the floor, but the dread doctors did not stop, as undeterred by the smog as he was. He grabbed one of their arms, kicking the other in the back as Malcolm fired. Bullets leapt against metal. Malcolm yelled something.

A fist hit him squarely on the jaw. He smacked back, just as hard, the mask bruising his knuckles.

Stars, his opponents were strong. The dread doctor programme hadn't started until after he'd left the palace, the job of collecting the dying falling to standard soldiers or simple guards. Beau, thankfully, had been spared the duty. He wondered what training the dread doctors underwent, if he knew them beneath their masks. They could have trained together.

Been friendly.

But not friends. Almost all his friends were dead.

He spied the doctor on the floor, slumped and unconscious. He was fairly sure he could get himself out of here, but only if he left her behind.

It had been a very long time since he'd thought of himself as any kind of protector, but leaving her just didn't sit right.

One of Malcolm's bullets hit something overhead, a stray coil of wire now spitting out sparks. Punching his foes back, Beau leapt onto the gurney and seized the wires, glad of his gloves, and drove them into the bellies of the dread doctors. They spasmed, thudding downwards.

Beau groped in the fog for Malcolm, but he seemed to have vanished.

His gaze dropped to Dr Thorne. No question of leaving her here, no time to think of something better to do. He levered her into his arms, tucked her against his shoulder, and fled into the night.

It was too dark for anyone to see them, and he was too fast for anyone to stop them. He sprinted down the backstreets and alleyways to the metal gate that led to the old underground. Few knew it still existed, fewer still had any course to go below. Homelessness was one of the few problems that didn't plague Petragrad; there were plenty of abandoned buildings if you were in need of shelter. Hot water, medicine, clean clothes, food? The lack of those is what would kill you.

He slowed as he ducked into the tunnel, stopping to check Dr Thorne's breathing. Her mask had come loose, displaying cool, perfect skin, the type unused to hardship.

Her entire life had just blown up in a single night.

And he was going to have to explain it to her.

He shouldered her once again and continued on his way.

He had ties to the Rebellion, a faction that lived outside the city dome, that occasionally travelled inside it to stir up much-deserved trouble and liberate supplies. They might be able to get her out of the city. Maybe.

She wouldn't want to stay with him, but the Rebellion didn't visit often. Mira would want her head. Where else would she be safe? She was a doctor; maybe she could get work in the makeshift infirmary in the lower ring until safe passage could be arranged? They wouldn't be able to pay her, but they could offer her food and shelter.

If they didn't sell her out for more of that for themselves.

Beau sighed.

"Quite the mess you've found yourself in, Doctor," he said to her unconscious form. "I really hope you have a way out of it."

4

BEAUTY AND THE BEAST

Asami woke to a curious, unfamiliar silence. A muted whir still rattled somewhere, but it was distant and far away. Everything was muffled, like her ears were stuffed with foam.

She sat up, rubbing her temples and the paste from her eyes. Her head was pounding, her throat parched. Her fingers found a glass of water by her bedside, and she drank thirstily as her eyes adjusted to the gloom.

Where am I?

Panic flared in her chest the second the need for water was abated, so sudden she choked on the dregs of her drink.

Breathe, a voice told her. *Assess the situation.*

Asami tried to listen, and counted her breaths, *in, out, in, out.*

She looked to be in some kind of converted train car, re-purposed into a bedroom. She was lying on a wide bed stuffed with musty sheets. A dresser was squeezed into one corner, a chair in another. Clothes hangers lined the bars on the ceiling, but they were devoid of clothes in favour of leaving them scattered all over the floor. There were a handful of books, too. A comb. Some cologne, dusty and unused. A personal room.

Wherever she was, her captor—or perhaps her rescuer— had not been expecting company.

She hoped that was a good thing.

She wasn't imprisoned. She wasn't hurt, or dead. Three good things.

Focus. One step at a time.

Her mind leapt to the safety of numbers, reminding her of the order of operations. *You have to divide before you subtract.* This was just another version of that. A terrifying, scary, real-life version. But the same principle applied. She needed to calculate the danger she was in before falling to pieces.

She took another deep breath and pulled herself out of bed, locating her boots. Her satchel was there, too, untouched, her goggles and mask resting atop them. She fumbled for her glasses and slid them on, revelling in the comfort of them. No one had taken the research, either.

She wasn't with Malcolm. Another piece of good news.

At least... she hoped.

Lacing her boots, she crept forward, out of the train car.

She was in an underground station, long since abandoned, coated in black grease. A scuttling of rats echoed around her, but she saw little in the faint green light other than the exits. She moved onwards, into a corridor stuffed with doors. One near the end was propped open with a fire extinguisher.

It was furnished with a wall of screens and wires, the kind of technology only the palace had access to, but there was nothing sleek and shimmery about the facilities here. Everything looked pieced together with rubble, a frankenstein of tech.

In a large desk chair of peeling black leather sat a huge, hunched figure.

"Um, hello?" Asami started.

The figure leapt to his feet. He was taller than she could have anticipated, with huge, broad shoulders. He whipped up the hood of his storm cloak before her eyes could settle on his face, but she caught a glimpse of his left cheek, of the distorted flesh there.

"You're awake," he mumbled.

Asami paused, taking in her surroundings. Her voice seemed to have vanished.

"You're all right?" he asked. "Not hurt?"

"No, no I'm not hurt." *Confused, very confused. Shocked. Definitely that. But hurt?*

"Good," he said. "That's… that's good."

"Where am I?"

"An abandoned underground military station," the man replied, as if happy to have an easy question to answer. "Off the records, more or less. You're… you're safe here, in case you were worried about that."

Safe. Asami wasn't sure she knew the meaning of that word, anymore. How could she be safe in this filthy underground lair, far away from everything she'd ever known.

Everything. Everything she'd ever had—

No, no, don't think about that. Focus.

One thing at a time.

"And... who are you?"

"An abandoned soldier."

Asami crept forward, as carefully as she could. Her legs still felt loose beneath her. "You're one of them, aren't you?" she whispered, her mind flicking back to the photos in Mortimer's lab, the ones in her satchel. "One of the soldiers from Malcolm and Mortimer's experiments."

"I am."

"They were supposed to have died—"

"Mortimer saved me," he said, and gestured to his hidden face. "Or what was left of me."

"And then you saved me."

He nodded, quiet and still.

"Why? You don't know me."

"You're a doctor, aren't you? You only save people you know?"

"I'm not that kind of doctor," she said. "But... no. You're right. Thank you."

He shrugged, although the movement didn't quite spread along both of his shoulders.

"Have you been down here for three years?"

"I go up the outer ring for supplies every now and again."

"What about your family?"

"They think I died on a mission."

"Right." Somewhere, in the back of her mind, was the stirring of a thought for her own family, for the life that had just obliterated in the past few hours, but it didn't quite reach her, not yet.

"How did you know? About me entering the lab? Were you following me, or—"

He shook his head. "I used to stalk the lab daily," he explained, although he didn't tell her why. "I keep an eye on things."

The dashboard behind him showed a series of images from all over the city, some moving. He clearly kept an eye on *everything.*

"You knew where the research was?"

"Yes."

"Why not..." *Why not release it? Why not use it to try and help yourself?*

"I don't understand any of it," he explained, as if reading her mind. "And the photos... I didn't much care to look at them."

His comrades. His friends, mostly likely. To have lost them, for his family to think he was dead, to have been down here so long by himself... She felt the tug again, the same one that had seared against her chest when she saw the victim of the black death in the alleyway. The desire to help.

Asami took another step forward. He shrunk back, hitting the edge of the desktop.

"It's all right," she insisted, "I *am* a doctor, after all. I've already seen the files. It seems silly of you to have to hide in your own... home."

Something in his shoulders relaxed, only slightly. He let out a low sigh, and peeled back his hood.

The left side of his face was covered in knotted flesh and

welts. His swollen brow almost completely overwhelmed the eye beneath it, which lacked the brightness of its cerulean twin. His mouth drooped in the corner, solid and unwavering. The malformations descended to his neck and ear, and, she suspected, down his arm; his left hand was almost twice the size of the other, a stiff-looking, lumpy thing.

But the right side of his face was smooth and unblemished, beneath a head of thick brown curls, although it was almost impossible to double it in her mind's eye, to imagine what he might have looked like before.

He tilted his face to one side, his fingers itching as if fighting the urge to pull his hood back up. "Pretty hideous, right?"

"Do they hurt?"

"What?"

"Your face... the disfiguration. Does it hurt?"

His flawless cheek tensed. "No. Not right now."

That answered her question, but not in the way she would have liked.

"What's your name?" he asked.

"Dr Asami Thorne."

"Asami is unusual for Petragrad."

"Yunasian mother, Toulousian father. It means love or beauty," she added, pulling on her sleeves. "I'm not sure it's a precise fit but there aren't any Yunasian names that mean intelligent, which is quite frankly rude. I'd rather be intelligent than beautiful, wouldn't you?" She clapped her hands to her mouth, suddenly realising her audience. She was so used to rattling off her thoughts on the name wherever she was asked, she hadn't thought—

But the man just shrugged. "Well, I think I'd sacrifice a *little* intelligence for beauty."

Asami bit her lip, holding back a laugh. "What's your name?"

He hesitated. "Beaumont," he admitted glumly. It was a Touslousian name. It meant handsome. "You can call me Beast. It's something of a nickname I've grown into."

"That seems a little rude."

He shrugged stiffly. "I really don't mind it."

"If you're sure..."

"Quite sure, Doctor."

"You can just call me Asami." Her eyes fell to his screens, displaying locations all over the sprawling city. She could never quite understand how technology like this worked, and seeing live images was... odd. She was familiar with picture-houses, with grainy films and music, but this was something different, almost unnatural in its newness.

Or oldness.

One of the images showed the middle ring, a street not far from her own. She caught a glimpse of the public gardens in the background. Home.

"I... I can't go back there, can I?" she whispered.

Beast shook his head. "There's been a warrant issued for your arrest."

"My arrest?" she shrieked. "For what?"

"Stealing state secrets, to sell to the enemy."

"Oh... *oh*." Her stomach caved. "My family is going to be so disappointed."

He blinked. "That's... that's what you're taking from this?"

"They're in Toulouse, so they won't find out immediately, right?"

"Still think you're fixating on the wrong thing..."

"Wait, they know I wouldn't do a thing like that. Will the government question them, do you think? Oh gosh, this is quite a mess. I hope they'll be all right. They don't know anything, of course, so—"

"You talk a lot."

"Yes, I have a tendency to prattle a bit when I'm nervous. Not... not at you, more the people-trying-to-kill-me thing." She paused. "Oh my, people are trying to kill me. The *palace* is trying to kill me. They want me dead. I *could* be dead. I could be dead!"

"There we go."

Asami sank into Beast's abandoned chair, head in her hands. "Dome above, this is awful."

Beast sighed, leaning against the dashboard, normal side towards her. "The best course of action is to probably get out of the city. I have ties to the Rebellion. They might be able to help, although it might take a while to—"

"The Rebellion?" Asami lifted her head. "You have ties to the *Rebellion*? Are you some kind of criminal?"

"The *government* is the criminal here," he said, affronted. "The Rebellion is just trying to—"

"They killed the king."

"That is the rumour, but honestly, does anyone really miss him? He was rather terrible."

"They killed the princess too. She was a *child*."

Beast shrugged. "It's all just rumour."

"Who *else* would have killed them?"

"I don't know if you've noticed, but our government isn't exactly the most trustworthy."

"They... no. They wouldn't. Not their own royal family. Surely?"

"Maybe not the government. But the queen?"

Asami blinked. "You can't be serious?"

"I'm just guessing. The point is, you can't blame the rebels for the rumours surrounding them when you *know* our government is awful."

"Well, that's true."

"Anyway, the Rebellion could help smuggle you out of the city. Toulouse would be risky, but anywhere else—"

It was too much. It was too much and completely ridiculous. Twenty-four hours ago, she'd had a tidy, neat little life, where she hadn't so much as cheated on a test. Now she was a wanted criminal, being advised to flee the city?

Where would she go? What would she *do?* Spend the rest of her life in hiding? Never see her family again? Hope someone else cleared this mess up for her?

She wasn't built for life on the run. That ruled out that option. She quickly examined her others, each more terrifying than the last, until, finally, she found the least terrifying of possibilities.

"No," she said.

"What?" He frowned, as if he thought she hadn't heard him.

"No. I'm not leaving the city."

"You... are aware of the danger you're in, right?"

"Myself and the rest of the military, if they ever try to recreate these experiments." Her mind flashed back to everything she'd ever seen Malcolm working on, every stray formula he'd tried to stop her from witnessing, and became suddenly convinced that he absolutely was trying to do just that. Mortimer was the pioneer. He buried some of his knowledge before he died. It could well be in the notes she'd seized. "I'm going to go through Mortimer's files and see if I can discover anything useful, or incriminating, and then somehow—not sure yet—I'm going to blow the lid on this cover up and clear my name."

"You sound remarkably confident."

"I've yet to find a problem without a solution." She knew she sounded more confident than she felt, because although she *hadn't* ever encountered a problem she couldn't solve, this was different. This was terrifying. She took off her glasses to clean them, forcing her fingers to do something productive, steadying. An old piece of advice her mother used to utter pulsed inside:

"Sometimes, Asami, if you can convince your enemy you've won, his own confidence will waver, and you can finish him."

This was invariably followed by her mother defeating her in chess, or stealing the last of something from her plate.

I hear you, Mama, she whispered internally. *Fear is my enemy. I shall pretend I have conquered him until I have.*

She pushed her glasses back up her nose. "Who knows," she said, "maybe I'll even be able to help *you.*"

"Me?"

"If there's a cure for what was done to you. I intend to

find it." If science made him this way, maybe it could fix him. Plenty was reversible.

"I... that's..."

"Unless you'd rather I wouldn't?"

"I... no." He paused, looking down at the floor. "Thank you. But, um... where do you intend to stay?"

"Well, here, if you'll let me. It seems the safest place. I don't take up much space. And I know I look like a prim middle-ring woman but I assure you, I can rough it." A complete lie, but he didn't need to know that. This place had the singular advantage of being available, and she found that was more than enough reason to stay. "Or at least, I think I can. I'm adaptable, I'll figure it out."

Beast snorted with laughter. "Sure. My underground lair is your underground lair. Make yourself at home."

"Excellent. One problem solved." She paused, and a yawn forced its way out of her mouth. "What time is it?"

He checked the pocket-watch attached to his plain, dark waistcoat. "A little after midnight. You were out for a few hours."

"I... I think I'd like to be out for a few more."

Beast half-smiled. "I'll find you something to eat. You can take the bed again. We'll work something else out tomorrow."

"If you're sure—"

"Your day has been considerably harder than mine. Please. I insist."

"All right," she said, and with that, shuffled off.

It was only after she'd inhaled a bowl of lukewarm soup

that her mind grew heavy with the magnitude of everything that had transpired that day, but she refused to let it suffocate her, refused to give into fear or nerves or horror.

She was alive. She had a job to do.

Everything else would wait.

THE CLOCKWORK
UNDERGROUND

Asami spent most of the next day in the train car, feeling as out of place and awkward as she had ever felt. The carriage was full of things that didn't belong to her. *Nothing* belonged to her, nothing but the few bits and pieces she had stashed in her satchel.

She laid out all her belongings on the bed. Her purse. Pens. A notebook. A pair of earrings. A small tub of hand cream. Mortimer's notes. Her ID for the palace, her mask and goggles. The keys to an apartment that probably wasn't hers any more, and a paperclip.

Nothing personal. Barely anything even *nice*.

She didn't want to clean up too much of the room, as it wasn't really hers and she shouldn't really be sleeping in it, but she wasn't sure what else to do. Beast seemed to have vanished, although he'd left some clean sheets on the step before he did so. She decided to explore the base instead, lacking the focus to work on decoding Mortimer's notes. She needed to know the limits of her new workspace, first.

Asami wriggled uncomfortably into her crumpled skirt and day-old stockings, wishing the floor were clean enough for her to walk around barefoot, and instead pushed her feet into her boots. There were no mirrors in the train car, but she could tell her hair was a mess by the feel of it. She braided her long brown locks as she walked, and ducked into the first door in the corridor.

It was a tiny kitchenette, basic and messy and piled with mouldy tins. Slices of burnt toast lay abandoned on the single clear surface nearby.

Suddenly hungry, she raided the cupboards and found a jar of oats and a tub of powdered milk. She was too hungry to second guess it, to spare a thought for iced buns and flaky pastries; her usual breakfast affair. She just wanted something—anything—to fill her up.

She lost her appetite as soon as she managed a few mouthfuls, washing up her utensils and stacking them by the side of the sink, although it seemed utterly pointless to clean anything in such a filthy place. She wondered if she should offer to clean, but she really wasn't sure where to start. She'd had a cleaner most of her life.

Instead, she opted to explore the rest of the base.

The next door along the corridor turned out to be an impressive storeroom, dusty but orderly, in contrast to everything else she'd seen so far. Her neat little heart did a leap just looking at the rows and rows of shelves and crates, all labelled and stacked by type. She had to resist the urge to take stock and evaluate whether or not everything was stored optimally, turning her attention to what she'd yet to uncover.

Aside from the lab, the train car and the kitchen, there was a dining room, a room that Beast had set up as something like a gym, several storerooms, a second carriage packed with furniture he must have moved out of the other spaces, and a rudimentary but oddly spotless bathroom. A broken mirror hung over a chipped sink, but everything but the glass showed signs of being scrubbed recently, cleaned within an inch of its life. There was nothing homely about the place, nothing warm or cosy.

He'd been down here for three years? How could anyone live like this?

She went back to the carriage to change the bedsheets, and tried to make a start on Mortimer's notes. It was a pointless task. She needed space to spread everything out and the carriage felt far too small. The more she spread, the more the walls seemed to shrink, until she felt like she was being pickled.

She went to the bathroom to wash her face, hoping it would clear her head.

The main door at the top of the steps banged open, and something loud grinded in the hall, a bark of gears. Asami jumped, toppling into a nearby bucket.

They've found me. Her heart raced. Malcolm and the dread doctors. They must have followed them, and Beast wasn't here. No one was here. She was alone, all alone, she'd always *be* alone.

Was she going to die alone, too?

Something thundered through the door, and Asami screamed, falling into the tub as a huge mechanical monster bounded towards her.

"It's all right," Beast rushed, appearing. "It's just my companion."

Asami inched upwards, just a fraction. "Your... companion?"

"Yes. Come in here, you mechanical mongrel."

Asami peered over the edge of the bath. A large, heavy shape clattered to a stop beside Beast's feet. It was a dog composed of scrap metal, clicking and whirring as he went. Two amber eyes stared under mismatched eyebrows of steel and bronze. Biological dogs were rare in the Mechanical Kingdoms, but clockwork ones were common enough. They never usually came this *large*.

The dog titled his head, dropped his jaw, and panted.

"His cooling systems are a little off—" Beast started.

"He's *adorable*," Asami said, clambering out of the tub, all fear immediately evaporating. She reached out to scratch under his chin. A leather tongue licked her cheek. "What's he called?"

"Pilot," Beast responded, blinking as if he'd forgotten Asami could speak at all. "Don't let him steal your food while you're here. He's got no idea he's not a real dog and I do *not* want to be cleaning jam out of his gears again."

Asami nodded, still patting the creature. Scrappy though he was, the animation was perfect. He let out a few grunts and happy wheezes. Beast, meanwhile, shirked back into the corridor.

"There's fresh bread in the kitchen," he said, not looking at her. "If you want it."

"Oh, thanks, I already ate."

"Suit yourself." He started off down the corridor, Pilot trailing after him. "Let me know if you need anything."

Asami stared after him, but only for a little while. She returned to the carriage, once more failed to focus, and instead found a small stack of well-thumbed books beside Beast's bed to flick through. There was an old gothic romance that was awful but in a rather fun way. It was the kind she would have lost herself in as a girl, about a young woman employed as a governess in a mysterious manor filled with demons. Sadly, it made the shadows in the train car jump too much for her liking, and turned the air stiff with cold.

She longed for noise and light, and tried not to think about how long it would be before she experienced either.

Beast avoided her for the rest of the day, and most of the next one, too. He made no attempt to reclaim his bed or speak to her in any way, shape or form.

She didn't go to him, either.

Towards the end of the second day, they bumped into each other in the kitchen. He leapt up as if he'd been found somewhere he had no right to be, eyes flicking towards the door.

"Are you nervous around scientists?" she asked. There had to be some reason he was avoiding her. *You've been avoiding him, too.* "Because of what..."

"Um, no," he said, gaze drawn elsewhere. "Not scientists. Mortimer was a scientist too, and he saved me. I'm mostly nervous around, well, people."

Asami blinked, not sure if she believed him. "Is this a recent thing? Since you came down here?"

"The isolation has not helped, but no, I've always been a bit nervous around... people."

Asami continued to stare. "I don't mean to sound impolite, but aren't you a trained killer?"

"Oh, it's easier to shoot people than talk to them."

She recoiled instinctively, shrieking, "That cannot be true!"

"Shockingly, it is."

Asami couldn't think what to say about that.

"Have I unnerved you?"

"A little," she admitted. She paused for a moment. "You'd really rather prefer to shoot people than talk to them?"

"No, no!" He waved his hands emphatically. "I'd prefer to do neither and sit in a nice quiet room by myself..."

"I think you might have chosen the wrong profession."

"Well, it doesn't bother me now..." He laughed half-heartedly, gesturing to his surroundings. "Sorry."

Asami dropped her gaze. "I'm not sure the avoiding thing is going to work, long-term," she said. "For starters, I can't work in the train car. I need space to spread out the notes—"

"You can go wherever you want—"

"I don't want to feel like I'm turfing you out."

"You're not! It's fine—"

"Perhaps it would help if we got to know each other a little better first?"

Beast cringed. "Twenty questions? Please no. I'm not very good at talking about myself."

"Me neither," Asami admitted. "In fact, this is probably the longest conversation I've had with a person outside of work since I moved here."

Beast tilted his head. "When *did* you move here?"

"Two years ago."

"Long time to go without speaking to anyone."

She raised an eyebrow. "Says the man who's spent three years underground."

"I'm not always alone," he admitted. "I have a friend who visits from time to time. And a few others…"

"Friends?"

"People I'm on friendly terms with."

"Why do they visit?"

Beast paused, as if this were not an easy thing to explain.

"It's all right," said Asami. "You don't have to tell me."

"Good," he said.

She looked at him sharply.

"I mean, um, because I'm not good at talking. Not because I don't want to Gears." He rubbed the back of his head. "I'm going to clean the kitchen and get something ready for dinner. Would you like to join me in a bit?"

Asami smiled. "I'd love to."

Thirty minutes later, she entered the kitchen to find Beast madly scrubbing the floor, a pot of overcooked beans burning on the stove. She sighed, removing them from the heat, and he spun around, brandishing the mop like he intended to run her through with it.

"Ah! You're here!"

"Here and *hungry*," she said, staring at the remains of the pot. "Would you like some help?"

"I was just... having a quick clean."

"You don't have to..." She looked around at the discarded tins, the dirty cutlery, the grime, inches thick. "Wait, no, you do. This place is *disgusting*."

He scratched the back of his neck. "I wasn't expecting company."

"I've been here a couple of days now."

"Honestly," he said, "I was expecting you to change your mind."

"I so rarely do," she replied, turning back to the beans. "Can I make dinner?"

"You can cook?"

"More than burnt beans."

At this, he laughed. "The supply room is next door. Help yourself."

Asami nodded, and went to raid the tins. She found another can of beans, some tomato soup, and a small supply of herbs and seasonings she could definitely make something from. Most of these were army issue, but the spices weren't. Someone had given them to him, someone with money.

She put the thought aside. It was one more mystery that would have to wait.

Back in the kitchen, Beast still cleaning madly around her, she added the ingredients together and put them over the stove to simmer. She sliced a few pieces of bread and toasted them, taking care not to burn herself. She'd ruined far too many clothes standing too close to the stovetop, and had a series of tiny burn scars on her wrists, mostly shrivelled up over the years.

Sakura used to call her a liability in the kitchen, but what she lacked in dexterity, she made up for in ability.

"Where did you get the bread?" she asked, wrapping up the remainder of the loaf.

"The outer ring market," Beast said, not looking up. "Sometimes I sneak up there for fresh supplies."

"The outer ring?"

"Easier to blend in, there."

"How do you pay for it?"

"I don't."

Asami drew back. "Do you steal from the poor?"

"No," he said, looking mildly affronted, "I steal from the middle-ring merchants who go there to exploit them. Or trade with the others, when I can." He paused, setting the mop aside. His next words were quiet and steady. "There will be consequences to what we do. Decoding Mortimer's notes. Going public. I'm not saying we should call it off. I'm just saying we should prepare for the inevitable anarchy and discord it'll cause."

"We?"

"Well, obviously I'll be helping you."

"Thank you."

"Let me know what you need."

She smiled, and he returned it. He cast his gaze over to the saucepan, and the ingredients surrounding it.

"What are you making?"

"A lightly spiced tomato-bean stew."

"Oh, you really *can* cook!"

"Cooking is just chemistry! And I'm really, *really* good at chemistry."

"What aren't you good at?"

"Anything physical. I have appalling hand-eye coordination. I'm very clumsy anywhere that isn't my lab."

"Endearing clumsy or threat to safety clumsy?"

"Threat to safety, definitely."

He almost smiled at that, and Asami moved past him, returning to the pot before it could burn. She spread the concoction thickly over the slices of toast.

Beast and Pilot shuffled forward into the corridor to a small dining room. It was less messy than the rest of the base, but only from underuse. It was heavy with dust.

"I'll clean this room next," Beast insisted, brushing down the surface with his handkerchief.

Asami did her best to look unperturbed, and passed him his plate. He tore into it like a starving animal, without a care for manners or propriety.

"You mentioned the Rebellion, the other day," she said, in between delicate bites. "They're friends of yours?"

"For the most part."

"How did you meet?"

"By accident. There's a tunnel nearby they used to sneak into the city," he explained. His words started slow, but they quickly picked up pace. "We ran into each other when we were both running from the dread doctors. Helped each other out, have been allies since. I wouldn't call myself one of them, exactly; we trade. Supplies for my assistance, usually."

Asami wasn't sure if she approved, if she'd abandoned every rule of her old life so quickly, but she was certainly curious. The rebels lived in the Outlands beyond the city borders, a place supposedly inhospitable. They must have lived underground, or had masks to help them breathe through the poisonous air.

"Why don't they help you?" she asked. "With exposing the government, I mean."

"They are, or they will. Their resources are limited."

"Have... have you ever been to the Outlands?"

"What?"

"I was just thinking, as a soldier, you must have been outside the city. What's it like out there?"

Beast paused for a moment, as if collecting his words. "Sparse. Bare. Barren."

"That much I know. Tell me more. Give me... details. Please."

"Details?" He shrugged. "There's some ruins halfway across the desert, remnants of a time long since past... there's an old church there. Little about the place has endured, but some of the walls are still painted, some old saint rendered by an ancient hand, artist forgotten, saint forgotten... but the image remains. It's been years since I saw it and I still can't scrub it from my mind."

Asami's mind drew pictures from his words, and for a moment she forgot to speak entirely.

"What is it?" He frowned at her.

"It sounds... strangely beautiful."

"Parts of it," he agreed. "There's beauty to be found in most places."

"Most?"

"Not all." He shoved another piece of toast in his mouth. "This is excellent, by the way. Best meal I've had in a long time."

She smiled, and decided against asking him about Sparta, and other things he might have seen outside the Dome.

"I'm happy to do most of the cooking, if we're going to be together for a while," she said. "But I may forget. I have a tendency to get absorbed in my work."

"I'll bear that in mind."

Shortly afterwards, Pilot went for Asami's toast, and Beast had to wrestle him away. Dinner over, he took the plates back to the kitchen, Asami made herself a cup of strong tea, and went back to the carriage to move her notes to the lab.

Tomorrow, the real work began.

The first order of the day was to try and get the *notes* in the right order. Some of them were dated, which helped, but so many pages merely ran on from the next it was difficult to tell where they belonged. There were about fifty pages, all in all, and she spread them all out around her, trying to make heads or tails of them. It involved a lot of reading and re-reading, and trying not to get too carried away with the formulas on one page while she was trying to focus on the order.

She wished she'd been able to grab all of them, but it was pointless going back now. Malcolm would have cleared the place out.

She tried not to think about what he could do, even with the handful he'd been left with. It was a thought that gave way to too much darkness.

Sometime later, after minutes and hours had trickled together, Beast came to find her.

"When you said you might forget about mealtimes," he said, placing a plate of crackers beside her, "I didn't think you'd forget so *soon.*"

Asami looked up. "It's lunchtime?"

"Passed two."

"Oh."

Beast shook his head, staring down at her neat piles. "I don't understand much of this stuff, but do you at least have an idea of where you're going with it?"

"I think so," she said, taking one of the crackers. "But I do need a break." Her eyes circled round the rest of the lab. Somehow, Beast seemed to have cleaned the entire place without her noticing. Wires were neatly roped together, crates and boxes neatly stacked, the dashboard dusted and sparkling.

"You're really good at cleaning," she said, somewhat dumbly.

"Of course I am," he returned. "I'm military."

She didn't ask why he'd let it fall into such a state in the absence of any company; the answer was right there in the question. After so long on your own, almost everything started to seem pointless.

Later that day, he gave her a box of large, crisp shirts, freshly laundered. "I don't have anything in your size, alas, but I think these shirts should be large enough to use as dresses when you desire a change."

"I would indeed," she said, lifting one from the box. It almost reached her knees. "Thank you."

She returned to the lab the following morning, wearing one of his shirts belted at the waist, sleeves rolled up to the elbows. It displayed a little more leg than she was usually comfortable with, but there was nothing to be done about it. Beast continued with his cleaning, giving her a wide berth. Pilot shunted in and out of the room, and kept her company when she returned to the kitchen to make good on her promise to cook. She mixed a couple of rations together and added some dried herbs to spruce it up. For the first time in a long while, she felt a little homesick, thinking of Toulouse, of the small courtyard garden of her childhood that smelled of rosemary and lavender in the summer, of her mother singing trilly as she cooked, of her father dancing with her in the kitchen. She could hear the scritch-scratch of her sister's pen at the table, the rustle of paper.

She tried to put it out of her mind, and not wonder if those days were gone for good. Her family had known it might be a long time until they saw her again when she moved to Petragrad, the travel being so expensive. But not one of them had ever thought that it would be forever.

"This is really good," said Beast as he dug into the meal.

"*Scienced,*" she said, and hid her thoughts behind a smile.

Beast cleaned up dinner while she returned to the lab, working until she was exhausted. She ran herself a bath, scrubbed herself raw with the soap, and cleaned her undergarments so thoroughly she was surprised she didn't rip them. She towelled herself down and pulled on one of the loosest shirts.

She headed back to the carriage.

A little while later, there was a knock on the door. "Asami? Do you have everything you need?"

She headed to the door to answer him. "I'm fine, thank you."

His eyes widened at the state of her undress, a hand going up to his hair. She caught his wrist; his palms were red and blistering.

"Your hands!"

"Ah, yes," he said awkwardly. "I might have been a little overzealous with the cleaning."

"Let me help you—"

"They're fine."

"I'll be the judge of that. I am a doctor, after all."

"Not *that* kind of doctor."

"No, just a smart one."

She steered him into the carriage and sat him down on the bed, which groaned under his weight. She'd located a medical kit earlier, and quickly started to dab with a clean rag and some antiseptic. Beast winced.

"Sorry," she said. "I can't believe you continued to clean with hands like this…"

"I can't believe you missed lunch."

She snorted softly, moving onto the second hand. The skin was tougher here, but still torn beneath the malformations. She could feel his eyes shifting away from her as she worked, as if it were too much to watch her touch him.

"Anything I can say to make you more comfortable?" she asked.

"Not really, no."

"I'll be as quick as I can."

"Thank you."

A minute or two passed by as she cleaned out the wounds.

"I heal fast," he said abruptly. "Happy side-effect, or one of the parts of the serum that actually worked. That's why I don't usually bother with minor wounds."

"Can you still feel pain?"

"Yes," he said slowly.

"Then you should bother." She finished doctoring the blisters, standing up to dispose of the rags and tidying the rest of the equipment. "I'm all done. I release you. You are no longer my prisoner."

Beast smiled, touching his wounds gingerly. "I'm not sure I'd mind being *your* prisoner."

Asami giggled, a sound that quite startled herself. She wasn't sure of the last time she *giggled* at someone, with a faint prickle in her cheeks. "My, Beast, we just met!"

Beast looked down, face flushed. "I'm sorry. I'm just... out of practise with socialisation. I won't... I'm sorry." He got up, inching towards the door. "I'll see you in the morning."

"You don't have to—"

But he was already gone.

6
GRINDING THE GEARS

While her mother and Sakura had been very accepting of her decision to move to Petragrad (despite the latter's initial remarks) her father was a little less understanding. He didn't say anything, of course. He didn't want to be unsupportive. But Asami could sense the quiet in him whenever the topic came up, the voluminous, silent unease.

She knew because she was exactly the same.

"Papa," she said one evening, three weeks before her departure, "it's OK to be nervous. I am too."

"Yes, but you are nervous for smart reasons, and I am nervous for silly ones."

Asami blinked, waiting for him to explain.

"I mean, obviously Petragrad is very large and industrious and they've got that whole murdering-their-king rebellion going on—"

"Papa…"

"But I trust you to stay out of that. I just… I don't like how far away you're going to be."

Asami's throat tightened. Her family wasn't exactly the emotional type (discounting the mild anxiety she and her father shared) and it was rare for any of them to be so up-front. She tucked herself under his chin, wrapping her arms around his waist like she'd done as a little girl, and breathed in the scent of coffee and peppermint. Papa. Home.

"I'll be fine," she told him.

He hugged her fiercely. "I might not be." He sighed, long and weighted, with a thousand other thoughts and fears she knew he wouldn't give voice to. "You're a good girl, Asami. You'll be fine. It's the rest of us I'm worried about."

Tears dusted her eyes that morning when she woke, stinging with the memory of her father's words. She got dressed quickly, keeping her eyes down over breakfast.

"Are you all right?" Beast asked her.

"I'm fine," she answered. She disliked the bitterness of the lie on her tongue, but she also didn't want to speak about her family, or even burden him with the festering mess of emotions inside her. "Is that tea?" she said instead, looking at the mug on the side.

"Only the finest for my Toulousian houseguest."

She took a sip, wincing.

"I may have been exaggerating the 'finest' part."

His words pulled out a smile. "How do you take yours?" she asked.

"Tea? No. Coffee. Black, with a teaspoon of sugar."

She shuddered, whilst thinking subconsciously of her father, who, despite being Touslousian, much preferred coffee to tea. Her mother would tease him about it mercilessly.

"What's your way of taking it?" Beast asked.

"Oh... don't laugh."

"I promise nothing."

"I like Earl Grey. Made with freshly drawn cold water boiled at 206°F, poured into a heated porcelain teapot and left to steep for four minutes precisely, strained into a teacup and flavoured with a quarter of lemon and two teaspoons of sugar."

Beast blinked. "You're going to need to write that down; no one will ever remember it."

"No one's ever made it for me before."

"No one?" He raised his single working eyebrow.

"Well, no one except my family."

He chewed his bottom lip, as if debating whether or not to ask about them. "I think we have some Earl Grey in the store room, you know," he said. "We've no lemons, but I'm sure we can find you something else. Let me have a look."

Before Beast could move, Pilot gave a sudden lurch and crunched against the floor. He looked up at them both, lamp-like eyes wide in surprise, before turning his neck to face his rear. One of his back legs was bent backwards.

"Gears," Beast hissed. "I've been meaning to take a look at that... Stay there, boy, I'll be right back."

Asami slid to the floor and patted Pilot's head. He didn't seem to be in any kind of distress, but it seemed the thing to do. She'd had a clockwork nightingale once, but its primary function was a glorified music box. Pilot was built as something else.

"You really are a lovely boy," she told him, and received another rough leather lick for her words.

Beast returned with a small toolbox, which he sat down between Asami and himself. He tugged out the leg gently, despite the unnecessariness of the softness, and inspected it.

"Could you hand me the spanner?" he asked, pointing at the box.

Asami opened it. It was meticulously organised, but half the tools looked the same to her. She passed over one of the long, thin items near the top.

Beast frowned as the object touched his palm. "That's a wrench."

"Is there a difference?"

"I thought you were smart?"

She narrowed her eyes. "And I thought you were kind."

Beast looked down guiltily, muttering an apology, and reached over to select the correct instrument. Asami went to take back the wrench, their fingers skimming hotly over the metal.

Beast dropped the tool. "Sorry," he said.

"No need to be," she said, plucking it up and handing it back to him.

How long had it been since she'd touched another person's hand, not out of necessity, but something more?

How long had it been for him?

"You don't need to help," Beast reminded her.

"And if I want to?"

His cheek twitched, not unpleasantly. "If you want to," he said, "I suggest you start by learning the difference between a spanner and a wrench."

Beau was not sure what to make of Asami Thorne, wasn't sure he knew her well enough to sum her up in words, or even if he enjoyed having her with him at all. He'd never lived with a woman in such close quarters, or at least, not someone he hadn't had a professional relationship with. Some of his squadron were female, but living together in the barracks or out on missions was completely different from sharing a space, just the two of them.

Asami literally slept in his bed. Not with him in it, admittedly. He'd given her fresh sheets the day after she arrived, and completely forgotten to come up with an alternative arrangement for himself for several nights running. In the back of his head, he'd been waiting for her to leave. Waiting for her to grow tired of darkness, or him.

But so far, nothing.

He wasn't used to the weight of her gaze, the strange breeziness of it, even when he'd first taken down his hood. Even Snowdrop, hard and unflappable though she was, had flinched, and he'd seen her weighing up whether or not to attack when they first met.

He helped out in the outer ring from time to time, pilfering supplies, giving them what he didn't need. He'd be-friended a few people, but even the kindest could be cruel with a look.

Asami hadn't been. Not a waver of a recoil when she saw him. It probably helped that she'd already seen the images of his comrades beforehand. Maybe she was just better pre-pared.

The photos. Nausea coiled in his belly at the thought of them.

He didn't have any photos of his team. Asami did. Photos he never wanted to see, faces he would never forget.

"Are you all right?" Asami looked up from her work, eyes large behind her glasses. They were warm and rich and bright, and he swore there were little chinks and flecks of honey and amber in them, though that may have just been the light.

Beau realised he was still staring. "Sorry," he said. "Just... thinking."

"Want to share?"

"Ah, no..." He got up abruptly, made an excuse about having something to clean, and went next door to the gym. Ash had helped him set it up not long after Mortimer found the place for him. Initially, it was a way of getting back into shape after weeks of lying on a bed, but Beau suspected Ash had encouraged the activity to convince him his body wasn't as ravaged as he thought. That it was still his.

He was right, of course. Beau's left shoulder and arm didn't move as they used to, and exercise had barely had an impact on their flexibility, but he was stronger than ever.

Too strong. He'd broken half of the equipment when getting used to his strength.

"You don't need to do this," he'd told Ash once as he helped him rehang the punchbag.

Ash, struggling to look casual in his ruffled shirt with the sleeves rolled up, crossed his arms, pouting. "And what if I want to?"

"Aren't you supposed to be at home right now?"

Ash clapped his hand dramatically over his chest. "And what if *you're* my home, dear Beaumont?"

Beau groaned at the ridiculousness of Ash's actions. "You can still call me Beast, you know."

Ash dropped his hands, his eyes finding somewhere else to rest. "It seems wrong, now."

"I don't mind. A name's a name."

His squad had given him that nickname after witnessing him in a fistfight. They'd previously found him quiet and reserved, not one to "rage out" as Jon had called it.

"Gent in the sheets, beast in the streets!" Sarah had announced, which made him blush ridiculously. Sarah had no idea what he was like in the bedroom, and never would. She was only teasing.

Ash had adopted the nickname too, after he'd met them. It made him more one of them, despite the difference in station and lifestyle. If he stopped calling him that now, if the name slipped away...

It threaded him to them, even now.

And Beau suited him even less.

"Please," he said to Ash, "Still call me Beast."

Ash nodded, seeming to understand, and gestured for Beau to come forward and test the new equipment.

"You can't stay here forever," he told Ash.

"Obviously not. But whenever I can be, I'll be here."

Ash was true to his word, visiting whenever he could. Sometimes political duties took him away from Petragrad, and it could be months between seeing him, but whenever he was in town, he came. And whenever he came, years evaporated, and Beau forgot he was different, forgot what had happened, and just for a moment felt like the man he had been.

It was a little like that with Asami, and the neutrality of her glances. She made Beau feel like the awkward boy at the school dance, wondering whether or not he should ask the pretty girl to dance.

He groaned, giving up on the punchbag, and went to raid the cupboards for tea.

7

WORKING IN THE RAILROAD

For three days, Asami worked on Mortimer's notes, ordering them, deciphering them, and trying to fill in the gaps. Beast skirted around her all this time, bringing her food when she forgot and cups of mediocre but well-meaning tea. He spent most of his free time swabbing the abandoned platform and scrubbing the tiles with a toothbrush. He took a trip up to the surface at one point to refresh their supplies, and came back with pilfered toiletries for her. Although against stealing in principle, Asami was willing to loosen her morals slightly for the sake of spare underwear, and reasoned that she was doing the public a favour with her investigation and therefore deserved it.

"I... may have taken the liberty of procuring you this, as well," he said, dropping a slightly squished lemon in front of her.

"Where did you—"

"Think nothing of it," he insisted, and slouched off before her mind could fully process the gesture.

Occasionally, Beast would settle into his big chair beside the dashboard. She quite enjoyed having him there, it was like having a colleague, and sometimes she'd break from her work to watch the world above on his screens, the images of the markets, the silvers of the shops, the trees on the boulevards.

"I miss the sun," she admitted. "Fake though it was. And the park, too. I miss the park."

"I haven't been there in years," admitted Beast, staring wistfully at the narrow scrap of it on one of his screens. "Even before... this. I hadn't been for so long because it was always there. Because I didn't appreciate it."

"I went every Sunday," she said. "But it was more out of habit. Never stopped to smell the roses." She sighed, fighting anything like a lump rising in her throat. "Something to look forward to when I've sorted all of this out."

She tried not to think about how long that would take, or what the next step would be after deciphering the notes, or all the dozens of things that could go wrong.

One step at a time, her mother used to say, guiding her through her school work. *Follow the sum until it leads you to the correct answer.*

Yes, Mama, she whispered inwardly, and for a moment, recalled her like one might the dead, like some vast uncrossable plain had stretched out between the two of them.

It had been so long, and she was so far away. Everything she loved was.

She turned her mind back to her work, and blotted everything else out, trying to ignore the wriggling feeling under her skin, like the dark had pincers.

A short while later, she looked up to find Beast's eyes still on her.

"Is there something the matter?" she asked.

"I'm trying to work out how you're still so calm."

"I'm calm?" said Asami, twisting the end of her braid.

"Well, you haven't fallen to pieces yet, which is pretty good going."

She shook her head. "I have work to do."

"I cried for about three days straight when I first came down here," he admitted. "And not because of… you know. It was losing everything, knowing I could be trapped down here for the rest of my life."

"Well, I'm *not* going to be trapped down here forever. And neither are you."

"It's all right to miss things anyway."

Asami swallowed, trying not to think of that, trying not to fixate on the small things. The big things, like her family, were always there, constant and loud. But the little things, like scented soap, feather beds, flowers and fresh tea and sunshiney evenings at the cafe on the corner by her apartment… those only scratched at her if she let them.

"Material goods don't matter," she said in response.

Beast sighed. "If only that were true."

*

The next day, Beast caught her muttering to herself as she crossed out another page of her own calculations.

"Need to talk it out?" he offered.

"The missing notes," she replied, still staring at them. "In some cases, I can fill in a trajectory, based on whatever happens next, but not if the next page was actually the results. Then I'm going in blind—"

"What do you need?"

"I'm going to need some rats," she said. "Quite a lot of them. I could try and design a trap, but—"

He shook his head. "Don't worry. I got you. Anything else?"

"A complicated list of chemicals and equipment?"

He snorted. "Write a list. We'll work something out." He placed a plate beside her. "In the meantime, eat something."

She did a mock salute, still not looking up. "Sir, yes, sir!"

Asami didn't particularly like the idea of using rats or any other animals, and she patted the mechanical hound as if he could absolve her guilt. Unfortunately, it was a necessary step, and it gave Beast something to do, although he held off collecting any whilst she wrote her list. Some could be stolen from stores and warehouses, but others were going to be trickier.

"I have a contact inside the palace," Beast assured her when she voiced her worries over dinner. "It'll take some time, but we'll get there."

"He'll need to have high-level clearance—"

"He's resourceful. He'll find a way. Have patience."

Asami usually understood that some things took time, that they could not be rushed, but that calm, rational side of her was having trouble staying afloat in the sea of... everything else. "How do you do it?" she asked.

He paused in the act of shovelling food in his mouth,

sauce dribbling down his lumpy chin. "Do what?"

"Stay calm and patient after… after everything."

"Well, I've spent three years like this, it isn't hard to be patient for a bit longer."

"How have you not gone a bit crazy in all that time?"

He grinned, wiping off the sauce. "I work out a lot."

"I noticed."

Beast paused.

"I mean, um, the gym. I noticed the gym. I haven't noticed anything about your, er… anything else. Because of the clothes. I'm sure you're more than… fine. Underneath." The hotness in her cheeks was painful. She stood up abruptly. "Um. I'm getting dessert now."

She unwrapped the sponge pudding steaming on the stove, a tinned monstrosity so thick with syrup it made her teeth ache. Beast devoured the whole thing noisily, in a manner that would have made her prim, mild-mannered parents recoil. She missed the light, dainty pastries of Toulouse, and dreamed of fresh cream as she helped him clean the dishes.

He winced as he passed her a plate.

"Something wrong?"

"Slight twinge in my shoulder."

"Here, let me—" She moved to his side, but he pulled away from her.

"It's fine," he insisted. "I just slept on it funny."

A sudden thought occurred to her. They'd planned to renew the sleeping arrangements after her first night, but they'd never gotten around to it. "Where… where have you been sleeping?"

"Um, my chair," he admitted guiltily. "I've been meaning to make a second bed since you'll be here for a while, but I keep getting distracted..."

"You can't sleep in your chair! You'll give yourself all sort of problems—"

"It's fine."

"Well, let me sleep in it tonight—"

"No!"

"That's because it's *not* fine, and well you know it!"

Beast sighed. "All right, I'll get started on another bunk tomorrow."

"And tonight?"

"What about it?"

"Where will you sleep tonight?"

"One more night on the chair won't do me any harm."

Asami narrowed her eyes. "It's clearly already done you some harm. No, I insist you take the bed. Doctor's orders."

"But... where will you sleep?"

"As I'm banned from the chair too, I suppose we'll have to share."

Beast's good eye widened, even the bad one straining incredulously against the weight of the meshed muscle.

"What? It's a very large bed. Plenty of blankets; we won't have to share anything. It'll be like we're sleeping in two entirely different beds. You must have had female comrades. I visited the barracks, once. Those quarters are *close*."

"Yes, but most of my comrades weren't..."

"Weren't what? Tiny, dainty little creatures?"

"I mean... yes, but—"

"Don't worry, Beaumont, I assure you that you shan't squish me in the night."

He chewed his lip, and she observed the way his shoulder twitched, the discomfort trying to convince him. "All right," he said. "But just for a night. I'll make up another bed tomorrow."

Satisfied, Asami went to remake the bed for two while he finished cleaning, undressing before he could arrive. They'd had dinner awfully late, her being lost to work again.

Sliding under the covers, she wondered if she'd made a mistake. The bed *was* large, but there was an intimacy to the action she hadn't fully considered when she'd suggested it.

You've shared beds with men before, she reminded herself. *You've had sleepovers with friends before. This is just... something between the two.*

But it had been a long time since she'd done either, and it must have been a long time for him, too.

He entered the carriage before she could think of a way out of it, his eyes widening as he saw her under the covers.

"Could you... Could I have the left side, please?"

Asami didn't ask why. Either he wanted that side because it was closest to the door in case of an intruder, or it was easier to sleep on that side, or it was because he didn't want to have her face his bad side. It seemed far too personal to ask.

"Of course." She shuffled over, turning her back as he stripped off his extra clothing and slid under the blankets she'd vacated. When she turned back, he'd folded his arms over the covers. The one facing her was roped with muscle. Hardly surprising, given his history. She tried to glance at the other; it was less distracting.

This bed sharing had been a terrible idea.

"I feel like we haven't talked a lot, despite our close proximity these past few days," he started, breaking the gathering silence.

"Sorry. Working."

"You don't have to apologise," he said, "but I feel we must talk about something or the awkwardness will only grow."

"Fair enough," she responded. "Beaumont. That name is Toulousian, but you're not, are you?"

"What gave it away?" he said, with half a crooked smile. "No accent?"

"*I* don't have an accent. Or much of one. It's not very strong—"

She'd gone to Toulouse's International Academy, the second finest school in the kingdom. All the students had been encouraged to adopt a "neutral" accent to help them get by in the highest circles of society. It had helped her adapt to life in Petragrad slightly, but in hindsight she felt it had rubbed away at the thin slivers of her culture, leaving little behind but a love of fine food and a tendency to drink excessive amounts of fancy tea.

"I like it," Beast interrupted. "Your voice. Your accent. Whichever. Both. It's… soft."

"You haven't complimented a woman in a long time, have you?"

"I have not."

Asami smiled, rolling onto her front. "So, the Toulousian name?"

"My mother was Toulousian."

"Was?"

"She died when I was fourteen."

"I'm sorry." She paused. "Were you close?"

"Yes. Very. And my father... he was nicer when she was around. Not that he was awful, but he became... harder, afterwards. I joined the military because I thought it might make us closer but it wasn't for me, if I'm honest."

This made sense to her. She'd known a few soldiers from the palace, but Beast didn't remind her of them other than his immaculately kept boots (the only thing that *had* been immaculate when she'd arrived) and his approach to cleaning when the occasion called for it. She couldn't quite put her finger on how he was different, precisely, or if it was merely his awkwardness, but he rarely reminded her of a soldier.

"Tell me about your mother," she asked.

Something softened in Beast's features. "Her name was Marie d'Bellcourt. She had flaxen hair and eyes like mine. She loved to sing and read truly terrible poetry. She liked to paint but she wasn't brilliant; she said she didn't need to be, that you could enjoy something you'd never be perfect at, but... well, she also said one bad painting was one step closer to a good one. That she'd spend the rest of her life getting better if she could."

His eyes lit up when he spoke of her, in a way they never had before. If there was pain, it was buried beneath love and admiration.

"How did she die?"

Beast swallowed. "Spartan bombing. I was in school at the

time."

Asami sucked in a shallow breath, imagining the suddenness of it, of having a mother one minute and not the next. She would prefer to have some warning, she thought, some time to treasure with them, prepare herself.

"Tell me of your family," he asked, severing the silence.

Asami knew it was only fair, and maybe... maybe it wouldn't be awful to talk about them. "Well, my mother is called Mina Sato. She is incredibly prim and proper—"

"Oh, not like you at all."

Asami scowled. "I like order, but Mama is... something else. There's an elegance to everything she does, from setting the table to drinking tea. She's so refined and sharp. She's a master tactician, but she has a great respect and admiration for the arts. That's how she fell in love with my father. He's a violinist."

"Any good?"

"Exceptional. He's played for the royal family. Alas, I have not inherited his musical talent, but my sister has. Sakura. She's a musical prodigy."

"Are you close?"

"I love her, but there's ten years between the two of us, so sometimes it feels like she was barely a person before I left to study."

He paused. "How old are you?"

"Twenty-four."

The pause stretched out for longer.

"What is it?"

"I'm just realising how exceptionally young that is for

someone of your skill."

It was much more of a compliment than the usual, 'you're too young to be a doctor.' Asami felt her cheeks heat. "I left home at sixteen to study. Achieved my doctorate at twenty-two. Second youngest to ever qualify."

"I bet you're really annoyed you're not the first."

"*Really* annoyed."

Beast laughed, and she laughed with him. A simple thing, the sharing of laughter, and yet it flickered against her chest. It had been a long time since she'd joked with anyone.

"How old are you?" she asked.

"Twenty-five."

"When did you join the military?"

"Seventeen."

"That's a long time to do something you hated."

"I didn't hate it all. Not to begin with. Not all of it, ever, really."

She rolled onto her side. "What parts did you like?

His chest heaved, sucking in a breath. A moment passed before he spoke again. "I liked the other soldiers and the sense of camaraderie. I didn't like the orders. The fighting. The... killing." A sigh slipped out of him, and his jaw tightened. "I would have been happier at home, tinkering with my wires and gears, finding out how things worked."

"Wires and gears?" She frowned. "Like... inventing?"

"More computers," he explained. "I'm quite good with them."

His family must have been very high up or influential to have access to that kind of technology, but that didn't seem to matter right now. Asami smiled. "Closet nerd."

"I guess."

"I like nerds."

The flash of a grin.

"If… if you ever want to talk about the things they made you do, I won't judge."

"That's the thing," he said. "They didn't *make* us do anything. I could have left at any time. So *I* judge myself. I judge myself for my misdeeds, no matter what anyone else thinks."

"Beast?"

"Yes?"

"Do you think you deserve this?"

A quietness settled between the two. "Yes," he said eventually. "I do."

Asami paused, gripped by his confession, the quiet tremble in his words. How could anyone have deserved *this*? Losing their comrades, surviving the thing that killed them, and being scarred forever by it? Having a freedom that others took for granted stripped from you?

Maybe he didn't stay down in the dark because of just his face.

And yet… he hadn't completely lost himself to that darkness, when many would not have blamed him.

She leaned across and kissed his cheek, lingering there for longer than she meant to.

"What was that for?"

"Because I don't agree, and I wanted you to know it. I think you've deserved very little of the bad luck you've received in life."

"Says the woman single-handedly trying to take down the government who tried to have her killed for whistleblowing."

Asami grinned, her eyes falling to his hand. She wanted to push her own along his palm until their fingers were linked together, but she didn't quite dare. The kiss on the cheek had been fleeting, easy to pull away from. Hands were harder to untangle.

It was *all* becoming hard to untangle.

"Not *quite* single-handedly, lovely Beast," she said, and watched the ghost of another smile dust that pale cheek of his. From this angle, it was easy to see what he once would have looked like, easy to mirror that half of him. Even in the low light, she could pick out the green flecks in his cerulean eye, the shimmer of his gaze.

No wonder he'd wanted the left side of the bed.

"I think I'm ready for sleep, now," she said, ignoring the slow tingle drifting inside of her.

"Me too." He rolled over. Pressed against the mattress, there was little knotted flesh, his misshapen shoulder barely noticeable. It was a good, strong back, the sort she wanted to reach out and touch.

What was wrong with her? She wasn't usually so easily swayed by a little muscle. Indeed, her past lovers tended to be slim, intellectual types, like herself.

And yet something in her stirred at the ripple of his skin, a hotness flushing through her, a dryness to her mouth.

Get a hold of yourself.

"Asami?"

She almost bolted in her spot, as if he could read minds. "Yes?"

"How *did* you know I wasn't Toulousian?"

"Your manners."

Beast laughed. "Goodnight, Asami."

"Good night, Beast."

8
RENOVATIONS IN THE RAILCAR

The next morning when Asami woke, Beast was gone, but there was the quiet rumble of someone moving in the next carriage. The door had been removed a while back, leaving nothing to separate it from its twin.

She pulled on her clothes and went to join him. He was moving boxes around and measuring a space between seats.

"Thought I'd get started on that bed this morning," he announced when he saw her.

"Why? Does your bunkmate snore?"

Beast glanced up. "No, no, it's not that. You're wonderful. I mean, um—"

"Relax, Beast. I'm teasing. You're right, we can't share forever." She helped him manoeuvre a box onto the other side of the car. "Can I help, at all?"

"How good are you at welding?"

"Um…"

"Hammering?"

"I understand the physics of it…"

He grinned. "Pass me that measuring tape over there."

They spent the morning figuring out the logistics of it, and then Beast sawed out the pieces while Asami made lunch. Afterwards, he asked for her assistance in holding the pieces while he welded and hammered. At one point, Asami asked to have a go herself, but quickly gave up after accidentally striking him in the thumb.

"Gears!" he swore, shaking his hand, "that's my good one, too!"

"I'm so sorry!"

"You're a liability!"

"I'm not very handsy..."

He stuck his thumb in his misshapen mouth. "To tell the truth, it's not my area of expertise, either." He shook the bed, which gave a little under the pressure.

"Really? But Pilot—"

"Is a bit rough around the edges, right?"

The dog, sitting patiently in the corner, gave something like a snort of annoyance.

"He was a gift," Beast continued. "I've fixed his outer parts a little myself over the years, but I've had to learn how to adapt everything myself, and it's not my proudest skillset." He tapped the bed. "Still, it'll do."

"I think it's perfect."

"You're only saying that because you hit my thumb and you feel bad."

"I am not!"

He shot her a smile. "Go back to your lab, Asami. Let me try and make this a bit more presentable."

Asami agreed, and headed back to her research.

By the time evening rolled around, the second car had been transformed. It was an orderly mess, but clearly a bedroom. Beast had hung curtains over the door and around the shoddy frame. He'd furnished it with pillows and blankets and built her a rudimentary bookcase. Two rolls of fabric stood in the corner, and a sewing machine at a desk created from a plank set across two chairs.

"In case you wanted to make yourself some more clothes," he suggested. "Or the bedding wasn't to your liking."

Asami, who liked everything matching and neat and organised, found she wasn't lying when she told him she loved it.

She loved his blush, too.

That night, she started on a new dress made of a fabric printed like a map, and read one of the books he'd left on her shelf. She wondered if he'd stolen it recently, or if some of the thumbprints were his own, if this book was a treasured companion he had gifted to her, and if that meant anything other than he was just being kind. She was, after all, the first person he'd spoken to in a long while. She'd probably be nice to *Malcolm* after all that isolation.

Well, maybe not Malcolm. But perhaps the kids at school who used to tease her.

Their new rooms being separated only by a curtain, she could hear him shifting around, and for a minute the intimacy of sound felt closer than they had been the night before.

"Are you all right?" he asked through the curtain.

Asami jumped. "I, er, how did you—"

"You've been standing in one spot for a long time."

She flung open the curtain. "How did you know that?"

He smiled, tapping his good ear. "Advanced hearing. Also training."

"Hmm…" she stepped into his car, curiosity piqued. "What else do you have?"

"Oh, the standard super-soldier skills. Slightly better eyesight. Strength. Stamina. Healing, as you know." He held up his unblemished hand. Asami appraised it carefully. "You're looking at me a bit oddly there, Doc."

"Sorry, resisting the urge to study you."

He put down his hand. "Please, resist. I've had quite enough probing for one lifetime."

"Sorry," she said, and her gaze circled up to his eyes.

He held it there, just for a moment. "You're all right, then?" he queried.

She nodded. "Just spacing out a little. Happens a lot."

"Right. Well. Goodnight, then."

"Yes," she said, inching back behind the curtain. "Goodnight."

*

She dreamt of an old memory, of her father designing pieces of music for his daughters. Sakura's was soft and bright and lovely, hers slow and serious. There were little bits where the rhythm would skip, "that's your mind, working" he'd said, his smile slight and sunny. She had a little of that smile, she knew, but mostly she took after her mother, pale-skinned and dark-eyed, with Yunasian features although tempered a bit by her father's genes. There were a lot of mixed cultures in Toulouse, especially in the International

Academy, but it was nice to see your face in other's. She'd liked sharing most of it with Sakura.

Sakura. Two years now since she had seen her. She'd just turned fourteen. Back at her apartment, her portrait sat in a gilded frame, a scrawny twelve-year-old, all elbows.

What did she look like now? What would she look like the next time Asami saw her?

She rose from slumber, unable to shake her thoughts. Attempting to be productive, she started unpicking one of the seams on Beast's donated shirts she was trying to turn into a nightdress. Quietly, so as not to wake him.

The level of darkness in the carriage was little different to that during the day. There was no false sun here to keep track of things, nothing but an endless, sweltering darkness, crawling under her skin.

She wanted sunlight, and the pictures on her nightstand, before she forgot either.

Something hot dripped onto the fabric in her lap. Rain? She glanced up at the ceiling, only to realise how ridiculous she was being.

Ridiculous. Foolish. Trapped.

And crying. Crying *hard*. Tears like vomit, streaming down her face.

She sobbed into the shirt.

Stop this, stop this, said a voice inside, but it reached her like a noise in a current, lost to everything else. *It's fine, it's fine, it's not forever—*

But what if it is?

Just focus on one thing at a—

But I can't.

They're fine, you're fine—

But I'm not.

"Asami?" Beau appeared in the doorway, rubbing his eyes. "What's wrong?"

"Oh!" she turned away sharply, hiding her face.

"Hey, it's all right," he said, stepping towards her. His hand brushed over her back, not quite touching. "Don't worry about it. Tell me."

"I miss my family," she sobbed. "I missed them before, and I miss them more, now. They're further away than ever. And the sun. I miss the sun, too. And I know it's silly and I should just be happy I'm alive and…"

"You don't have to be happy about having so little," he said softly, and this time, touched her back. "Honestly, when I first brought you down here, I thought you'd be shut up for days. Miserable forever, or until I could get you out of the city." He swallowed. "I was alarmed when you wanted to stay. But… I'm glad you did."

She sniffed. "Because I can help you."

"No," he said, his voice a ghost of a whisper. "Not because of that." He shook his head, leaning against the bed frame. "You get to miss your family. You get to miss whatever it is you want to miss."

She dabbed at her eyes. "What… what do you miss?"

He sighed. "Sun, like you said. Restaurants. Fresh coffee. The view from the palace. People." His throat bobbed. "I'm forgetting their faces, I think. My comrades. The ones who didn't make it. I can't remember if Sarah had blue eyes or grey, or if Mariah's scar was on the left side of her face or the right, and I can't quite remember the sound of Matteo's laugh. But I remember that he laughed more than any of us. I remember Jon's shocking puns, and Adam's sleight of hand; the way cards seemed to jump in his hands as if animated. Great cook, too. He used to take plants we'd find in the wild and flavour our food with them. The first time he did that, Jon panicked, certain he'd poisoned us all. We teased him about being frightened of plants after that, never lived it down."

Asami breathed carefully. "I'm scared I'll forget my family's faces."

Beast's eyes met hers again. "Some things fade, but the important things... those stay with you. Faces aren't memories. Faces aren't even people."

Asami stared at him, and the glassiness in his eyes, bluer and greener than she had ever seen them. "How do you do it?"

"What?"

"Keep going. Having lost all... all of that. It can't all just be exercise."

"I keep going badly," he admitted. "You've caught me at a rare good moment."

"It can't be that simple."

"Mostly I try to focus on what's still there," he said. "Half a decent body. The handful of friends I've made, the one I still have. And when that fails... I just tell myself how incredibly pissed off they'd be if I dared to let all that be in vain. Doesn't always work, though. Sometimes you just need to wallow."

Her fingers trembled, and she reached out towards him, towards his cheek. He buckled, flinching away from her. "It's all right," she said softly. "Faces aren't people."

He stilled, nodding, offering her silent permission, and her fingers slipped to the matted flesh of his left cheek, his swollen brow, the hard side of his mouth. "Studying me, Doctor?"

"Yes," she said, "but not your face."

People weren't faces. People weren't even really flesh. For all she admired the human body, its flaws and intricacies, its construction and secrets, people were made of something more than bone and blood and muscle. She hated not knowing *what* almost as much as she liked almost being able to see what precisely it was beneath Beast's flickering gaze.

He took her hands, laying them flat on top of his. Even his right dwarfed hers. "You have soft hands," he remarked.

"You have a…" She stopped, unsure of precisely what she was going to say. "I'm not sure *what* you have," she said, "but whatever it is, I like it."

The next morning, Beast wasn't in the adjoining cart. She found him in the main room instead, constructing what looked like a desk by laying a plank over some well-stacked boxes. Nearby were a series of smaller containers housing paper and pens.

"You made me a desk?"

Beast buckled, startled by her sudden appearance. Evidently he'd been far too focused on the task.

"Ah, yes, well, it seemed silly you sitting on the floor all the time... It's not really a desk. Just a bit of wood lying over—

"It's a desk, it's lovely, and so are you."

She slid into the seat he'd found for her and began to sort through her notes. He hung at her side, good cheek pink. The exercise, no doubt, or maybe it *was* due to her comment. It might not mean anything. She blushed at many a person she wasn't attracted to. Maybe she'd just made him uncomfortable.

"Should I leave you to it?" he asked. "I can always set up the desk in one of the store rooms if you'd prefer quiet. Properly convert it for you—"

"Don't be silly," she insisted. "Sit down. Do your own work. I actually quite like the sound of the keys; reminds me of the lab."

Beast shuffled towards his dashboard.

"Unless... I'm distracting you?"

He paused.

"Beast? Am I distracting you?"

"Nothing I'm doing is important enough that I mind it."

"Maybe I should—"

"No," he said. "Stay."

Of course he wanted her to stay. Of course after all the silence, any distraction would be welcome. It didn't have to mean anything.

Did she want it to?

Stop this, said a voice inside her that sounded suspiciously like her mother's. *You have a task to do. There is no time for anything else.*

All right, she told the voice, and turned back to her work.

Beau spent almost two hours in the gym pounding himself into exhaustion, trying to blot out thoughts and not doing a particularly decent job.

"Am I distracting you?" She'd asked.

Frequently, and with little reprieve.

This was hardly the first time Beau had found a woman attractive, and definitely not the first time he'd been nervous in front of one. But there was something... disarming about Asami. Something that crawled under his skin in a slightly more pleasant way than the dark used to when he first came down here.

He'd had a couple of girlfriends before. A school sweetheart which had run its course shortly before he joined the military, and a woman he'd dated a few years afterwards. Maintaining a relationship when he was hardly ever in the city, and although they'd tried for almost two years in total, it had eventually fizzled out too.

To be honest, it might not have lasted so long if he *had* been home. He was bound to have annoyed her with his bad habits sooner rather than later.

And he'd developed a lot more bad habits over the years, along with other, less desirable qualities.

He stopped punching the bag, stretching his fingers out in front of him, the left stiff and awkward as ever.

He was not built for someone like her. He was not built for anyone at all.

Beau gave up on the bag, the weights, the bench, everything. He'd worked up a fine sweat. He banged across to the bathroom, ignoring the mirror he'd broken in a fit not long after arriving. Ducking out of its glare was automatic, now.

Stripping off, he climbed into the tub and turned on the taps full blast. Voices screamed out with the water, probing and teasing.

"Looks like our little Beast has a crush!" Mariah, loud, hard, joking.

"Aww, how sweet!" Sarah.

"Going to make the beast with two backs?" Jon.

"Go on, Beast! Do it for us!" Matteo.

More voices, turning harder, crueler, each becoming more indistinguishable from the last.

"If I was alive, I'd make the most of it... pity you were the only one to survive."

"You don't deserve her. You don't deserve anyone."

"You could never make her happy."

"Worthless."

"Disgusting."

"Monster."

Beau ducked his head under the water, and started to scream.

Beast had been flitting in and out of the room all day, even forgetting to come and get Asami for lunch. When she grew hungry enough to notice, she went to find him. He wasn't in the kitchen or the gym, although the latter showed signs of being used recently. She turned back towards the kitchen just as the bathroom door opened, and he stepped out wearing nothing but a towel.

For a few seconds, they faced each other in stark, empty silence.

Then Beast turned sharply on his heels and dived back into the bathroom, slamming the door behind him.

"Beast—" Asami pressed the door.

"Don't come in!"

"I won't, I won't, I promise."

She kept her hand flat on the door, trying not to think about those few seconds, and all she had seen—all the knotted flesh and twisted skin, and the precise, unblemished muscles of his abdomen beneath. The scientist in her wanted to examine the imperfect join, the woman in her had a more sinful curiosity, but the human in her...

The human in her just wanted him to come out, to not be ashamed.

"No tail, then?" she said, she said quietly, pressed against the door.

"What?"

"A tail. You don't have one."

"Are you trying to be funny?"

"I thought I was succeeding."

Silence met her, thick and full. Perhaps she should just go somewhere else, let the awkwardness dispel on its own. But… she didn't want him to be alone with his thoughts any longer than he had to be. He had spent too long alone with them.

"I forgot you were here," Beast's voice came through the door, little more than a whisper.

"What?"

"I forgot you were here, when I got out of the bath. Just temporarily. I don't usually forget you're around. Although you do move very softly when you're not tripping over your own feet."

"Would you like me to wear a bell?"

Silence again.

"*Would* you?"

"I… I don't like being sneaked up on."

"I can announce my presence more loudly, if you like? Perhaps I can hum. I can't sing. That will be *much* worse, trust me."

A faint snort of laughter drifted through the door.

"I could strip, if you like. Partially. Even the score."

The silence thickened again, only for a moment. "That is not a fair comparison and you know it."

Asami chewed her lip, pulling on her sleeves. "You know, I really don't mind."

"Let me guess, *you don't see it.*"

"I do see it," she said, "I just don't care. I know that doesn't necessarily make it suddenly all right for you, but... you should know it. This is your home, and—"

"It could be your home, too."

Now it was Asami's turn to pause.

"I mean, I know it's not what you're used to, and it's not ideal, or what you want, but—"

"No," she said. "It isn't, but... thank you. I'd like it to be my home. Well, not as much as I want a comfortable apartment in the middle ring, but I'd like it nonetheless."

They lapsed into silence again, but softer than before.

"I'm going to get something together for lunch, now," she said brightly. "You can join me in a bit, if you like."

There was a non-committal murmur, and she turned her back to the door, making a loud show of entering the kitchen.

Fifteen minutes later, Beast joined her in the dining room. He was fully dressed again in his frayed waistcoat, dark trousers and fingerless gloves, although he'd rolled the sleeves up to the elbow, displaying the mottled red of his forearm. She said nothing about the slight adjustment to his wardrobe and slid a plate towards him. They chattered amiably before parting ways, and she returned to her research.

Her eyes wandered to a section of notes and photographs which detailed the patients' reactions to the serum. She hadn't read them before; they'd been dated and easy to place, not to mention difficult reading—she was in no mood to know the finer details of what had taken place there.

But Beast lived with the consequences of these words, bore them on his face and body, and she was a coward indeed if she let herself avoid them.

She took a careful, steady breath, and moved to the first entry.

Six hours after administration, none of the subjects appear to have experienced any side-effects. Ten out of twelve report feeling high levels of energy. All vitals normal.

Twenty-four hours after administration. All subjects experiencing increased strength and heightened senses. Blood pressure slightly elevated in eleven out of twelve.

Forty-eight hours after administration. Subjects' endurance has increased threefold. Malcolm's detailed report extremely promising. Her Majesty keen to widen distribution. Have advised further observation.

Fifty-two hours after administration. Subject seven is complaining of severe stomach cramps. Have supplied morphine. Two others complaining of nausea and headaches. Elevated heart rates in seven out of twelve.

Sixty hours after administration. Ten out of twelve have been hospitalised with a range of symptoms. Vomiting, severe pain, migraines. Red welts are beginning to appear on eight of the ten. Remaining two under observation.

Four days after administration. Patient eight in respiratory distress. Three others suffering from heart failure. Remaining two now hospitalised.

Five days AA. No. 9 died this morning of cardiac arrest. Two more remain in critical condition. Have applied for morphine; we ran out in the night. The welts have increased in mass, and now appear tumorous. Subject one is almost completely covered and cannot move.

One week AA. Three more have died. Four more in critical condition. The protrusions over the skin have resulted in blindness for one of the patients. Attempts to remove the masses have been unsuccessful.

Ten days AA. Only five of the patients remain alive. We have managed to stabilise four of them, but the malformations are extreme.

After that, Mortimer's notes slid into something else, less like a report and more like a diary. He'd stopped caring whether his notes were being viewed.

I sat beside patient three today. She asked to see her mother. No one knows what we have done here; Dome knows what their families have been told. Her stats not being good, I told her she was on her way. I told her anything and everything until her heart stopped beating. Her face was unrecognisable, but the only monster in that room was me.

What have we done?

Asami skipped over the next parts, detailing the painful ends of the rest of the subjects. Mortimer said nothing about how he had sprung Beaumont from the facility, or who had helped him, but there were detailed notes on how he managed to improve his condition.

And how Beast had begged for him to end him, to follow the rest of his comrades, not to leave him to live this way. He spoke of pain like fire inside him, of a darkness worse than death. He screamed for it, and many times Mortimer wondered if he shouldn't just give him what he asked for.

Though her eyes stung with tears, Asami wrote out the important information for her own records, and forced herself to continue.

Two months now since subject was exposed. Although he has improved significantly and appears to be in a stable condition, subject occasionally suffers from bouts of chronic pain that render him completely immobile. Morphine eases the symptoms somewhat, but there is presently no known cause or solution.

Asami's heart thudded. He hadn't mentioned anything about chronic pain—had it cleared up in the years between Mortimer's notes and the present? It seemed unlikely.

She remembered his response to her asking if the malformations pained him.

No, he'd said. *Not right now.*

Oh, Beast...

Somehow, he'd dragged himself out of that, but she wondered if the scar it left behind wasn't worse than everything else altered about him.

There was a quiet rap on the desk, and she looked up with a jolt. Beast was hovering over her, holding out a plate. The good side of his face was lit by a smile, and the other, the other full of hard, knotted flesh that couldn't move...

She saw both sides of him in a way so stark it was almost painful.

She leapt into his arms, throwing her arms around his neck and clinging to him like she might cling to a raft in a storm, fingers bunching in his clothes. Never in her life had she felt something like this before. It was more than guilt and anger and pity and horror. She felt like she was bleeding, that Mortimer's words had sliced across her chest, and Beast was the bandage, the only way of plugging up the wound.

Don't let me go. Don't ever let me go.

He froze at her contact. "Asami—"

"Don't say anything," she begged. "Just don't. Don't ask what I read. Don't ask what I *saw.* Just... let me hold you for a moment. Please."

He said nothing, but his arms slid around her back, pinning her closely to his chest.

9

A RUMBLE OF GRIEF

Despite coming from a prestigious military family, Beaumont had no wish to follow in the footsteps of his father and grandparents, no matter how much his aged grandmother barked over the dinner table that it was an obligation and an honour to serve their glorious kingdom. The United Nations had been formed some forty years beforehand, and all that talk of war and honour seemed superfluous during a time of peace.

Then there were whispers of unrest in the South, of Sparta expanding their territory.

Sparta was a kingdom Beau knew little about. His affluent relatives had plenty to say about Toulouse, Firenze, Navarra, Yunasia and Ismael. There were books in the school library on all of them. But Sparta was closed off, secretive, secular. They didn't allow visitors.

Beaumont hadn't asked many questions, but he knew it troubled his father and grandparents.

His mother told them all not to worry.

"Out of mind, out of sight," she'd say breezily. "Some

people just want to be left alone. I say we let them."

Beau couldn't remember if she'd said something differently the day she died. He couldn't remember much about the morning at all. His mind would scramble for details later, to remember exactly the shape of her smile, the sound of her laugh, the crinkle of the tablecloth in the manufactured breeze as they ate their final meal together.

He would remember nothing.

But he would remember the shudder of the bombing for as long as he lived, every other tremor he felt jolting a piece of him back to that day.

11:45am. History. Vlad Kostanov was flicking spitballs across the room, trying to hit their teacher on the back of his head. Beau didn't want to laugh, but he also didn't want to be left out.

So he laughed, even though he knew it was wrong, laughed with the others. Did as he thought he was supposed to.

He was laughing when the shudder crept through the classroom.

He was laughing when his mother died.

The bombing was far enough away that the rumble sounded more like distant thunder, but it rattled the walls of the room, just a fraction. No more than a group of people running loudly on the floor above might have done. The teacher spun round, glancing upwards, as if the answer would reveal itself.

"Odd," he said, and continued with the lesson.

A few minutes later, the screaming started on the streets,

the shouting, the yelling, the calling for aid.

Everyone abandoned their seats and raced to the windows. They could see nothing of the damage, nothing except civilians racing one way, and guards another.

A thin plume of smoke emanated from the shopping district, and Beau thought with a lurch of the gallery where his mother worked.

He started to run. He was not the only one. Half the class had family that had reason to be in that part of the city, half the class had lives that had just been obliterated.

Not that they all knew it at the time. At the time, there was just this deep, raw fear, this cold heat inside all of them as they hurtled towards the school gates and into the streets.

Not all of them kept running, not when they heard the screaming up close. You never forgot the first time you heard a real scream, one not born of minor fright, flimsy pain. In years to come, other details would go hazy, the images pixelated by grief. He would remember thin snippets; the smelling of smoke and burning flesh, the coppery tang of blood in the air, of stone and flesh meshed together.

But mostly, it was the screams he would remember. Screams of terror, like throats torn in two. Screams of pain, of bodies broken irreparably. And screams of grief, of hearts and families eviscerated in an instant.

He stood in the street, watching the chaos unfold, for a period of time he couldn't quite measure. None of his classmates had run on. All of them were standing by the gates still, as if waiting for it all to vanish. A few were crying.

Beau was the first to move. Maybe the only one. He ran towards the centre, not caring if it was dangerous, not thinking about whether or not the explosions had stopped. Not thinking about anything but his mother, and making sure she was fine.

Because she had to be. She had to be, didn't she?

Because if she wasn't... if she wasn't...

She couldn't be dead. She couldn't be.

He knew what the human body needed to survive, the vital organs required for survival. He was equally sure he couldn't survive without her, that she was some other, separate, inexplicable organ that he required for survival.

Mother, mother where are you?

He ran until he couldn't breathe, until his chest hurt, until his sides caved. Guards and soldiers swam around every street corner, expunging fires, pulling people from the wreckage. He knew some of them. Father's friends, subordinates.

"Ensel!" he yelled, recognising one of them. "Ensel, have you seen—"

Ensel turned to face him, his face losing all colour in seconds. He opened his mouth, his eyes darted instead to the end of the street, where a blockade had been set up around the gallery. Beau could see his father there, standing by the doors.

One of which had been blown off.

Along with the side of the building.

People were being carried out on stretchers, loaded onto transport, bandages and sheets staunched with blood. Some screamed, some moaned. Some were past all that.

Beau abandoned any hopes of his mother not being hurt, but he prayed she was just injured. So many others were. There was no reason for her to be—

"Father!"

His father turned with a slowness that would etch into Beau's heart, like the rusty turning of a clock.

He never had to speak the words, but the second his face settled on his son's, Beau knew. It was whiter than the sheet covering the body at his feet, and papered with agony.

He tried to speak his name, but Beau was screaming too hard to hear it.

10

WINE IN THE RAILS

Days bled together, their routine sliding into sync like clockwork. Asami missed a hundred things, but her new normal was not unpleasant. Having her own space to sleep and her own space to work helped. Having someone to talk to helped.

She liked her new room, crammed though it was. She liked the curtains and cushion covers she'd made for it, and the way her dresses hung from the rails. She liked spending mealtimes with company, biting her lip whenever Beast tried to modify his table manners for her.

She liked Beast, or Beau, as she had taken to calling him in her head. She wished they'd met in other circumstances, but she liked him nonetheless.

I wonder if we would have been friends if we'd met in the world above?

The barracks were next to the Imperial research facilities. They shared a cafeteria. She'd conversed with soldiers before, albeit briefly and with little to report.

She hadn't really paid them much attention, though,

thinking them more brawn than brain, with little to talk about.

Would *he* have looked at *her*?

"What are you thinking about?" he remarked over lunch.

"Whether you and I would have been friends if we'd met at work." It was nice to tell him the truth. How often in the last two years had she been so truthful with anyone, when every 'I'm fine' was dusted with dishonesty?

Beau smiled. "Doubtful. I was always very awkward around women who weren't fellow soldiers."

"You still are."

"Thanks, Asami," he said, looking down.

"I'm teasing," she said. "Sorry if I'm not doing it right. It's been a long time since I had anyone to tease."

"No friends above?"

"No *time* above, outside of work. There's a few back home, but... well, hard to tease through a letter."

He nodded, and a short silence passed between them. "Shall we have a drink tonight?"

Asami blinked, certain she'd misheard him. "A drink?"

Beast's face buckled, flushing in seconds, as if his words had been just as much of a shock to him as her. "I just thought, since you've been working so hard, it seemed like a nice way to end the day. If you don't want to—"

"No, I want to," she said. "It's just..."

"Do you not like to drink? It's wine, but I could find something else."

"I'm *Toulousian*. We love wine almost as much as we love tea. I just... never mind. Yes, wine, please."

He shot her a half-grin, and she was glad that the right side of his face had been spared, that he retained that crooked smile of his, that dimple.

She wondered if his other cheek had a dimple once, too.

"I'd offer to cook tonight to complete the gesture," he continued, "but I'm rather afraid that would backfire."

She smiled easily at this. "Let's have a sort of picnic dinner."

"What?"

"Let's roll out a rug and cushions and have dinner on the floor and watch something on your screens and drink wine and forget all our worries."

"I... only have the one bottle."

"Yeah, it won't take much for me. Find some pillows. I'll make dinner."

That night, they seated themselves on the floor of the lab, surrounded by more rugs and soft furnishings than was quite frankly necessary. They dined on tinned sardines, crackers, dried fruit, nuts, and flavoured rice balls.

"Sorry dinner's a bit eclectic tonight," Asami said, portioning out the rice balls onto the tin plates. "Picnic food is a bit hard to do with military rations."

"You're apologising for being able to make something palatable out of the supplies? I should be applauding your kitchen wizardry." He popped a rice ball into his mouth and grinned as well as he was able.

"Kitchen *science*," she insisted. "No magic, just logic."

"If you say so, Doc." He poured out the wine—a deep, luscious red in a faded bottle—into two chipped cups. It was a horrible way to drink wine, and she could see both her parents recoiling in her mind's eye.

Luckily, the warm, silky texture more than made up for the poor presentation. A soft murmur slithered out of her.

"It's good."

Beast necked it back like a stiff whiskey. "Hmm. Not bad."

Asami flinched. "Please, never do that again."

"What?"

"Wine needs to be *sipped*. Savoured. Enjoyed. You can't just swallow it!"

He caught her eyes, the readable part of his face simmering with something like mischief. "There's a dirty joke to be made there, but I'm not going to make it."

"Gross, Beast." She wasn't as disgusted as she made out. In fact, she quite liked this part of him, the funny, mischievous side. "When did you get so bold?"

"Military humour. It hasn't left me completely." He finished his drink in one long, steady gulp.

Asami narrowed her eyes. "I hate you." She took a careful sip, savouring the taste. For a moment, she longed for home, for her parents' smelling the wine before drinking, commenting on the subtle notes that Asami had never been able to distinguish.

"Mind go somewhere?" he asked.

"I miss my parents."

Beast stilled. "We... we could send them a letter," he told her. "It might be a bit dangerous. The government could be monitoring them, waiting for you to make contact. But if you just wanted to let them know you were safe—"

Asami shook her head. "How could I ever stop there?" There was also the chance, of course, communication between the kingdoms being generally poor, that they hadn't heard. That they were safer, happier, if she said nothing. Her throat tightened. "Isn't there anyone you miss from your old life?"

His jaw tensed. "Most of the people I miss are dead," he said. "But yes, there's one or two. It's just been a long time. It dulls, over time. The missing people. You don't notice it so much." He took another drink. "Let's think of something else to talk about."

"All right," she said. "What would you like to talk about? Childhood friends? Past lovers? Embarrassing memories?"

"Pass, on all."

"One of the people you miss isn't a lover, right?"

He raised his good eyebrow. "Why do you ask?"

"Just trying to get a picture of your life before."

His face fell, just a fraction, and he turned away from her. "It wasn't much of one, to be honest. I spent a lot of time at the barracks or outside the Dome, or travelling to the other kingdoms. I was rarely ever on leave, and when I did, I stayed with my father. I didn't have a place of my own. I lived for the day, the mission. I never thought more than a few weeks ahead. I was never lonely, never bored."

"This must have been quite the change."

"Quite."

"Why stay?" she asked. "Why not go to the Rebellion, if you're allies with them?"

"I don't know," he said, but with a twitch in his temple

that made her wonder if he was telling the exact truth. "What about you? What was your life before like?"

"Quiet," she told him. "But busy. I was never bored enough to be lonely, either."

He cocked his head. "And now?"

"Now..." *Now I have you.* "Now I still have the work, don't I?" she said instead. She took another long sip. "And your delightful company when that exhausts me."

"Ha! Glad I can offer some form of amusement."

Several, uttered her traitorous mind, and her gaze fell to his bare forearm and the parting of his shirt. Her mind flashed back to that moment in the corridor a few days ago, his naked chest. Her memory seemed to dispel the twisted flesh, creating something more like the body he might once have had...

Not that this one was terrible, clearly.

"Plenty," she said, and finished her cup. She held it out for a refill. "Tell me more of the other cities. I've only ever been to Toulouse and Petragrad."

Beast smiled, and told her everything. He told her of Navarra and Firenze, the two kingdoms known for their agriculture, where there were great fields and meadows and forests. He told her that the false sun there was warmer and thicker, that it made the grass gold. He described scents he had no words for, things she'd only dreamed of.

He spoke of the towering city of Yunasia, a place her mother talked of often, but with a freshness to his words not thinned by years. She had family over there, but they had never visited themselves, their stately grandparents little more than characters in a story, existing on paper and portrait. It was too far away, too expensive.

His words brought the buildings into their lab, unfurling glistening markets and fine foods.

He'd skirted Sparta, of course, but he spoke little of that, instead telling her of Ismael in the East, a land of spice and colour, and the cool, cold lands to the north, thick with ice and snow.

As he spoke, she drank, and ate, and drank some more, imbibing far more than she would usually and occasionally offering him what she hoped were witty remarks. She wasn't sure. He laughed, but she couldn't remember her words. There was definitely a "that's what she said," somewhere in there, and maybe a, "bet that's not the first time you've been told that."

Oh dear.

By the time he had finished, Asami had sunk to the floor, staring dreamily up at the ceiling as if she could spy stars.

"You all right, Doc?"

"I have something to tell you," she proclaimed.

"What is it, pray tell?"

"I have a really, really, really, *really,* exquisitely low tolerance for alcohol."

He smiled, and it was the sort of smile she wanted to rip from his face. "I *might* have gathered that already."

She crawled back into a sitting position, glaring at him. "I'm sorry, but some of us aren't giant six-foot-eight genetically engineered super-people, all right?"

"I'm six-foot-four…"

"You're *huge*. And like, genetically enhanced. Me? I am not genetically enhanced. I am *tiny*. I hate being tiny. You get stepped on. People think your mind is as small as your form but my mind is a *giant*."

"It certainly is."

"Are you judging me?"

Another irritating smirk. "I wouldn't dream of it."

"Well, excuse me, Mr Beast, I may not be a super-soldier or wizard-technician, but I am proud of what I am."

"And what is that?"

"I," she said, pausing with what she really hoped was dramatic effect, "am a *scientist*."

Beau laughed. "You're certainly that," he said, and then his voice seemed to transform into something else, soft and felt-like. "You're really something, Asami."

"You know what else I am?" she said, inching towards his shoulder, closer and closer by the second. It was nice to be this close to someone. Why didn't people spend more time being attached to one another?

Beau's eyes widened, and she found herself curiously drawn to his good one, to the fringes of his dark lashes. "What's that?" he asked, and his voice had a strange, wavering quality to it.

It was probably just the alcohol.

"*Tired,*" she said, and promptly passed out.

Asami was sitting at the dining room table, doing her mathematics school work, only the numbers kept jumping around the page. She grabbed a sum with her fingers and held it up to the light, only the figures morphed into nonsensical words instead. They babbled around the room, repeating an old nursery rhyme.

A ring-a-ring-a-roses,
A pocket full of posies,
Ashes, ashes!
We all fall down.

"What a shame," said her mother calmly, counting cards in the corner. "That's the only thing you were ever good at."

Her father's violin picked itself up from the corner, and started to play the tune. Her sister's voice accompanied it, her expression stark and empty, eyes like a doll's. The strings began to crack and bleed, and still the haunting song wore on.

"Papa!" Asami called. "Papa, *please!* Stop it."

"I cannot," he said, appearing by her shoulder. "Can you?"

We all fall down.

The violin cracked in two, and the splinters formed into flesh, into horrible, twisted, malformed faces.

No song, now. Just Mortimer's words.

What have we done, what have we done, what have we done?
He begged for me to end it.

Asami woke crying.

A dream, all a dream. Or most of it. She hugged the blankets to her chest as the fear abated, waiting until her breathing returned to normal.

She was back in her bunk, although she couldn't remember getting there. She was shoeless, but fully dressed, and tucked under the blankets.

Beast must have brought her back.

It was doubtful she'd have drunk enough to have blacked out, which meant she wasn't conscious. He hadn't helped her stagger home. He'd have had to carry her.

Oh dear.

Her mouth was dry, and she tumbled out in search of water, only to find a glass already at her bedside. She smiled, trying not to imagine what it must have been like to be tucked against his chest, her cheek pressed to his neck...

Asami guzzled, pushing back her thoughts.

It's been too long since you were with anyone, she told herself. *You're creating fantasies. Just... read a book.*

Or... get it out of your system.

She downed the glass and wished in hindsight she'd saved some to splash her face with. No, she wasn't going to go there with him. They lived together. They could be stuck together for a long, long time. It would only make things awkward. She wasn't very good at relationships and a fling didn't suit this kind of living arrangement.

Put it out of your mind.

She wrapped one of the lighter blankets around her shoulders and shuffled out of the train car, towards the bathroom. She relieved herself, splashed her face, and had another drink. On her way back, she heard voices inside the lab.

She paused. Beast talking to Pilot? No. There was definitely another voice. Maybe he was speaking to something through his screens, or on a telephone? The palace had such technology. Maybe he did too.

And yet the voice… it sounded real, no distortion, although she couldn't quite make out the words.

Until they moved towards the door.

Asami bolted into the kitchen, ashamed of even the mere notion of eavesdropping.

"I thank you for your assistance, as always. I know how much you risk—" Beau's voice.

"You don't need to thank me, you fool."

A hint of a laugh. "Now you sound like the good doctor."

"This doctor. Is she pretty?"

Beau's voice went rigid. "I am disinclined to comment."

"Afraid I'll steal her from you?"

"Not commenting on that, either."

A laugh passed between the two of them. Asami froze behind the door, wondering who this person was, why Beast trusted him enough to tell him about her, and whether that was dangerous.

And wondering why she was more interested in whether or not he thought she was pretty.

Priorities, Asami. Readjust them.

"I'll see you to the door."

"Worried someone will assault my virtue on the way out?"

"I… don't have a response for that."

"Well, that's…"

Their voices faded off down the corridor. A short while later, she heard Beast returning. Remembering her promise to announce her presence and realising how creepy it would be to walk into a dark room and find someone standing there, she quickly turned on the lights and started banging around, going through the actions of making herself a cup of cocoa.

Beast entered the room, frowning at her appearance. She wondered if he'd forgotten she lived here again, even if he'd just been discussing her with his guest.

"Asami." He blinked.

"Hey," she said. "Did you have a guest just now? I heard—"

"Yes. An old friend."

"He knows about you?"

"He helped Mortimer rescue me. Brought me down here."

"He's military?"

"Sort of."

She frowned. "You won't tell me?"

"It's… complicated. If anyone found out he was helping me, things would not end well for either of us."

"You can trust him with my identity but not me with his?"

Beast raised his brow. "You were listening."

"I… I caught the end of the conversation. And don't change the subject!"

He sighed. "I don't *want* to keep things from you, but I won't lie, either. It's not safe to tell anyone. So, please, don't ask me to."

Asami chewed her lip, tugging on the end of her braid. She wanted to know, she wanted him to trust her, wanted him to *like* her enough to trust her, but she also saw the logic of what he was saying. It wasn't fair to force it, to him or this mysterious person.

"All right," she breathed.

"Thank you." He turned his eyes to the start of her cocoa. "Too much alcohol keeping you up?"

"Ah, the great thing about getting drunk so easily is that it's quickly out of my system. I'm right as rain."

"So what's keeping you up?"

"Nightmares," she shivered.

He added the hot water to her mug and started to stir, not meeting her gaze. "I have those, from time to time. What are yours about?"

"Oh, not being able to count. Creepy songs. Fairly standard." She paused. "Yours?"

Beast's lips thinned. He passed her the mug. "You don't want to know."

"I probably don't," she agreed. "But would you like to share?"

Still not meeting her eyes, he poured himself a drink. As he stirred, he spoke, his voice far softer than his words.

"It's common for soldiers to dream of things they saw in action. Acts of violence. Death. I see that, sometimes. But mostly I dream of those few days after we were all given the serum. I was one of the last to fall ill, you know. But I saw the others. I... I heard them. When Petyr's lungs were filling with blood, I heard him. When Vlad, who was always the toughest, screamed for morphine, I heard him too. Sarah asking for her mother. Matteo turning blind. I saw and heard it all, and I still see it, and still hear it, and even though it's less than before, even though I've found ways of coping, I wonder if they'll haunt me for the rest of my life."

Asami paused, breath hard against her chest. Beast sipped

his cocoa as if he'd been discussing the shopping.

"What do you do to cope?" she asked.

"Oh, exercise. Make sure I'm tired before bed. Reading. Cocoa." He held up his mug, trying for something like a smile.

"The next time it happens, come to me," she said. "I don't care what the time is. Just come to me. We'll talk about something utterly mindless until you're ready for sleep. Understood?"

"Only if you tell me about your demon sums."

Asami put her head in her hands. "I'm regretting telling you that."

"Don't," he said. "I like it when you tell me things."

"Good," she said, leaning beside him. "As I like talking."

They were only a few inches apart, but she didn't dare reach out. Instead, they sipped their drinks and spoke of nothing, until Asami felt ready to sleep.

THE TALE OF ASH
AND BEAU

Beau didn't follow Asami to bed, although his eyes watched her until she left the room. He did not yet feel like sleeping, his mind pained and slightly fuzzy. He had a headache coming on, even though he hadn't drunk very much. It was enough to keep him up if he didn't dispel it.

He made himself another warm drink and took the last of his painkillers, making a mental note to get some more. He hoped it really was just a headache and not another episode; he had not yet explained those to Asami, and he really wanted to avoid her seeing him like that, especially as he was quite sure they were friends now. He didn't want pity to swallow that up, for her to see him as some invalid.

He was far too fond of being her friend.

At school, Beau was one of those people liked by everyone, befriended by no one. He was quiet and reserved and got on well with most people, but he tended to fall a bit on the shy side when talking to people one-on-one, and he overall just felt slightly awkward socialising in general.

Which meant the parties at the palace he was forced to attend with his parents were something hellish.

As soon as he could behave in public—which was very young, because he generally always did what he was told—his parents would force him into a fine suit and parade him in front of the glittering court, to be ogled at by their friends and superiors, some of which would pinch his cheeks and ruffle his curls and make him feel even more on display than ever.

It was enough to make him want to misbehave in the hopes they left him behind for future events, but public spectacles were not his style and he didn't want to disappoint them.

So he gritted his teeth, endured it, and snuck off as soon as he was able.

It was during one of these awful parties that Beau first met Ash. He was about twelve at the time, Ash a little younger, but he was already tall and slim and easily passing for a teenager. Beau had some time ago discovered the kitchens at the palace were more than willing to part with their leftovers in exchange for a bit of dishwashing, and he ended up sitting in the corridor just outside with a plate of misshapen macaroons when Ash came by.

He was dressed in a red suit lined with gold, tiny studs arranged in the shape of suns clustered on the cuffs and collar. He was all soft fabrics and sharp edges, looking even more uncomfortable than Beau.

His eyes widened when he beheld the plate of treats.

"I swear," he said dramatically, "I shall give everything

that I own in return for one of those confectionaries."

Beau blinked at him, not fully understanding who this boy was, or why he was talking to him. "They have canapes at the rest of the party…"

Ash sighed, slumping against the wall and sliding down beside him. "Mother insists I not stuff my face before a suitable hour and I am so, *so* hungry." He batted his fawn-like eyes at Beau, in a manner the older boy later realised was supposed to be endearing. *"Please,"* he said desperately. "I'd give my right arm for a pink one."

Beau held out his plate. "Help yourself," he said. "But I don't want your right arm."

Ash had laughed. Beau remembered thinking that even his laugh was a bit silly, musical and flippant and yet older than his years, the type of laugh he'd learnt from copying adults. A laugh to be summoned whenever the occasion called for it. "My eternal gratitude, then," he said, grinning as he took one of the pastries. Every movement he had was refined and delicate.

"I'm Ash," he said. "The least ridiculous of the many names my mother heaped on me. You?"

"Beaumont. Beau."

"A pleasure to meet you, Beaumont. Which macaroon is your favourite? I promise to eat as few of those as possible."

Beau had never had a friend like Ash before. In fact, it wasn't until he'd befriended Ash that he realised he hadn't really had much in the way of real friends at all, just a lot of people he got on with. Ash was only in Petragrad for a couple of weeks when they first met, but they got into an awful lot of trouble together during that time, sneaking around the palace and out of it.

Ash liked playing harmless tricks on people, hiding insignificant things, swapping around the nobles' shoes with ones too big or too small, retuning the princess' piano after every practise, and once changing her sugar to salt.

Beau didn't see him pull that one off, but the next time they met he had a gash on his forehead. "She threw a teapot at me," he said, grinning like his injury was a badge of honour.

Beau had never gotten into trouble before. After the initial fear wore off, it was quite exhilarating, and if his parents were disappointed, they didn't show it too much; likely tempered by Ash's station and the fact he would be returning to his own city very shortly, too far away to be a bad influence.

But they kept in contact through letters, and met whenever Ash was in town.

When Beau's mother was killed two years later, Ash came back with his entire family, as a show of support for the bombings as a whole. Ash had slipped straight from his parents' side and arrived at Beau's door dishevelled and breathless.

"I'm sorry it took so long, and that I'm an utter mess," he rushed upon gaining admittance. "I've quite the story about how I snuck away. Daring. Brave. Most dashing. Also disgusting and—" he stopped, spying Beau's face. "I'm sorry," he said softly. "Really, truly sorry. I have… I have no idea what to say. I don't even know why I'm here. I'm just… oh, Beau." He took him in his arms, and Beau had sobbed until he couldn't possibly sob any more.

It was the last time he let someone else see him cry.

Ash stayed for two weeks, and after that, he had to return home. For weeks afterwards, Beau felt almost as lost as he'd felt in those first few days without his mother, as if Ash's presence had plugged up the wound. But now it was bleeding steadily again, and he had no idea how to stitch it back together. There were others at school who'd lost people, but they hadn't lost *her.* Grief, he discovered, was different for everyone, isolating even when you should have been able to share it.

His father didn't speak of his mother for months after the funeral, and never at length. It was years before he would say her name again. She hung in the air between them, a voiceless, palpable ghost, an unspoken presence. Beau wanted to give her life by speaking about her, but the few times he tried, his father stiffened so much it felt like twisting a knife.

So he stayed quiet.

Her ghost grew louder still.

When Ash visited again, he took him to visit the family plot where she was interred. Ash spoke about her like a fond friend he hadn't seen in a while.

The dead were never so dead as when they were ignored. His friend brought her back to life, just a little.

Ash's visits to Petragrad grew longer. The servants at the palace twittered that a marriage alliance was being considered between him and Princess Ivory, but Ash never gave weight to them.

"Let them talk," he'd tell Beau whenever he asked. "And let

my parents entertain the idea, if it gives us longer together."

Beau didn't know the princess well, but Ash spoke about her a lot, even if he rebuked the rumours. Mostly he spoke about how stuck-up and irritating she was, as if those weren't traits he also embodied.

"She has a foul temper," he remarked one day.

"I'm not sure you dislike that as much as you pretend," Beau would tease, digging him in the ribs.

He didn't give much thought to the princess, or Ash's relationship with her, until the assassination.

He'd managed to weasel his way out of the party by going to talk to one of his father's colleagues about the possibility of enlisting. It had been weighing on his mind for some time, ever since his mother's death. Lots of others from his class had already enrolled. School talked about it like it was an honour, a duty. Some of his classmates said he should do it for his mother, for revenge.

But they hadn't known her, hadn't known that for all she'd married into a military family, Marie loved peace and forgiveness. *"An eye for an eye would make the whole world blind,"* she told him once, quoting some ancient scripture.

His mother would not have wanted him to fight at all, least of all for her.

But his father wanted it, and he was the only parent Beau had alive to impress.

The bomb that tore through the balcony where King Nikolai and his daughter Ivory were standing reverberated all the way to the barracks. Like the shudder that had stolen his mother, Beau bolted at the murmur of it, and had to be held back by two of his father's comrades. He remembered over-powering them, but not how he did it.

"Gears, he's strong!" said one of them, as Beau wrenched free of his grip.

By the time he arrived at the palace, the shaking had stopped, all the nobility had been removed, and guards were questioning the guests while others were dug from the rubble. Beau raced through the rooms until he found where Ash was being kept, and battled through the guards to get to him.

Ash had looked up from the chaise where he was sitting, soot streaked across his clothes, fabric torn and crumpled. He had a gash across his forehead which someone was trying to doctor.

"Beau," he said shakily, "Beau, Beau, she's—" He did not get much further than that, the words tangling on his tongue.

Ash's family survived the attack. So did most people, apart from the king and his daughter. Beau sat beside him all night, and stood by his side at the funeral, and understood even if Ash never said it that he'd lost more than a casual acquaintance that night.

And, like Ash for him, Beau had no words to give.

Aside from those two incidents, the friendship between them was easy and simple. For all that the younger boy could be over the top and ridiculous, he *talked* to Beau about things. Real, true, big things, like how he felt about taking over from his father and how much, sometimes, he hated his life.

"Do you ever wonder who you'd be if no one ever expected something of you?" he asked him one summer some years later.

Beau nodded, unable to talk, because he did wonder, and he didn't know. "I'm joining the military," he said instead.

Ash had been furious, or as furious as Ash got. He danced around the room making wild motions with his hands, wittering on about how it was an utterly terrible idea and a waste of his beautiful brains.

"Brains aren't beautiful," Beau insisted.

"Oh, but they *are,* Beaumont, and yours is the finest!" He shook his dark head, sighing. "Well, I hope the military makes good use of your mind, and you take good care of that pretty face…"

They would see each other a few more times over the years, and each time they did, it was like all the months between the last visit melted away. There was an easiness between the two of them Beau had never found with anyone else, even his comrades, where it took being shot at a few times to properly bond.

Ash was at the palace again when Beau took the serum. He didn't try to warn him against it. Indeed, he supported the idea. "A chance to make you even more handsome and stronger than you are, dear Beast? I say you take it!"

They were placed into isolation after that to monitor for side effects, and Beau wasn't supposed to talk to anyone. Even his own father had been banned from the room.

But Ash had a way of getting into places he wasn't supposed to, and hearing things he shouldn't have known.

He came to visit after most of Beau's unit had been hospitalised.

"I hear it's not going well."

"No," said Beau stonily. "It's not."

"But you feel fine?"

"So far."

Ash gritted his teeth, and something like anger had flashed across his face. "If things go south, I swear I will do everything within my power to save you," he said. "Everything that I own. Whatever I can do."

Beau swallowed, not wanting to digest those words. "And if you can't do anything?"

Ash's face tightened further. "There's always something that can be done."

Ash was right. Beau had never been quite certain what precisely had saved him from the fate that befell the rest of his squad, whether it was science, a natural resilience, or all the money Ash had thrown at Mortimer to equip his facility in the outer ring. But Ash was true to his word. He'd done everything he could to save him, even when Beau had begged him not to.

He remembered little of the journey from the palace to the outer ring, drugged out of his mind. But he started to come to not long after they arrived, returning to consciousness feeling like his flesh was melting off his bones and screaming for it to stop.

Ash grabbed his hand as Mortimer fiddled with the morphine, and brought out his pocket watch.

"Time is passing, Beau," he'd said. "This will too. Just hold on a little longer."

Three years later, in the underground base Ash and Mortimer had sourced and furnished for him, Beau felt that pain again, the burning flair that spread across muscle and skin, pain that no drugs or money had ever been able to dispel. His hands shook, seizing in front of him, and there was nothing and no one to hold onto.

He hit the floor, eyes rolling in their sockets. He searched for the sound of a ticking clock, for the reminder that everything passed eventually. *Everything passes.*

But not the worst kinds of pain.

Like losing his mother, his squad, Mortimer.

Like being thrown down here into the mechanical underbelly of the city, to rot unnoticed by the rest of the world.

Like dragging Asami into this darkness with him.

Asami.

He felt like calling for her, but at the same time, he wanted to wrap himself away inside the darkness and fall apart. He didn't want her to witness this, didn't want to see it reflected in those eyes of hers.

Pain festered good thoughts, making gloomy ones worse.

Just let it take me this time, he prayed. *Just let all of it be over.*

THE PAIN BENEATH

Asami slept in the next morning, curled up under the covers, too comfortable to move. The sheets felt warmer and fresher than before, and if she didn't open her eyes, she could imagine she was back in the middle ring. The air held that clean, soft quality, the crisp smell of freshly-cleaned bedding. She thought of her gossamer curtains, swaying in the filtered breeze, of plush carpets underfoot and the papery aroma of hot books.

For a strange, shard of a moment, she imagined someone else was with her, a warm body in the bed beside her. A rare kind of longing, as fine as it was fleeting.

She shook it away, burying her face in the pillow.

Eventually, worried about being labelled a sloth, she pulled herself out, dressed in one of Beast's shirts with the new dress she'd made out of the map fabric, and skipped along to the kitchen.

Beast was nowhere to be found, so she busied herself making breakfast, waiting for him to emerge.

When he didn't, she finally went in search of him, loudly humming as she did so.

"Beast? You up?"

He wasn't in his carriage bedroom, and the pristinely made bed showed no signs of being slept in, although it was possible he'd remade it and had an early start…

Odd.

She checked the gym next, a part of her secretly craving to catch him in a compromising position, but the room was quiet and cold.

"Beast? Where are you?"

Maybe he'd gone back to the lab after their late night cocoa, and fallen asleep there. Maybe he'd had more wine than she'd assumed.

She opened the door, and found him lying on the rug, utterly immobile, Pilot crouched beside him. The dog let out a whine as she approached, an oddly pitiful scrape of gears.

"Are you still asleep?" she asked.

Beast let out a low, hard moan. Not one of sleep, or annoyance.

One of pain.

Subject occasionally suffers from bouts of chronic pain that render him completely immobile.

Asami ran forward, skidding down on her knees. His face was scrunched together, distorted in a new, horrible way, his entire body curled inwardly as if trying to suck his limbs back into his body.

Her hands hovered above him. "Tell me where it hurts," she whispered, aware of the brittle quality of her voice.

"Everywhere," he rasped, "it hurts everywhere."

If she had her lab, she could do something. If she had drugs, she could do something. But she had nothing, nothing at all.

Never in her entire life had she ever felt so powerless.

She placed a hand on his arm. His muscles were tight beneath her touch, wire twisted to the point of breaking. "Does it hurt more when I touch you?"

"No," he hissed, teeth gritted together.

"I'll be right back."

She hurtled back to the train car, fetching blankets and a pillow, eyes scanning about the room for something, anything more. She thought of old medical textbooks, of everything she'd read. Pressure on a wound could reduce pain, but he wasn't injured. She'd paid little attention to old remedies in any case, certain in the power of medicine to heal.

She dashed back to slide a pillow under his head. There was no question of moving him, no question of doing much at all. The only thing she could do was keep him warm.

With that in mind, she slid in next to him, and pulled the blanket over them both. "Heat might help," she told him, pressing her tiny body to his back. "I can talk, if that helps? I'm sure I can find something to witter on about."

A shudder. "Please."

She tried to do what he had done last night, with his beautiful stories of other places. She was no traveller, so she took him on a journey through her memories instead while she poured her heat into him. She told him of the day Sakura was born, of her parents coming home from the hospital, how in an instant this tiny little creature had obliterated the steady quiet of her life. There had been difficult moments, of course, anger and biting and hair pulling, but for the most part, Asami had adored her from the start. She told Beast about her father reading this big book of fairytales to her whilst Asami sat nearby, politely correcting the ridiculousness of the plots.

"Why doesn't she just climb down her own hair?"

"I don't think I'd like a talking frog in my bedroom, either."

"I don't think it's a good idea to marry men who imprison you."

"The witch *cuts out her tongue?* Papa, are you sure you should be reading this to her?"

"He kisses a corpse? That's not very hygienic."

She told him about watching her mother play chess, about falling in love with numbers, about friends she'd made at school. She spoke of university, of finding like-minded people, of moving to Petragrad and letting the work absorb her. She told him of her little apartment, the bland joy it brought her, and whispered of the palace gardens and catching Prince Nero with his latest conquests.

He managed a sound almost like a laugh about that.

She told him every last detail of de-coding Mortimer's work, and following the breadcrumbs, and coming down into the metal belly of the city, and barely being afraid, because she'd met him.

"I don't think I ever properly thanked you for that."

He murmured something about not needing thanks. "I just thought… I wanted you to know that whatever I've lost,

I'm very glad to not be dead, and that it took so long for me to break because just having you around… I don't know. You made it less terrifying."

She spoke until the words turned gummy, and his body relaxed, and he slowly turned to face her, ignoring how close she was to his awful, ruined, lovely cheek.

He stared at her, eyes wide despite the pain.

"What?" she asked. "Something on my face?"

"No, not your face."

"On what then?"

"On your soul, perhaps."

"My… soul?" she frowned.

"Do you believe in souls?"

"I'm a scientist," she said primly. "I believe in things that I can measure."

"How unromantic."

"You're hardly a poet, Beau."

"I believe in souls, I think. I believe that some things cannot be measured, that there's more to the world than what we can see, and hear, and touch…" He gave a hard shudder, breathing slowly through his teeth. Asami pressed into him, as though her closeness could force away the pain. She held him hard until the worst of it passed.

"Do you think you can move, yet?" she asked. "It can't be good for you to lie here on the floor like this."

"At least the company's better than usual…"

Asami smiled, but her lips felt tight and wrong. "All right, I think you're good to try and move." She wriggled out of the blanket, ducking under his arm and tugging him upright.

"Lean into me, but not onto me. If you crush me we'll both be in trouble."

"Wouldn't... dream... of it."

She hauled him to his feet, arm tight over her shoulder. His rough cheek pressed against her head, but he seemed incapable of caring. Pilot hovered by his other side, gears creaking as he nudged his thigh. Beast steadied himself against his head.

"We can go as slowly as you like," said Asami. "But you need to tell me if you're going to fall. Gently now, carefully."

It was a long, agonisingly slow walk to the train car. Several times they stopped, Beast's eyes glazed over, his entire weight resting against her, or the wall. He couldn't always issue a clear or quick enough warning, and ended up slumped against her, breathing hotly, painfully against her neck.

"I'm sorry, I'm sorry..." he whispered.

"It's all right," she told him. "It's fine. Don't rush it."

Finally, eventually, they reached the bed. She hauled him into it, pulling the covers up to his shoulders. She placed her fingers to his head. He was warmer now, but not feverish. "Can I get you anything?"

He looked at her. "My pocket watch," he said. "Can you bring it?"

She located it on his dresser. It was a beautiful, intricate thing, burnished gold, weighty and polished. Easily the most well-kept thing he owned.

She placed it beside him.

"Can... can you open it?"

Asami did so, trying not to look inside, worried, for a moment, that it might include the portrait of a beautiful woman, although she knew such a thing shouldn't bother her.

It didn't. There was an engraving of some sort, a string of initials, but too many to take in. She tilted the clock face towards him.

"Is that all right?"

Beast's eyes flickered, rolling almost as quickly as the hands. "Time is passing…" he murmured, before falling fully into the pillows, eyes white in their sockets.

There ought to be something she could do. If he was bleeding, she could bind the wounds. If he was hot, she could cool him down. But this? There was no solution to sucking pain from bones.

"There must be something I can do…"

"Isn't," he hissed, shuddering through something else. He uttered a quiet curse under his breath, turning inwardly on his side. "Oh gears, oh gods…"

She rubbed his back and grabbed his hand, unsure whether either action was particularly helpful. Her fingers crushed under the weight of his grip.

"It won't… it won't let up quickly," he said, as a little of the pain abated. "You can't stay by my side all day. Go do something."

"But I—"

"You can't do any good here. Maybe in your lab."

She wondered if that was a hint, a plea, *go back to your notes and find a way to fix this.* "Call me if you need anything, you hear?"

"Will do."

She patted Pilot's head. "You stay here with him, all right? Be a good boy."

"He's always a good boy…"

Readjusting the covers one final time, she headed out of the car and along to the kitchen, propping open the door in case he needed her. She hoped she could hear him so far away.

As she opened the cupboard door, she heard a long, painful moan, the kind that coiled along her chest.

She could still hear him. She just wasn't sure she wanted to.

Her fingers shook as she filled the kettle, so unsteady she almost burned herself brewing the tea. She took a few moments to calm herself, sipping away, before making him a cup and taking it to his side. She waited until his groans had subsided, so that they could both pretend she'd heard nothing.

He pretended to be asleep when she entered. She pretended she believed him.

She raided the medical supplies, but although well-stocked with bandages and antiseptic, there was nothing for pain. Of course there wasn't. He'd used them long ago.

Dejected, she returned to her lab and tried to work. She lost hours reading and re-reading, taking nothing in. She took a break and tried to fix herself something to eat, breakfast long since spoiled, but she had little appetite.

She imagined Beast didn't either, but she brought him something anyway.

"I can't," he said, groaning at the sight of it.

"Well, I'll just leave it here for when you can."

She stroked his good arm, wishing for drugs, for better understanding, or that magic was a thing and she had it.

I'd believe in nonsense, for you. If that's what it took to fix you.

"How... how long does it usually go on for?" she asked.

"A couple of days, maybe? Three, at most."

"Days? Gears and garters, how do you cope?"

"I don't have a choice." He shifted up in bed. "I need to—"

"You need to just lie back and let me try to take care of you."

"Um, while that's nice, I, er, need to use the bathroom..."

"Oh," she said, "well..."

She tumbled out of the car, fetching a copper bedpan that she'd seen in one of the store rooms. She brought it back to his side and held it out to him.

"I'm not sure you'd make it to the toilet."

Beast gave another groan, different from the others. "This is horrifically embarrassing."

"Oh no," she said, sliding the bedpan under the covers and letting him deal with rest, carefully avoiding his eyes. "Embarrassing is this time I went up to collect a much-deserved award in front of my entire school and tripped on the steps on the way up."

"That doesn't sound too bad."

"Oh, no, that's not the whole story. See, I collected the award and started going back to my seat... only to realise I'd left half my skirt behind on the steps. I'd been so focused on getting the award that I didn't notice! I was mortified. Cried all night long."

"That *is* embarrassing," he agreed. "What was the award for?"

"Hardest worker."

He grinned weakly. "Much deserved indeed, then." His jaw tensed. "I'm... I'm done now."

"Right." She pulled the pan from under the covers and gently placed the lid back on. Beast wriggled uncomfortably under the blankets. "You have a better bedside manner than most medical doctors I've encountered. I wonder why you didn't follow that path."

"Oh, me? I'm not great with blood."

There was a good reason she'd never gone down that route, but she couldn't explain it to him now. She hadn't even been able to tell her parents.

Beau barked a laugh, feeble though it was, and even though it was a lie, she felt it was the right one.

"I'm just going to deal with this," she said, gesturing to the pan. "I'll be back."

"You don't have to—"

"I'll be right back."

Contents of the bedpan dealt with, she returned to try and force him to eat. He seemed willing to try, but his appetite was worse than hers.

"Sorry," he said, giving up after a few mouthfuls.

"You don't have apologise."

"I'm not accustomed to being taken care of."

"Well, get used to it, because I'm not going anywhere." She

carded her fingers through his locks. "I wish there was more I could do. I'm not used to uselessness. I'm usually very good at fixing things."

"You don't have to stay."

"See, I rather think I do." She leaned across and kissed his lumpy forehead. He blinked up at her, eyes wide in surprise.

"How are you not disgusted?"

"I am disgusted by many things," she said. "Your table manners, for example. But not *you*. Never you. Just... try and rest, dear Beast. The worst will be over soon."

The worst was not over soon. Although they got through the day, she woke in the night to his muted cries, and found he'd stuffed the pillow into his mouth. She tried to comfort him, but he vomited with pain, rousing out of it only enough to sob that he was sorry as she cleaned him up. She stroked his hair and told him it was fine, and stayed with him until he fell back into a bitter and exhausted sleep.

That night, Asami dreamt she was back in Toulouse, playing with her sister in the park. They rented a couple of penny farthings and went whizzing off to the deepest part of the green, where the trees grew dense and dark. Sakura, who was far more imaginative than she was, started singing a song about dragons and trolls, of wicked faeries lurking in the velvet dark.

Asami was tired and cross, annoyed at having been saddled baby-sitting, and was finding it difficult to humour her.

"There's no such thing as faeries," she snapped.

Sakura stopped pedaling and scowled. "Well, I wish there wasn't any such thing as *sisters.*"

Asami laughed at her childish fury, at her cross little face, which just made Sakura more annoyed. She tried to stamp her foot, but it went straight past the pedal, causing her to lose her balance and topple straight over into a pile of nettles.

Sakura barely had time to scream before Asami had leapt from her own saddle and yanked her from the undergrowth.

"Ow, ow, ow!" her little sister howled, lip trembling as Asami set her down on a clear bank nearby. She scrambled amongst the long grass, pulling out a series of large, leafy fronds and rubbing them over the white welts bubbling along Sakura's skin.

"Dock leaves," she told her shortly. "They'll suck the pain away."

Sakura stopped sniffling. "Really?"

"Absolutely," she said, rubbing it more frantically. "Feel that?"

Sakura paused. "I... I think so."

Asami smiled. "Good," she said. "But we've some antiseptic at home that will be even better."

Sakura's lip trembled again, then stopped. "And ice cream."

"And ice cream. Shall we go?"

Sakura put her arms around her sister's neck, and that, her father would tell her later, was the best medicine of all.

Rumex Obtusifolius, better known as bitter dock, was, of course, a placebo. Asami already knew that. There *was* a suggestion in one of the books she'd read that the moisture released from any leaf might have a minimal soothing effect, but that the dock itself had no special medicinal properties. The size made it better for rubbing. That was all.

Asami watched Beau, and knew he needed more than leaves.

She brewed him a tea and told him it might help, pretending it was a creation she'd invented from their supplies.

It did not help. Nothing did.

For two days he remained more or less trapped in the bed, relying on her for everything, too weak to be ashamed. There were moments where he practically writhed, lit by pain, and she wondered if he would have screamed if she wasn't beside him. She kept him warm and held his hand and stayed, hoping her presence offered him some kind of balm, that there was something in her father's words. Touch could heal.

Irrational. Unscientific.

But all she had.

"You're all right," she told him, time and time again, as she stroked his hair and kissed his swollen knuckles. "You're all right."

But she wasn't. Watching him like this was an agony of its own.

"Beau," she whispered, "Beau, I'm here. Just listen to my

voice. Don't focus on anything else."

"That name doesn't suit me," he said.

"Yes it does," she insisted. "You are beautiful, Beaumont."

"You're blind, Doctor."

"You know I'm not talking about your looks."

"Who's the poet now?"

She sighed. "You're making me irrational and illogical and I don't like it," she said, her fingers brushing his cheek, "but I like *you,* Beau. I like you a lot."

He said nothing to that, and a little while later, his eyes were fluttering with sleep. She wondered if he'd remember that when he woke, and if she wanted him to. At the moment, she didn't care what he knew about how she felt about him, if it brought him any kind of comfort, but she wasn't sure what she'd want when he recovered, or what she wanted for herself.

Nothing complicated. Nothing that could ruin their friendship.

It had been a long, long time since she'd had a real, true, close friend. The kind she thought she'd tell secrets to, if she had any.

She woke in the night, parched, eyes sticky with sleep. She'd dozed off beside him again. She'd tried sleeping in her own bunk, but her sleep was punctuated with his low moans, and she'd found it easier to be nearby and be useless than be further away and be useless still. She fancied he was quieter this way, too, but perhaps he was only controlling it more for her sake.

Foolish boy.

He was sleeping now, still and sound, and the sight stilled the constant ache in her chest that had burned inside her these past few days. She watched the steady rise and fall of his chest, his gentle breath, and fancied that his damaged side didn't look nearly so bad in the low light of the night lamps.

Her throat demanded water. The jug beside the bed was empty, so she trudged towards the kitchen to fill it.

Halfway along the corridor, she heard a sound up ahead. She froze, waiting for it to go away. A loud rat, perhaps? A vagrant seeking shelter?

It occurred to her she had no idea how far away from the streets they were, how far below the city. She'd never once been tempted to venture out. But the door was rarely locked; Beau clearly wasn't scared of discovery.

Before she could hazard a guess as to what could be out in the tunnel, the door at the top of the base banged open.

Sound stilled inside her, and she leapt into the first door she reached: one of the supply closets.

She pressed her ear to the gap, heart pounding. Was it the dread doctors? Had they found her? Something was clicking and clacking—a weapon? She scanned the room for anything she could use to defend herself, but all she had was a couple of mops and brooms. She'd never fend them off with those, and Beast—Beau—

He couldn't move.

Could she leave him, even to save herself?

Someone tripped on the final step. "Oww! Stars, can we not turn on a light?" A voice, young and male. Probably too young to be a guard, although she couldn't be sure.

"I'm looking for it…" Another voice, older.

"Let's not startle him like we did the last time…"

"It's the middle of the night," said a third, female. Hard and sobering, despite the volume. "He's probably asleep."

"He won't be for long," said a final one, older and deeper than the others. "Not with the racket you three keep making."

Asami stilled, breath tight in her chest. At least four people, three male, one female. Nothing else she could discern except they were moving with something mechanical.

She pressed her fingers to the door, wondering if she should close it, or run for it, or hide on the shelves, or search for another way out—

Silence pressed back.

"Hunter?" the female whispered. "What is it?"

"Ssh," he hissed.

Asami trembled, hugging her arms, hardly daring to breathe.

The door wrenched open. A torch flashed, and someone grabbed her by the arms. Half a scream was lost under the clatter of mops and buckets, and she was yanked out into the harsh, white light.

13

THE REBELS ON THE RAILROAD

"Hunter!" yelled the woman.

Fear pulsed inside Asami as she found herself hauled against a wall by a huge, bear-like man. His tanned skin was half-hidden by coarse black hair, covering most of his face and streaked with silver. The scent of oil and woodsmoke clung to his thick, worn clothing, and as much as he wasn't dressed like a soldier, he had the strength of one. His grip felt like iron.

"Who are you?" he demanded.

"I'm... I'm..." The words crumbled on her tongue, mind numb with panic.

"Dome above," said the girl. "Hunter, she's just a small woman—"

"*You* were a small woman, once. You were far from helpless."

"She's dressed for bed, for Stars' sake. I don't think she's a palace spy! Put her down."

Hunter's jaw tensed, but he followed her instructions. Asami slid to the floor, scrambling away from him. Her heart thumped madly in her ears, and yet she felt she might choke on it, her throat closed with fear.

The woman crouched down beside Asami. She looked a little younger than she was, but her pale face carried a hardness to it that went beyond her years. Blue eyes glimmered in the faint light, and black curls tumbled around her shoulders.

"I'm sorry," she said. "Ignore Hunter. He tends to smash first, ask questions later. Are you all right?"

Asami massaged her arms. "I... I think so. Just shaken."

"Can you stand?"

"Who are you people?"

Hunter snorted. "You first, girl."

"*Doctor*," said Asami, anger tempering her fear. "Doctor Asami Thorne. I was a researcher at the palace."

Hunter raised a black brow, and Asami wondered if she'd just made a terrible mistake. What if there was a reward out for her capture? She had no idea who these people were—

"*Was* a researcher?" he probed.

"I discovered something I wasn't supposed to," she said. "And, well..."

"You discovered what happened to Beast, you mean?" offered the woman.

Asami could only nod. "Are you the Rebellion?" With their mud-streaked clothing, and their familiarity with the place, it made the most sense.

It was also the least terrifying option, which is why she hoped she was right.

The group shared a look.

"Part of it," the woman said, ignoring the disapproving looks from the others. "Where's Beast?"

"He's… not well."

Something in the woman's expression flickered, a shard of discomfort. "I see. That's unfortunate. We're in need of his assistance."

"He's probably got most of the info written down that we need," one of the others said. Not Hunter, not the young one, either. A man around her age, with hair like painted silver. "Let's check the lab."

"Good thinking."

They all walked off without another word, leaving Asami to follow after, amazed at the flippancy of them, their ease with this place. They slipped into the lab and towards the cabinet beside Beau's dashboard, revealing folders and binders stuffed with maps and notes, timings of trams and guard duties, all beautifully compiled.

She had to admire the presentation of the notes, even if his handwriting left something to be desired.

"What are you all—" Something small whizzed past her ankle, and she looked down to reveal the source of the earlier clicking and clacking; a small automaton the size of a cat. It looked like a couple of rodents meshed together, with two wheels in the place of back paws. A handful of similar hybrids circled around the space, making it hard for her to focus.

"Don't worry about them," said the woman again, meeting her gaze. "Or *us*. We'll just collect the info we need and be on our way."

"But what are you looking for?"

She tapped her nose secretly. "I'm Snowdrop, by the way. The other two are Dandelion, Clover and Hunter."

"Snowdrop, Clover, Dandelion and... Hunter?"

"They're code names, obviously. Would you like one?"

"I'm... I'm sorry," Asami steadied herself against the wall. "This is all rather a lot."

"Hence why I think it's best we clear out." Snowdrop chewed her lip uncomfortably as the men sorted through the sheets and maps, making quick notes. "I'm sorry about Beast. I know it can get bad at times. Doesn't like that I know, of course, but... can't exactly be hidden." She shuffled off the bag on her back, a messy canvas thing, frayed and patched, like the rest of her clothing. Her bodice seemed to be several poorly stitched together, flashes of fine red and purple fabric beside scraps of faded blue and brown. Her trousers and shirt were torn and streaked with mud, and the thick outer layer of her cloak was as dark and wrinkled as bark.

Snowdrop set down her back pack, and took out several objects: knives, twine, bullets, rope, tiny parcels and pouches.

Finally, her hands closed around a small leather bag. "There's some herbs here that do well as a tea for pain relief," she said, tossing it over. Asami fumbled with it. "It's not much, but it should take the edge off."

Asami sniffed the package, wrinkling her nose unconsciously. "Herbs?"

"What's the matter, Doc?" said Snowdrop, brow furrowed. "All your fancy chemicals come from somewhere."

She was right, of course, but usually medicine that came from plants had been refined and concentrated. She squeezed the contents of the pouch hesitantly. "Where would you even get this stuff from?"

Snowdrop held out her hands. "Where indeed, right?"

"Snow? You ready?" Hunter boomed, even his whisper loud. "We think we have everything."

"What, already?"

"The man keeps good records."

"Clearly! Well, Doc," Snowdrop turned back to Asami, offering a gesture half like a bow, "thanks for having us. Sorry to drop in so unexpectedly. We'll be heading off now."

"If you're sure…" she mumbled, wondering if she wanted them gone or wanted to ask a hundred other questions first. Should she offer them tea? A bed for the night? Wish them good luck?

What were they even *doing*?

Snowdrop mimed the tipping of a hat. "It's been a pleasure, catch you around."

They were gone without another word.

For a long while after they left, Asami stood in the middle of the floor, stunned by the silence they'd left behind, trying to make sense of what had just happened.

Her shaking fingers closed around the pouch of herbs. With nothing else to do, she went to the kitchen to brew it, setting the tea beside his bed for whenever he woke, and crawled back into her own.

A little while later, she heard him wake, heard him scramble for the tea, curse and hiss with pain, and fall back into a fitful sleep. Certain he was sleeping again, she tip-toed out of bed, watched him lying in his own, and took the dregs of the cup back to the kitchen.

It was almost morning, and she suspected sleep was likely impossible. She returned to the lab, hoping to get in a couple of hours of work before he rose again. The rebels had left the folders spread out over his desk in their haste to leave, so she busied herself tidying them up.

The red binder depicted all the times the trams carrying medical supplies docked in the city, and her eyes scanned over all of them, processing the information instantly.

One was coming today, in just a couple of hours.

Asami paused, thinking.

She wasn't sure how much she believed in the power of herbal tea, and she wasn't sure how much longer she could watch him suffer.

It's almost been three days, she reminded herself. *It should be over soon. He just needs to endure a little longer.* You *need to just endure a little longer—*

But episodes like this would happen again, no telling when. And it was intolerable that he had had to suffer for so long already.

Don't do this, said the voice in her head. *It isn't worth it.*

But he was.

A plan started forming piece by piece in her head, built from Beau's excellent notes and her own past knowledge. She knew the tram docked in the middle ring just after 9am. The guard presence was fairly light, but there was a last-minute inspection before it went up to the palace. There were always, always scientists on board. If she was careful, if she was quick, if no one looked too long at her face, she might be able

A ROSE OF STEEL

to sneak on board and grab something before slipping away into the crowd.

She still had her white coat and palace ID. As long as no one stopped her... or scanned her...

She was pulling on her clothes before she could think twice.

I'll just go and investigate. If it's too guarded, I won't try. What's the harm in checking it out?

She made up another tea for Beau, just in case, and left it beside his bed. She thought about writing him a letter, in case things went awry, but what did you say to someone you'd only known a few weeks, even if they'd become the first real friend you had in the city?

More than a friend, she thought desperately, eyes gazing in his direction. *Whatever we are, we are more than that.*

And for that reason alone, it was impossible to say goodbye.

She bent over and kissed his brow instead, saying nothing, and slipped up the steps with a map in her pocket.

It took far, far too long to find her way through the winding tunnels of the underground, but eventually faint sunlight drifted overhead. She arrived at a slatted door which gave way into an alley in a street at the edge of the outer ring.

Asami pressed against the door, and pushed it open.

The sunlight hit her like a sledgehammer, and she raised her hands to cover her eyes, blinded by the glare. She had forgotten how bright the world was, how *loud.* Even in this narrow, forgotten street, noise crawled around her. The rumble of the trams, the whirring of the gears, the steady throng of people on the main road making their way to work.

She took a few moments to acclimatise, then left the map behind in the tunnel in case she was apprehended, pulled up her hood, and slid into the crowd.

Two streets later, she saw herself.

Asami stopped abruptly, irritating one of the people behind her, and stared at the dirty brick wall where a faded print of her face was plastered on a poster.

It had blackened and crisped through exposure to the fog, and no one had replaced it. Did that mean they weren't looking any more, or just that this one had escaped attention?

Her heart pounded in her chest.

"Wanted for Treason Against the Crown. Reward: 50 Silver Pieces."

Fifty was a lot for anyone in the slums, but was an insubstantial sum for others. She felt a little miffed she wasn't worth more.

This is a good thing, she told herself. *It means they don't think you're that important. It means less people will be looking for you.*

She made her way carefully through the narrow, winding streets, keeping an eye out for any further posters. She only came across a handful, all equally ignored. Perhaps the palace decided that she was likely dead, or had quit the city.

She'd taken off her glasses and let down her hair, both staples of her appearance that might have made their way onto any wanted posters, but as soon as she hit the middle ring, she slid into a boutique on her journey and applied a little make-up from the free testers. Just enough to make her look different without drawing too much attention to herself. She thought of the brothel workers the night all this started, with their immaculate faces, how much better they'd be at this than she was.

She thought of that night, too.

If you could go back to that moment... if you could turn around, ignore the trail of breadcrumbs, return to your life, none the wiser... would you?

Ignorance was easy. Easy to live under. But not easy to return to.

And you wouldn't have met Beau.

She swallowed her heart. It was too soon to work out which path she would have preferred.

Her pocket watch let her know that time was slipping away, that it was only twenty minutes now until the train stopped. Thankfully, she saw no more posters of herself as she bustled through the crowd to the station, keeping to the shadows where she could, trying to think like someone, anyone else.

I am a spy, a soldier. A heroine in a tale. I am not a lone little scientist way out of her depth.

I am, I am, I am...

If any of the guards clocked her, what she'd be was dead.

Dead. She could be dead.

This was crazy, mad, ludicrous.

You can always turn back, said the voice inside her, reason and logic personified. Mama's voice. *Assess your surroundings. Make no sudden moves.*

It was just chess, she told herself. It was just strategy.

She just needed to observe, check her foe's movements. She would be careful, calm, considerate.

Beau's shivering body, twisted with pain, rushed through her.

Careful, she reminded herself. *Don't lose your head.*

And not over a boy. Don't you dare.

Finally, she reached the platform. She trembled in the shadow of a nearby cafe, tucking herself into the dark as if she could disappear. She wondered if spies still felt this fear, or if it had ghosted away with the experience. Did Beau feel this way when he was stealing, or had he grown used to it in the military?

Beau, Beau. Please be OK.

She steeled herself, breathing carefully.

Two bored-looking people guarded the carriage in their crisp palace uniforms, as it stood motionless on the platform. They were chatting lightly to one another, not expecting a robbery in broad daylight, not expecting a robbery in the middle ring at all. She still didn't dare walk up to them. She hadn't the confidence, or the strength in her legs. She'd only be able to risk it if another scientist approached first...

She couldn't do this. She couldn't. Beau wouldn't want her to. His pain wasn't worth her life. She should turn back.

Her life. She was risking her life. What was she thinking?

A cart selling flowers overturned on the corner, spreading blooms all over the steaming streets. The male guard rushed to assist—likely swayed from his post by the very attractive flower seller—and the female groaned at his absence, stepping forward a few paces.

A strange, dizzying boldness gripped her, and Asami seized her chance. She walked forward, flashing her card to anyone who might still be paying attention, and slid into the carriage.

The door clicked shut behind her. Her heart skidded against her chest. She hoped she hadn't just made a terrible mistake.

The carriage was lined with shelves and crates, in little order other than what fitted in what space. It was going to take forever to sort through, and she only had minutes until it started moving again.

Quick, quick, Asami.

She started at one end, searching for morphine, nemean, anyxatol, cofedren, opatrex, methylene—anything for pain relief or numbing. Dimly, in the back of her whirring mind, it occurred to her that now might be the ideal opportunity to steal the rest of the ingredients she needed to recreate the serum, if she could remember what they were. Her usually perfect recall was stumbling.

Think, think!

The door clicked open, and Asami dived behind one of the crates.

The female guard tumbled into the carriage, wrapped in the arms of a brown-skinned gentleman wearing a red corset jacket embellished with studs in the shape of a stag. He pressed his grinning face to her neck.

Asami stifled a gasp.

The gentleman was Prince Nero, heir to the throne of Firenze, distant cousin of Queen Mira.

"Your Highness—" whispered the guard breathlessly, "if we're caught—"

"Hush, love," he murmured against her neck, "I'll take the blame..."

"I could lose my position!"

He hoisted her onto a nearby crate. "Let me worry about your... position." His fingers slid to her thighs, and her objections stuttered into murmurs.

Asami's heart lodged somewhere in her throat. What was she going to do? In a few minutes, the train would restart. Nero probably didn't have to worry about being found here, and even the guard had less reason to worry than she did, but for her...

It was taking her back to the palace. To the military. To Malcolm.

Her breathing grew heavy. She reached out to grab something—anything—to steady herself, and her fingers slipped on a nearby canister, sending it crashing to the floor.

I really am 'threat to safety' clumsy...

The sounds of kissing evaporated.

"What was that?" asked the guard.

"Something fell over," said Nero indifferently, "as it is apt to on a *train*."

"We're stationary," said the guard.

Asami heard her shuffling upright, likely gesturing to the prince to be still and silent. She stared at the canister. Should she grab it? It was heavy enough to use as a weapon, but against an armed guard? Nero was by the door. There was no escape. She could pretend she was supposed to be here, that she'd heard them come in and gotten embarrassed...

Was that believable?

Was this it?

Her mind juddered with all the things she could have told Beau.

Thank you for saving me.

I'm really glad I met you.

Stay safe.

You are worth the risk I take.

I'm sorry, I'm sorry, I'm sorry.

Something outside the door exploded. The guard leapt back towards Nero, pushing him to the floor. "Your Highness, stay down!"

"Excellent advice."

She raced out into the fray. Asami couldn't see what was going on. If she left her spot, Nero would spot her.

A smoke bomb burst into the carriage, obscuring everything in seconds. She pulled on her goggles and mask, the crates swimming with white. Nero was coughing nearby, stumbling against the shelves. She turned back, sightless, scrambling. Now was the perfect opportunity to get what she came for—

The guard skitted back into the carriage.

"Your Highness! Your Highness, where are you?"

The door to the adjoining carriage banged open. Someone let out a shot. The air crackled with grey and gunpowder. Cries and shouts skidded about like metal insects, and people were everywhere.

No, not just people.

A small automaton appeared at her ankles, some sort of bird-cat. It looked oddly familiar.

The crate behind her lurched. Someone threw open the lid.

"Grab as many as you can, quickly. Dandelion, don't forget the—"

A face appeared above her, goggles of green and bronze framed by black curls. A shake, a sigh. "Didn't have any faith in our herbs, eh, Doc?"

Asami didn't reply. A second later, Snowdrop had wrenched her to her feet and was stuffing her satchel with supplies. One of the automatons—a tiny bird-like creature —buzzed around the rebel's head. Snowdrop leaned into the sound, listening attentively.

"Reinforcements," Snowdrop snapped. "Let's get clear."

She smashed in one of the windows with the butt of her pistol, knocked the shards aside, hurled another smoke bomb into the crowd, and leapt over the ledge. She held out her hands to Asami, who didn't object. One of the other rebels— Dandelion or Clover, she couldn't remember—flung himself out afterwards, his backpack fit to breaking.

She didn't wait to see who was following. She kept close to Snowdrop's side as she burst through the people and the pouring smoke, pistol down but still in hand. A guard rose out of the smog, sword extended, but she shot his arm and kept running.

The screaming was everywhere.

The smoke dispersed.

Snowdrop wheeled into a nearby alley. She shoved Asami

against the wall and wrenched off her coat, flinging it into a nearby bin. She pulled off her own cape and turned it inside out, the deep purple lining disguising the rough green outer. She shoved it round Asami's shoulders and yanked off masks and goggles, twisting up her own hair, pulling on a blue scarf.

Asami stared at her all the while. "The others—" she said eventually.

Snowdrop shook her head. "They'll meet us at the rendez-vous. We're less noticeable travelling alone. Come on. Look frightened."

"Not hard," Asami said numbly.

Snowdrop grabbed her arm and pulled her back into the throngs. Guards lined the street, casting eyes over every-one, but Snowdrop's quick disguises worked and it was clear no one was looking for Doctor Asami Thorne today. They walked briskly, their pace increasing once they were clear of the chaos. A few streets later, they boarded a tram. Asami knew better than to ask where they were going.

"Why didn't you tell me you were going after the medical train?" she asked eventually, her heartbeat now slowed. "I would have waited if I'd known!"

Snowdrop glared at her. "I don't know you," she replied. "And I'm not in the habit of telling strangers our plans. Why didn't *you* sit tight and just use the herbs?"

"Why give me herbs at all if you were robbing a supply train?"

"Because I knew we'd be gone for hours, and I didn't want Beast to suffer any longer than he had to."

At that, Asami stilled. "Oh."

"Precisely." She looked out the window. "Outer ring. Come on."

14

THE INFIRMARY

The guard presence had thinned considerably by the time Asami and Snowdrop left the tram, and no one seemed to care much about two women making their way to the dregs of town. Asami said nothing else as they walked, too ashamed of how stupid she'd been, how reckless and foolish.

And for what, a man?

No. Not just any man. Someone who needed you.

She bit her lip. Much good she'd done him. He'd have been furious with her if she died. He would never have wanted her to do that for him.

Although she was fairly sure he would have done it for her.

Of course. He's a trained soldier. You are not.

She kept imagining her parents' disapproving looks, the slow shakes of their heads. *Idiot, idiot, idiot.*

She should never have left the lab. She should never do anything bold or adventurous or reckless again. She should—

"We're here," Snowdrop prompted.

Asami unscrewed her gaze and lifted up her head. They were so far into the outer ring that the black wall beneath the glass of the Dome was visible right behind the tall building of crumbling apartments that towered overhead. Most were empty or boarded up, but a few washing lines hung across the street, cluttered with damp, soot-stained clothing. The bottom floors housed a row of garages, and one was rolled open.

The rest of the rebels sat inside, crowding round a rudimentary table, doctoring their injuries. Hunter, sporting an excellent gash across his forehead, got up to put his arm around Snowdrop when she materialised.

"Not like you to be late," he said.

"Someone slowed me down."

Asami pulled at the cuffs of her shirt. "I'm sorry," she said to the floor. "Thanks for getting me out of there."

"No problem." Snowdrop shrugged. "I'd like my cloak back now, though."

Still feeling foolish and guilty, Asami tugged off the cloak and handed it back. There was a bit of a bite to the air, and she missed her coat, more than for just the warmth. It was one of the few things she'd brought with her into the underground. One of the few things still *hers*.

Snowdrop and the others were tearing through the equipment they'd stolen, including the ones stowed in Asami's bag. They separated everything into piles while Dandelion kept watch outside.

"Why rob a medical train at all if you have access to herbs?" Asami asked.

"Medicine lasts longer, and there's more of it," Snow replied, not looking at her.

"What do you even need it for?"

Hunter scoffed. "What do you think?"

Before Asami could ask what she meant, a small figure appeared at the door. Asami's immediate thought was that it was a child, but although the thin, rakish woman standing there had the height of a youth, she was wrinkled with age, grey and gaunt and waifish. A puff of steam could have blown her away.

"We're nearly ready, Grandma," said Snowdrop.

"Grandma?"

"Code name," the old woman coughed. "What's yours?"

"I'm—" Asami started.

"She's not one of us," Clover said shortly.

Grandma raised an eyebrow. "Then how do we know we can trust her?"

"I'm no friend of the palace," said Asami, just as curtly.

"You'll find few here that are."

"Dread doctors!" hissed Dandelion from outside. "Look sharp!"

Everyone, including Grandma, hurried into the garage and rammed the door shut. Clover leapt to an open tin in a corner of the room and sprinkled a strange, grey dust over the entrance. It fell slowly, like tiny shards of metal clinging to the air.

"Their goggles have heat sensors," Snowdrop explained to Asami. "Took us a while to figure that out. The powder seems to confuse them."

A shadow passed under the narrow gap of light at the end of the garage, and time stuttered to a stop as it lingered there. Asami's breath tightened in her chest, and she wondered how it was possible that her heart seemed to have slithered up to her ribcage.

The shadow moved, dull, heavy footsteps descending down the street.

The group gave a collective sigh. Snowdrop shuddered, as if freeing herself from a spider's web. "Dread doctors. Those guys really give me the chills."

"Not their biggest fan either," Asami agreed. "I wish they weren't called doctors."

Clover and Hunter lifted the garage door, the little bots squirming about their feet. Grandma squeezed out afterwards, barely looking around, as if she'd lived too long to be afraid of dread doctors or didn't really care one way or another.

The others repacked the supplies. Asami opened her mouth to ask if she could have some for Beau, but it was bundled up before she could, everyone moving again. She wasn't used to this kind of *speed.*

"You coming, Doc?" Snowdrop asked.

"Asami," she corrected. "And where are we going?"

"You'll see."

Hunter at the lead, the rebels traipsed through the streets, automatons clicking behind them. Few gave them any notice, or even raised their heads at all. So many gazes screwed to the ground, so many bent bodies and skin etched with coal. Asami wondered how Mortimer had coped, coming home to this after the glitter of the palace. A few hours here, and the faces twisted into her, a raw, festering guilt alongside them.

Asami knew guilt. It was a feeling she'd been plagued with since childhood. Guilt at lying to avoid disappointing her parents. Guilt at disappointing them anyway. Guilty for the handful of times she hadn't studied her hardest before a test, or the rare times she'd snapped at someone. Guilt for forgetting birthdays because she was too tied up in her work, for missing things.

She had never felt a guilt like this, one that came from ignorance, from living beside them and *above* them, and never thinking of them at all.

It was enough, for a while, to dispel her thoughts of Beau.

After twenty minutes or so, the group came to the door of a basement underneath an old warehouse. Grandma was posted at the entrance, nodding people in, keeping an eye out. Asami descended with the rest in a thud of heavy boots and clanging of gears, the little bots jumping down the steps.

The steps led to a large, dark room, filled with bunks and chairs, screens and tables. Dozens of people lay or sat around the space, some still, some sleeping, some thrashing. Some moaned, some coughed, some were quiet. A handful of other people moved around, changing dressings, administering rudimentary aid, changing sheets... and pulling them over stiff, still forms.

A hospital. Or what passed for one, in the outer ring.

Dandelion and Clover moved to a station in the middle of the room and started to distribute the medicine to the other volunteers. Hunter stood in the corner, like a general surveying the aftermath of war.

Asami hung back, beside Snowdrop. "It's for the poor," she said quietly. "This whole trip… it wasn't for the rebels at all. I had no idea the Rebellion did things like this. No one ever—"

"No one ever talks about it? Well, they wouldn't, would they? Doesn't exactly fit the narrative the palace wants to portray."

"Why?"

"Why do we have this whole Little-Red-Riding-Hood-thing? Stealing from the rich, giving to the poor?"

Asami frowned at the reference, thinking back to her childhood fairytales. "Is that right?"

Snowdrop shrugged, and strolled forward. She plucked a vial of liquid morphine from the table, and handed it to Asami. "For our dear Beast. Sorry I can't spare more."

Asami folded the vial away. "Sorry I didn't trust in your herbs."

"It's all right. I get it. Took me a while to believe in them, too."

Asami wondered who Snowdrop had been before she joined the Rebellion. She carried herself well, and there was a freshness to her complexion that made Asami feel she hadn't started life in the slums. But she decided not to pry, not to push. People's stories were their own.

She glanced at the door.

"You know the way back?" Snowdrop asked.

"I think so, but…" Her eyes circled back to the other patients, to the people lingering at their sides. What made

Beau's pain more important than theirs, other than she felt it more?

At least Beau had the tea.

"Some of these people have the coal sickness, don't they?" she said.

Snowdrop nodded.

"Why not just let them—"

"Once you go into the palace infirmary, you come out in an urn. And you die alone. No one wants that. At least this way, they get to be with their families."

Her gaze drifted to an old man lying on his side in a bed, his wife gripping his hand. Only, at second glance, Asami realised they weren't that old. Fifty, maybe. It was hard to tell under the dirt.

"When I die, I hope I have someone with me who loves me like that," Snowdrop whispered, almost to herself.

Asami shivered, because the thought of dying like that— or watching someone die like that—was too horrible to contemplate. She hoped her end was quick and painless and no one had to suffer with her.

"I'll stay and help for a bit," Asami said, pushing such thoughts away. "It's the least I can do." She rolled up her sleeves, marching to a corner of the room where someone had hung up aprons.

Snowdrop followed her. "I didn't know you were that kind of doctor."

"I'm not," she said, tying on the apron. "But the basics are simple. It's not surgery. It's just care."

Snowdrop looked at her, and it was different from her

other glances. No annoyance or frustration or mild indifference. Asami couldn't quite put her finger on what.

"What can I do?" Snowdrop asked.

Asami wasn't sure her smile quite reached her mouth, but she felt it nonetheless. "Follow me," she said, "and I'll let you know."

For hours, Asami worked with the volunteers to administer aid, dishing out medicine, making the patients as comfortable as possible, and sorting the remainder of the drugs for distribution. She assessed each patient, trying to calculate their weight to maximise the effectiveness of the drugs, leaving detailed instructions of how much to give them, and when.

Most of them, she suspected, would be dead within a few days.

She cleaned the spare beds, helped Clover swab the floors, re-organised the kitchen supplies and discussed with Grandma how to arrange the beds optimally. She expected someone to be annoyed with her suggestions, this outsider coming in and telling them how to run things, but if they felt any annoyance, they kept it to themselves.

"You can come again," said Grandma, stuffing a pipe with herbs during a break.

Asami didn't want to ask what they were.

Exhaustion began to pull at her bones by the evening, her fingers chafed from the cleaning. She thought of Beau, alone. He might be worried about her, if he was conscious. Or maybe he'd think she'd finally abandoned him, or just found somewhere else to be where she didn't have to watch him.

That last one was half right. It was easier to watch these people suffer than him. Why was that? When had that started?

Snowdrop came to fetch her, pushing a bowl of something warm and tasteless into her hands.

"Thank you," said Asami. "I think I'll head back soon."

"Probably wise. You look tired."

"And what about you? What will you do now?"

"We've got a couple more jobs to do," Snowdrop explained. "Can't tell you much more. Just in case…"

"In case I get captured and tortured into revealing information?"

"Yes."

"Great." Asami shivered. She did not imagine she would last very long under interrogation.

"To that end, Clover is walking you back to the tunnels."

"Am I?" He looked up from tinkering with what Asami suspected was a bomb of some kind, hopefully devoid of the explosive elements.

Snowdrop shot him a look.

"Oh, I am, apparently. Jolly good. Right." He stood up sharply, pulling on his cloak and mask. "Off we go, then."

They walked back briskly through the darkening streets, melding into the shadows, keeping an eye out for dread doctors. Awkward as the silence was, Asami was grateful for the company. It dispelled a fraction of another kind of gloom, and saved her from getting lost.

"How long have you been with, er…" She wanted to avoid saying 'Rebellion' in public, not certain they were safe. "Snowdrop and the others?"

"Four years," he said.

"Four?"

He barely looked out of his teens, with wild sandy hair, large grey eyes, and tanned skin unbeaten by the harshness of years. In fact, Asami thought he might be as young as sixteen. People aged faster in the outer ring, and she suspected something similar occurred in the Outlands, too.

"Black Death took both my parents by the time I was thirteen," he explained. "I have a little brother and sister. Couldn't stand the thought of the same thing happening to them, or me, and them having no one. My little brother's lungs have never worked right. When the Rebellion came through here looking for more people, I volunteered."

"They took you? A child? And… your siblings too?"

He shook his head. "Hunter said I was too young, even though Snow was barely any older. So I made myself invaluable—learned how to make bombs. Helped them out. Convinced them it was safer for us in the Outlands than down here. Took a while. But it worked."

"And is it?"

Clover paused to frown at her.

"Safer, I mean? In the Outlands?"

He snorted. "You'd be surprised."

You could see glimpses of it from certain points in the palace. A great, wide desert, the sharp peaks of mountains, a dense woodland around it. The Cold Desert, they called it, the remains of an empire pulsed to grains of sand. It held less life than a graveyard, for even graves carried echoes of life once lived. The sand was a phantom.

She wanted to ask more, but she sensed she'd get little from him. Shortly after, they reached the door to the tunnel.

"Need any more help?" Clover asked.

Asami fished out the map she'd left behind. "I think I'm good."

He nodded, tipping his goggles in lieu of a hat. "Thanks for your help earlier, Doc."

"Anytime."

"Be careful. We may just take you up on that."

He gave a quick wave and disappeared back down the alleyway with a swish of his long, green coat. Asami hugged her arms and descended into the tunnel, closing the door tightly behind her.

She stumbled back through the winding passageways, so exhausted that several times she took a wrong turn and had to double back. Finally, she reached the door leading down the steps to the base, and made her way to Beau's room.

He was sleeping soundly beneath the covers, curls tousled, hiding his malformed eye. Asami brushed it back, running her fingers over the lumps and contusions. They had never been frightening to her, never revolting, but now they were something else. Something less. She couldn't explain it.

She leaned forward and kissed his head, lingering there for longer than she would have done if he'd been awake, and marvelled at the beautiful, unspoilt parts of him, the softness of most of his mouth.

Beside him, on the chair she'd been using, was a basket of fresh food, supplies, and painkillers.

A small note was scribbled on the top.

Dosed him at 4pm. Give him another in the morning. Sorry I can't do more.

It was unsigned, written in a deft but scrawled hand. Asami didn't have the energy to wonder about his mysterious benefactor. Actually, she was suddenly surprised she'd managed to summon the strength to get this far. Her muscles were taut and trembling, her head heavy, and fatigue pulled at every crevice and sinew.

She folded the note back into the basket, yanked off her boots, and tumbled into the bed right beside Beau, too exhausted to care about the mess she was in, or the intimacy of the action. Too exhausted to feel anything but a shocked, dazed relief, that he was safe, and so was she, and she was home.

15

THE HEART BELOW

Although she knew it was impossible, a feeling like the morning dawn roused Asami from her sleep. For a second, before she opened her eyes, she was home in Toulouse, and filtered, perfect sunlight was spilling through the gaps in the curtains. She thought of apple blossoms and raspberry pancakes, and that heady time before the seasons switched, half spring, half summer.

Large, careful fingers were stroking her hair, and warmth washed over her skin.

She opened her eyes, and found Beau staring down at her. The slight smile on his face seemed to melt every other part of him away, every other part but the softness of his gaze and the gentleness of his fingers. Asami smiled back, warmth pooling through her, spreading from the centre of her belly to her toes.

Beau drew his hand away, breaking the thin threads growing between them, leaving the air between them fuzzy with something else she could not name. It trembled like the fragments of the powder Clover had used the night before. "You don't have to stop," she said.

At that, Beau smiled again.

"How are you?" she asked.

"It's passed," he said. "I'm fine."

Asami launched herself from her spot and into his arms with such fervor that she rolled him back against the mattress. Beau gripped onto her, tugging her against him.

"That was horrific," she whispered. "I was so worried."

"I'm sorry."

"You don't have to be sorry for that," she said, peeling back. *Somebody else needs to be sorry for that.* She took his face in her hands and marvelled at the brightness of his eyes. "Breakfast," she declared. "You've not eaten for days. And then a bath. And then I'll stop fussing."

"Almost a shame," he declared. "But I'll follow your orders, Doctor."

She stood up, not troubling with her boots now he'd cleaned the floors so diligently, and scooped up the basket on the seat.

"Your friend brought us quite the care package."

"You spoke with him?"

She shook her head. "He was gone by the time I got back."

"Got back from where?"

Asami cringed, stilling on her way to the door. "Ah, yes, that."

"Asami?"

"So, I may have gone above ground and got involved in a *little* bit of a train heist with the Rebellion." No need to tell him she'd been foolish enough to go alone.

"You *what?*"

She marched on, down the platform, towards the kitchen and away from his gaze. "Don't you dare get cross with me. You go above all the time."

"I'm not public enemy number one!" he said, hurrying after her. "Everyone thinks I'm dead! And I'm trained to avoid detection—"

"Well, perhaps you better train me, because I was *awful...*" She shook her head. "Don't worry, I'm in no mood to try it again, and nothing happened. Met some of the rebels though. Hunter is a bit terrifying. Snowdrop seemed nice." She paused at the kitchen door. "She was worried about you."

He shrugged. "She's a nice person, sometimes."

"So you and she..."

"What? No. No. Nothing like that."

"Right."

"Asami..."

"Yes?

"I haven't been with anyone since this"—he gestured to his face—"happened."

Asami had suspected such a thing, but no relief came with it, just a dull, heavy feeling, the weight of a loneliness that wasn't hers. "It's been a year, for me," she said slowly. "I had a brief *thing* with one of the scholars from the palace. It never amounted to anything and I didn't expect it to. And before then... well, not much worth talking about."

There had been a semi-serious relationship at university. First love. It had burned bright and short and when it ended, the heartbreak had been minimal. She'd moved on readily enough, but no one held her interest long.

Was it the same with Beau? Would it short out, if she let it spark up? At her centre, she wanted to say no, despite her track record.

She pulled at the end of her braid. This is why she preferred numbers. There was always one right answer. People were not sacks of numbers, no matter how much she sometimes wished they were.

"You don't need to tell me this," Beau told her.

"I'm just letting you know you need more than just a pretty face to meet people."

"Ah, so it's my personality that's the problem." He smiled weakly. "Good to know."

"I like your personality, Beau."

"You're still calling me that?" he said, looking down.

"I like it," she said. "Honestly, I didn't like calling you 'Beast'. It felt very rude."

"I doubt you've ever said a rude thing in your life."

"If you really don't like Beau—"

"I like it," he said, "when you say it."

At this, she felt her cheeks prickle, but a few moments later they stretched into a yawn.

"You still look exhausted," Beau said. "Maybe you should go back to bed."

"You going to carry me there again?"

Beau scratched the back of his neck. "If I did wrong—"

"Not at all. You can carry me any time you like."

She dipped finally into the kitchen, pulling out tins and bowls. Beau hung in the threshold, as if reeling from her words.

"I don't mean to make things awkward between us," he started, stepping over to the table, "but for the sake of clarity... are you flirting with me?"

"Yes."

Beau gulped. "But... why?"

"*Why?*"

"Why are you flirting with me? Is it just a pity thing, or a proximity thing, or—"

"It is *not* a pity thing!" she insisted, resisting the urge to kick him in the shins.

"Then a proximity thing? Forced together in a high-stakes situation? Because statistically speaking—"

"Don't bring statistics into this if you're trying to convince me that I don't like you. You know what numbers do to me."

Beau did not smile. "You're avoiding answering the question."

"That's because I'm not sure," she said. "I *think* I would like you regardless of how we met, but yes, I understand the logic of enforced proximity."

"I... I need you to be sure."

Her jaw tensed. She fiddled with her cuffs. "I understand that logic, too." She paused, not meeting his eyes. "Go clean the dining room for breakfast. It's grown dusty in your absence."

Everything slid easily back to the way it was before, and if any awkwardness existed from her semi-declaration, it was shelved or dispelled, to be discussed never or later depending on whether she could make up her mind or not. Their old routine quickly shuffled back into place, and if Asami became unfocused at times, staring at the intense look in Beau's eyes as he surveyed the city, it was only once or twice.

She understood him wanting to be sure. She understood proximity infatuation, too, or infatuation born of an intense situation which fizzled away as soon as the situation was over.

But she wasn't sure she could understand a future where everything was normal again, and she and Beau lived separate lives.

What would be normal about that?

Distracted, or clumsy, she accidentally broke two of his mugs within a twenty-four hour period. The first time, he merely sighed. The second time, he got a bit short with her.

"I think I'm regretting saving you."

"It was only a couple of mugs!"

He pointed to the stack of dirty plates beside her, and the discarded paper she'd yet to clear up because she was too drawn into the project. Tidy though she usually was, she certainly had her moments where everything else stopped around her, waiting until she re-emerged.

She glared at him indignantly. "This place was filthy when I showed up!"

"Well, it's not filthy now, and it also doesn't have any mugs!"

Beau shifted off grumbling, and Asami returned to her work, twinging with guilt.

The next day, he presented her with wine after dinner, served in steel glasses he'd clearly crafted himself. He'd gone for a design something like flower petals. They were clumsy and rough and Asami loved them, so much so that she couldn't stop staring, watching as Beau drank from his own.

"Something wrong?" he asked.

Asami shook her head. "It's just... did I tell you I wanted wine glasses?"

"Maybe? Not sure. You cringed every time you drank from a mug. I put two and two together."

Asami stared at him. She wasn't sure anyone she'd ever known had been quite so observant. "Thank you."

"It's nothing," he said. "Sorry I snapped at you the other day."

"Sorry I broke your mugs." She took a sip and paused. "I'm sorry I don't have anything to give you."

Beau opened his mouth, but shut it quickly. After another second, he rushed, "I wouldn't worry about it."

But Asami did. Later that night, she whipped out the spare fabric Beau had secured for her, and started cutting out a waistcoat for him. She stole one of his others from his room to get the best fit, and got so caught up in sewing it together that she fell asleep halfway through the task. Beau found her there the next morning.

"What are you doing?"

Asami looked down and realised where she was. "Oh, bother. I suppose the surprise is ruined now." She held up the unfinished garment.

"You made me a waistcoat?"

"I was trying to."

He stared at her, as if waiting to wake up. "Why did you do that?"

"You made me the glasses!"

"It's an exchange?"

"It's supposed to be a nice gesture." She narrowed her eyes. "If you don't like it—"

"What? No! Gears, Asami, I'm sorry. I'm just so unused to anyone making anything for me I quite forgot how to accept a gift. I love it, I'm honoured, thank you." A smile ghosted his cheek. "Perhaps you better not wear your dress at the same time, though. Wouldn't want to match."

"Why not?"

The smile turned tense, but it did not slip away. She tugged the garment back.

"It shouldn't take long to finish. Think you can manage breakfast today?"

Beau gave her a long, lingering look, hard as stone and soft as feathers. She couldn't work out for the life of her what it meant. "Of course," he said, and shuffled off to the kitchen.

An hour or so later, she presented him with the finished waistcoat and wrestled him into it. It was a good fit, and he grinned long and hard.

"Want to see it in a mirror?"

His face fell. "Not particularly."

"Right," she said. "Of course."

"I'm sure it looks splendid."

"You do."

Half a blush dusted his good cheek, but then he muttered something about getting back to work, and they spent the rest of the morning doing just that. Asami wanted to say something to him, but she couldn't quite think what. The silence wasn't precisely uneasy, but neither did it hold the companionable warmth it used to.

"Have I unnerved you?" she asked eventually. "Or upset you?"

"You disarm me," he admitted, "and sometimes I have no idea what to say to you. Is the silence making you uncomfortable?"

"No, no! Well, yes, a little. But only because I wondered if you were upset—"

"I'm not, I assure you—"

Pilot raised a steel ear, and emitted something like a bark.

"What is it?" Asami asked, heart clenching.

Beau wheeled towards his screens, eyes darting across them. Something—someone—was thundering down the tunnel. Asami barely had time to see who it was before the door at the top of the stairs slammed open.

Hunter fell down the steps, covered in blood.

16

PRISON BREAK

Beau hurried towards him, but Hunter was already stumbling to his feet, Clover fast behind, half of the bots whirring at his side.

"I tried to tell him to slow down—" he yammered, looking wildly at Beau and Asami.

"She's gone, she's gone, they've got her..." Hunter muttered, as Beau steered him into a seat in the lab. Asami raced to get a medical kit, returning to pry off his jacket. He waved her away. "No, don't worry about me, I'm fine..."

"You're covered in blood," she rushed. "Stars, is that a bullet wound?" She examined a hole in his shoulder, pulsing with red.

"It's fine, but Snow, Snow's—"

"Mission went wrong," Clover explained. "Snowdrop's been taken into custody."

Beau froze. "And Dandelion?"

"Keeping eyes on her. At the moment, they're holding her in one of the lower rings. If they move her—"

"She can't be taken to the palace," Hunter muttered, his words as slippery as his blood-soaked chest. "She can't be. I need to get her—"

He tried to rise, but both Beau and Asami pushed him back.

"You've lost a lot of blood," she said. "You're not going anywhere."

"I have to get her back—"

"*We'll* get her back," Beau insisted. "But you're staying here, soldier."

Clover glanced at Asami. "Can you help him?"

"I'm not a surgeon. I can clean and dress the wound, but anything else—"

"You're not leaving me here!"

Asami sighed. "Clover, can you run along to the train carriage and fetch the basket beside the bed, and the sewing kit from the adjoining car?"

Clover did not ask twice. He raced off and was back before Hunter could protest too much. The basket was still packed with all the medical supplies Beau's mysterious friend had left; she had not yet had the opportunity to organise it. She whisked through the vials now, measuring out a large dose into a syringe, taking a rough guess at Hunter's weight.

"Something for the pain," she said, administering it into his arm.

Hunter stared at her, his body relaxing. "It's fine," he insisted thickly. "I'm fine…"

His chin slumped against his chest, his breathing slowed. He was out cold.

Clover's eyes darted to the wound, as if worried he might have passed out from blood loss. Beau merely raised an eyebrow at her. "You knocked him out."

"Do you blame me?"

"No, I'm just wishing I thought of it."

Asami bit back a smile. "Clover, please go and put some water on to boil and then come back and explain everything."

Slowly, Clover did so, and Asami listened patiently, pausing only to fetch the whistling kettle. She doctored Hunter as best she could while Clover continued with the story. A robbery of some sort. More guards than they were expecting. Details that didn't really matter apart from the final one; where Snowdrop was being held, a facility in the lower ring.

"We… we can get her out, right?" he said tremorously, sounding very young. "We *have* to get her out."

"We'll do our best," said Beau, already moving to the maps.

Asami watched him work, watched his eyes race over blueprints, plans, notes about guard rotas and securities. She could almost see the gears in his head turning, running through a dozen ideas, possibilities, scenarios.

She imagined she might wear a similar look when she was working something out, but she couldn't imagine it stirring up anything inside anyone.

He really was astonishingly attractive when he was being smart.

Clover peered over his shoulder. Asami pried her gaze from the intense look in Beau's eyes to the plans, trying to work out whatever it was he was seeing, but her mind didn't work through strategies as well as it worked through numbers.

For a second, she thought achingly of her mother.

"Clover," said Beau eventually, "how tall are you?"

"Um, five eight?"

"Hmm." He put his hands against his shoulders. "Might be too wide."

"What for?"

"There's a couple of ways in. Safest would be to climb through one of the tunnels underneath the prison, and liberate a key. It's far too tight for me, though. Probably you, too."

"We could send one of the bots?"

"Risky. They're a bit loud, and fiddly things like this—"

Clover sighed. "Too many margins for error."

"What about me?" interrupted Asami.

Both men turned to stare at her. "No," said Beau. "Absolutely not."

"Why not? You said it was the safest option."

"Safest for…"

"Yeah, Beast, why not her?" said Clover smugly.

"If I just need to sneak in and grab a key—"

"It's a bit more than that, and no. I won't have it. I'm not putting you at risk."

"But I'm fair game? Not going to lie, that hurts," said Clover, clutching his heart. "Come on, man. She wasn't totally awful when we were running from the palace guard."

"Thanks." Asami glared. "Please, Beau. Let me help. I don't *particularly* like the idea of waiting around while you run into danger, either."

Beau's jaw tensed, his fingers tightening into fists. "Fine.

But you're in and out."

"Sir, yes, sir!" She gave him a salute.

"That was terrible."

"So was breakfast, and yet I did not complain."

Clover started to empty his bag and draw weapons from the wall, taking inventory. "When you two have finished bickering," he said, "please tell me what we need?"

Beau went through the plan as they packed, hastily pulling together equipment, forcing the two of them to memorise the layout of the complex as well as they were able. He quizzed them as they moved through the tunnels, swift and sharp. Asami babbled back precisely, impressing him with her memory even as she tripped over in the darkness. She'd changed into her loosest skirt, which she'd sliced at the sides to allow for freedom of movement, but she really wished she'd had access to a pair of trousers and a set of decent walking boots.

Beau caught her as she stumbled.

"It's the footwear," she said. "Not the nerves. Promise."

"I don't like you doing this."

"You've made that very clear. But you can't keep me safely locked up at home whilst you go gallivanting off. It's not fair, and you know it."

Beau paused.

"What?"

"You called it home."

"Well, what else would I call it?"

"I'm not even sure I've called it that in three years."

She paused too, her fingers trembling at her side, but the few inches between them suddenly seemed like miles. "But you would now, right?"

"Yes," he said slowly, in a confession that sent her heart racing, "I would."

"Tunnel's coming up!" Clover yelled from ahead. "I'll go report to Dandelion."

He raced on into the darkness, half of the little automatons scurrying after him. Beau and Asami were alone once more. She saw the 'tunnel' he spoke of, a narrow gap several feet above the ground. She hoped she wasn't shaking.

"Want to run through the plan again?" Beau asked.

"No. I'm fine."

"Right. Of course you are."

"Beau?"

"Yes?"

"I'll *be* fine." She rose up on tiptoes and tugged his face down to hers, placing a kiss against his cheek, savouring the warmth of his skin against her own.

She pulled away, and for a second, she imagined Beau wanted to say or do something else, but instead he linked his fingers together and held them out for her to climb on, posting her into the space.

It was just as filthy and greasy as she anticipated. It would have to be, for it to lie forgotten like this.

"Grab the key and open the door," Beau repeated. "Set off the smoke bomb. Get out."

"I haven't forgotten."

"I know, I just..." he sighed, with a breath that seemed to shudder against the tunnel. "Stay safe. Don't do anything foolish."

"Rarely do."

"Have you forgotten how we met?"

Her cheeks warmed. "Never, Beau dearest. I'll see you on the other side."

Her confidence wavered in seconds, if it had ever been there to begin with. It was the equivalent of him trying not to scream in front of her.

Don't be scared. You can do this.

Beau's footsteps disappeared.

Shuffling forward, inch at a time, grinding against the dirt, Asami crept up the tunnel. Clover would never have fitted; she barely did. She imagined the original architects had not planned the tunnels for human occupation.

It was horribly, impossibly dark. In some ways, it was better not being able to see the filth all around her. In others, it was worse, the darkness pressing down like an iron. She was drowning in it, choking in it, and she had to wade forward, onward.

Her heart trembled in her chest, sucking air from her lungs, and several times she had to stop to steady herself, even though she could feel the seconds trickling away.

They could not afford to delay. She could not afford to stop.

She forced herself to think of the blueprints Beau had shown her, counted down to the turns, metre by metre, inch by inch. Her estimations were off at several points, but the numbers brought normalcy to her journey, reined in her fears.

Ten feet, right turn. Twenty, left. Incline by 15%. Left after thirty-five feet.

I'm not cut out for this, I'm not cut out for this, I'm not cut out for this—

Twelve feet, right turn.

Finally, blissfully, a light appeared ahead, a faint trickle against the dark. The sound of voices, too, emanated down the tunnel.

Asami crawled forward, into the dim light.

17

PRISON BREAK II

"So," said Clover, after they'd filled Dandelion in on the plan and stood in the shadow of a nearby building, waiting for Asami's signal, "good to see you up and about again."

Beau did not take his eyes off the barred window, where, any moment now, they should spot her signal. How long would it take her to crawl through the vent? She'd been fairly certain about her estimations, but she'd never been in a situation like this before. She wouldn't have made allowances for fear or panic.

Be safe. Just be safe.

He shouldn't have let her suggest this. He should have found another way—

"Beast?" Clover nudged his elbow. "You sure you're fully recovered? You look… um…"

"I'm fine," Beau snapped.

"Right." Clover dug his hands into his pockets, and rocked back and forth on his heels. "So, Asami. Is she single?"

At this, Beau scowled. "You're too young for her."

"Yeah, but you're not." He shot him an impish grin, which

made Beau's stomach coil further into tight, constricting knots.

Too old for her, he was not. But everything else—

It had been a long time since anything like this had elicited any kind of fear in him. If anything, the odd heist and the clever bit of stealing gave him a rush of elation, a sense of satisfaction. Nerves over such events had long fizzled out.

Nerves over talking to women hadn't gotten much better over the years, though. It turned out there were scarier things than being shot at.

And nerves over actually feeling something... well, that felt completely new.

This was all new.

"Hey," said Clover, sensing something in Beau's demeanour, "I was just trying to lighten the mood."

"I'll lighten up," Beau said through gritted teeth, "when she's safe."

"We're not talking about Snow, are we?"

"We are not."

Clover sighed. "That's cold, man. You've known Snowdrop for what, two, three years? Then a few weeks with this pretty doctor and poof—"

"Don't tease him," said Dandelion. "One day, you'll fall for someone, and I will tease you back threefold."

Fall, fall, fall. The words buzzed around Beau's ears. He'd fallen in love before, but never did the word seem more appropriate than this. *Fall. Verb. To move from a higher to a lower level, rapidly and without control. To lose one's balance. To collapse.*

The sickening feeling of falling had wedged itself permanently inside his gut, and there was nothing to drag him back upright again. He could only fall further, further into the dark.

It doesn't need to be dark. Not if she's with you.

But she couldn't be. She *wouldn't* be.

"You won't need to tease me," Clover insisted, deaf to Beau's silent screaming. "When I fall for someone, I'm not going to beat around the bush. I shall tell them immediately."

Dandelion rolled his eyes. "I'll remember that, when your time comes. I don't think it will be as smooth as you imagine it."

Clover snorted and muttered something else to him. Beau didn't notice. His eyes were trained on the building, watching, waiting, imagining the hundred things that could go wrong.

Asami's brain worked a bit like that, he knew, constantly calculating a thousand possibilities. It was no wonder she was a bit scatterbrained and clumsy elsewhere, with so much going on inside her head.

When did he start thinking about her brain?

He gulped. *When you wondered if her brain was thinking about you.*

She'd made no secret of her attraction to him, but he couldn't quite make sense of that, because it was ludicrous. She barely knew him, and she wouldn't be the first person to fall for someone she was forced to spend time with. It would fizzle out if he left it long enough. It had to.

Because the alternative…

What's the worst that could happen?

She could change her mind and crush what little self-worth you have left.

Dandelion clicked his tongue, checking his pocket-watch. "The train will be coming soon," he remarked. "If she doesn't signal us soon—"

"We *can't* let them get Snowdrop," Clover insisted, voice wavering. "We can't."

Smoke erupted at the window, and Beau bolted forward.

The worst that could happen is something happening to her.

As expected, all the guards turned towards the smoke, giving the men the split second of surprise they needed. They dropped into the open, racing towards them, grabbing them by the throats. Fingers pressed to nerves, dropping them into unconsciousness.

They raced into the building. Bullets flew overhead. Several of the guards had taken refuge behind one of the desks, but Beau wrenched it off the floor and smashed them against the wall, holding them in place as Dandelion and Clover disarmed them, weapons clattering to the floor.

More firing, this time from behind them.

Reinforcements.

Shit.

"The door!" Beau hissed at Dandelion. "Get the door!"

Dandelion sprinted across to the main entrance, slamming it shut. Clover looped rope over the three guards still wedged behind the table.

A horrible, old, bitter thought rose inside Beau. *It would be quicker to kill them.*

Sounds crawled from the room along the corridor where Asami was, and he dropped the desk instinctively. One of the guards wriggled away from Clover's binds and hurtled towards it, grabbing a weapon.

Beau rushed after, but his feet were yanked from underneath him. He crashed to the floor.

"Idiot!" Clover hissed, scrambling out of reach of the freed guards.

Shots slammed against the door Dandelion was holding. They were outnumbered, they weren't holding position, and the three guards were spiralling in multiple directions.

One was heading towards Asami.

Asami.

Beau hauled himself upright, but a truncheon smacked him in the back. He just had time to roll and grab the weapon as it came crashing towards him, splintering it in his grip.

The guard's eyes widened as Beau's hood came loose, exposing his twisted skin to the grainy light.

"Monster," the man whispered.

Beau punched him in the face. "I get that a lot."

He snatched the pistol from his belt just as the back door blew open.

THE RETURN TO BELOW

The tunnel ended with a grate installed under a fitted bench. Through the slats, Asami could make out a small room with a line of cells, although she couldn't see too far into them. There was a desk at the corner and a row of keys on the wall behind. Opposite that was a door.

Asami's job was to get the key, open the main door, set off a smoke bomb, and get out. She was not to wait around. She was not to search for Snowdrop.

She stared at the door, and the row of keys. It would have to be the big one; the others looked too small for the locks.

She could understand Beau managing to steal the blueprints, but how had he known where the keys would be kept? Had he broken in here before?

Then it occurred to her that Beau hadn't broken into here before at all. He'd been one of the guards, a soldier on duty.

How strange that she couldn't imagine him as one, despite how swiftly he'd taken charge, how clear and commanding he'd been. Yet she couldn't imagine him as one of the guards because already she saw them as the bad guys, and him...

Him as something else.

And what does that make me? she wondered. A few weeks ago, the guards had made her feel safe. She thought she knew right and wrong, and found it largely clear cut. Yet here she was, freeing someone the palace decreed an enemy of the state.

And while she knew she was almost certainly doing the right thing, she hated the idea that it was also criminal.

A silly concept. Made-up, really. But she did not want to die as one.

Asami took a deep breath, and tried to move the grate. It did not budge, but carefully, she went into her pocket, and removed the smallest of the bots. It was no larger than a mouse.

"You know what to do?" she whispered, holding it up to the metal panel.

The metal mouse-hybrid made a sound almost like a squeak, clamping onto the corner, and started to whir. Asami hoped the noise was attributed to the dozens of other mechanical sounds in the great, roving metropolis, although it didn't look like anyone else was in the room to notice.

Maybe they *should* have sent the bot.

The main door opened, and a thick-booted guard clunked into the room. Asami saw him turning a key and sliding it into his pocket. Her stomach plummeted; was that the key? It was clearly *one* of them. Maybe none of the others worked on the door at all? Perhaps protocol had changed since Beau had been on duty here—

"How much longer?" barked a voice from the desk.

Asami startled, not realising there had been a guard behind it the whole time, parked just out of reach.

"Not much longer," the heavy-booted one replied. "Train's arrived. Just been checked."

Asami's stomach plummeted further. *No, no.*

"What happens if we can't get in through the main door?" she'd asked Beau.

"Then we'll have to intercept them before they get Snowdrop onto the train. We don't have the forces to attack them after that."

"The station's pretty far away, I recall. Would it not be easier to try getting to her then?"

Beau had grimaced. *"The facility, small as it is, is connected to the underground rail. If they try to move her, we'll be in trouble."*

A few minutes. A few minutes and they would have lost their gap. What then? Asami didn't want to think about that, but she could barely think of anything else. The bot was done with the grate and back in her pocket, but that hardly mattered. Two guards stood between her and the key.

The booted guard turned towards the cells. "You look kind of familiar," he called into the dark. "Have I arrested you before?"

"Believe me," said a calm, clear voice, "you'd remember me if that had happened."

Snowdrop.

"Pretty smug for a prisoner," returned the guard, annoyance lacing his voice. "There's no trial for rebels, you know. The Queen will have your head."

"I don't doubt it."

There was a rumble far off. The train? Reinforcements? Asami wasn't sure. But their gap was closing by the millisecond. She had to act. Quickly.

If she set off the smoke bomb, it would signal the others. Maybe, just maybe, with the element of surprise she could snatch the key and get it to the door to let them in before they caught her.

Because they would catch her. She wasn't swift enough or strong enough to escape. They would grab her before she could squeeze back into the tunnel.

She glanced at their belts. No pistols, only truncheons. They could incapacitate her, but killing her would be hard.

And the others would come, right? It would only be a bit of pain.

She thought of Hunter, stumbling into the base, covered in blood, desperate for help. She thought of all those in the infirmary, refusing treatment for the sake of a little longer with their families. And she thought of Beau, writhing in pain for days and trying not to scream for fear of alarming her.

She could handle a few minutes.

She pulled down her goggles, pressed the panel open, and took a long, steadying breath. Her fingers trembled against the cold metal of the smoke grenade. She clenched them, and her teeth, together.

She yanked out the pin and threw it into the room.

While the smoke was still dispersing, before the guards

could even cry out, she scrambled into the space and dived towards the one with the key, hand straight into his pocket. She snatched it back before he understood what was going on, narrowly missing one of his flailing arms. Snowdrop was banging on the bars, yelling expletives, disorientating them further. Asami barely heard. She hurtled towards the door and slammed the key into the lock, turning just as a pair of hands grabbed around her chest.

"The door!" the guard hissed to his colleague. "Get the door!"

Asami screamed as the second one stumbled forward, a grey blur in the smoke, arms searching for the lock. She lashed out with her feet, kicking and screeching. By luck rather than any real ability, her heel caught on the end of the key. She kicked again, dislodging it, and sent it skittering into the mist.

Snowdrop had given up yelling expletives and was now singing.

"*There was an old guard from Petragrad,*
Who tried to catch rebel,
What an arse, he slipped on the grass,
Now look at him tremble."

"Will you shut up!" snarled the guard.

"*He caught a mouse, a tiny thing,*
And then he appeared to rejoice,
But one thing the guard did not know?"

Asami felt the guard's back smack against the bars of one the cells, and an arm shot round his neck. When Snowdrop next spoke, her words were low and dark.

"I'm really good at throwing my voice."

The guard dropped Asami, fingers grappling at Snow-drop's arms. He gargled and rasped, flailing and desperate. His eyes looked like boiled eggs.

A crash from outside. Shouting, firing. The other guard vanished.

Asami knew she should run, like Beau had told her, but all energy seemed to have abandoned her. She could do nothing but watch as the guard struggled, growing limp.

Finally, he crashed to the floor.

"Is he dead?" she squeaked.

"Maybe," Snowdrop returned, her voice bland. "I'd rather not stick around to check. Can you find the key?"

Something in Snowdrop's words tugged Asami to her feet, and she stumbled forward into the dispersing mist, search-ing for the desk, the board, the keys. She'd memorised the lay-out well, but she tripped twice, half blind, fully clumsy. Her fingers grasped at the cold metal stems and she yanked them free of their hooks, wading shakily back through the mist to-wards Snowdrop's cell.

The rebel took the keys from her, trying them one by one. "You didn't come alone, I take it?"

Asami shook her head.

"The others OK? Hunter too?"

"I dosed him up and left him behind. He's scratched up but he'll be fine. He was worried about you."

A smile twitched in her cheeks. "Hunter worries."

A bang went off behind them. Asami yelped as Snowdrop knocked her to the floor. Another guard advanced into the room, but a second later a dark shadow cut across the threshold.

Beau.

The guard sprung backwards, raising his pistol towards the imposing form. Asami screamed, but Beau dived behind the thick metal door and tore it from its hinges, flinging it at the guard as if it weighed little more than cardboard.

He crashed against the floor, and Beau turned to Asami, relief darting in his expression despite the hardness of his brow. "I thought you were supposed to be getting out?" he said, offering her his hand.

"Fate had other plans."

A cry from outside.

"Reinforcements!" Clover yelled. "Hurry!"

Snowdrop located the right key and smacked open the door. Beau handed her a pistol with a curt nod. "You good?"

"Better than ever."

Asami hovered between them as another shot went off. "Don't I get a weapon?"

"You can barely walk straight; I'm not trusting you with a gun." His tone was soft despite his words, and he raised his hand as if to go to her cheek, but thought the better of it. He turned his back. "Stay behind me. Snowdrop, take the rear."

"You know, I don't think I've ever seen you give orders before," said Snowdrop, taking up the position. "It's attractive. You should do it more often."

Beau said nothing, but moved back towards the door, peering carefully around the corner, an arm flung out behind him, covering Asami.

"I'm sure *Asami* would be into it."

Asami twisted her head round to stare at her. "Are you… flirting with him, on my behalf?"

"Girl's got to have some fun."

"We're being shot at."

"I'm multitasking." She paused as a shot fired overhead. "Are you two wearing matching clothes?"

"No." Asami tugged her soiled cloak tighter. It had been the only dress loose enough for her to move easily, and it was probably ruined.

A crash sounded.

Priorities.

Beau charged ahead, through the crackling of gunfire and the swirl of smoke. Guards slumped around the room, furniture in tatters. Copper stung the air.

Don't look, don't look.

She focused on Beau's back and willed the rest of the room to blur away, forced it too, *begged* it to. She couldn't look for Clover or Dandelion or any of the bots. She couldn't look at the guards' eyes and still chests. She couldn't think about trying to save anyone.

She couldn't think of them as enemies, either. Not fully. Not now. Most of them were only here to do a job.

They spluttered into the outside. Shots reigned down from the rooftops, impossible to tell who was one of theirs and who was someone else. Impossible to tell anything, really. Gravity itself seemed blurred and bendy.

"Stay back!" Beau hissed, clearing a path through the guards, swiping every opponent away with a massive sweep of his arms. Snowdrop fired overhead, keeping them covered.

A sourness reached Asami's stomach, and she wondered if she shouldn't have tried squeezing back down the tunnel. She was nothing but a liability, here.

"Close your eyes!" Clover hollered.

There was crack, and a bright, burning light burst across the street, a light that seared against the back of her brain. Asami paused, blinded, but Beau seized her hand as the shots stifled, and hauled her into a back alley.

At the last second, the firing resumed, and something sharp snipped across her skin. A yelp ripped through her, but she didn't stop. She didn't dare. She didn't even breathe until the light disintegrated into darkness, and they slid into the cold, dark passageways beneath the clockwork city.

19

A DRAIN FULL OF DREAMS

Asami clutched her arm, her whole body numb and tingling, connected only by those shreds of pain. She held only a dim awareness of the blood trickling down her arm.

Beau scanned the rest of them. They were all there, all present and correct.

"Anyone hurt?"

"A few minor scrapes," Clover muttered. "Nothing serious. Dan? Snow?"

"Bruised, but fine."

"Ugh, nothing a bath can't cure…"

Beau's eyes circled back to Asami. "You're bleeding."

"Yes," she said quietly, her voice feeling sticky, "and I'd like to say it's just a scratch, but it really hurts quite a lot, actually, so if we could just get back—"

Without a word, Beau lifted her into his arms, keeping her injured one outwards, the rest of her pressed against his bad side. Not that Asami thought any part of him was bad. He was good, all good, all perfect…

It was possible she had lost too much blood.

She tried not to focus on the searing pain in her arm, tried not to focus on anything at all but the smell of his neck and the softness of his shirt against her cheek. It was a much better distraction.

"She all right?" asked Snowdrop, keeping pace with them.

"I'm fine, mostly," said Asami. "Beau's overreacting."

"Hmm," she said coyly. "Not usually one of his traits..."

Eventually, they reached the base. Beau slid Asami down into her chair in the lab, and went to fetch the supplies still in the basket beside Hunter, who was just regaining consciousness.

"Snow—" he started, launching shakily to his feet.

"Steady, steady old man," Snowdrop said, steering him back down. "Take it easy."

"You're all right."

She shrugged. "Nothing I couldn't handle."

Dandelion coughed.

"With a little help from my friends." She went quiet for a moment. "Thank you for coming to get me."

"Any time," said Dandelion, clapping her back. "But just not *all* the time. It's my turn to get arrested next."

Beau was still shaking his head as he rolled up Asami's sleeve. "You should never have volunteered," he seethed quietly, the anger pressing inwardly, towards himself. "We could have found another way."

"It was a good plan. It worked pretty well."

"You could have been hurt. *Really* hurt."

"So could everyone else."

"But you have people that care about you!"

"Rude," said Snowdrop from Hunter's side. "I get that you're not talking about us and are doing your own thing, but still, rude."

Beau scowled.

"She's right, you know," Asami said. "Everyone has someone that cares about them."

Beau's face was white and frantic. "Not like…"

"Beau?" she prompted, when he remained mute. "I care about you, too."

Beau said nothing to this, although his good cheek prickled. He turned back to her wound. "It's just a graze," he said. "Nothing serious."

"So you didn't need to pick me up at all?"

Beau didn't respond to that either. He started to clean the injury with water Clover had diligently prepared. Her flesh stung, and she dug her fingers into her thighs, trying not to wince.

"I'm all right, Beau," she said softly. "You don't need to worry."

"I'm afraid I don't have much of a choice." He sponged away the blood. "It's shallow. It doesn't need stitches."

"I know," she said, giving it a cautionary glance.

Beau frowned for a second, but didn't stop. He started to wind a bandage around her arm. "So, I cannot help but notice, despite you telling me you were squeamish about blood, that you seem remarkably calm and level-headed."

"Ah," said Asami, her cheeks heating, "I might have lied about that."

He raised an eyebrow. "Then why didn't you become a

medical doctor?"

Asami sighed, squirming in her seat. It was something she hadn't ever really told anyone, even when she could see the silent disappointment grazing in her parents' eyes when she explained her chosen field. She had been worried about revealing the full truth to them, like exposing a wound, anxious it made her seem unstable, weak, foolish.

But she didn't mind so much, telling Beau.

"Pain is infectious," she started. "It's a disease. It digs its claws into the people beside you and won't let go. I want to fix pain, to slow that epidemic. If I was a regular doctor, a healer, I'd spend much of my time watching people die, delivering bad news. I couldn't do that. But as a researcher… I'm only ever going to save people."

A long, drawn-out pause followed. "Why didn't you just tell me that before?"

"Well, it seemed funnier to say I was squeamish…"

Beau fixed her with a disbelieving stare.

"You were in pain," she replied. "I didn't want you to know how much that affected me. You might have told me to go—"

"Why wouldn't you?"

"I couldn't," she said, and for a moment was about to tell him it was like how she couldn't turn away from that hospital in the outer ring, either. But it wasn't like that. With them, once they were out of sight, it was easier. With him, it was worse.

Everything was worse with him.

And better. *So much better.*

"So," said Snowdrop, arriving at their side, "I'm sure I'm

not the only one who's absolutely ravenous. Dandelion's a fair cook, can he raid your supplies? Also, I'd love a bath, but I think you call dibs, Asami. Do you need a hand getting out of your clothes?"

Asami raised her bandaged arm, but quickly realised she'd struggle even without the wound. Her whole body felt stiff to the point of painful. "Please," she said, aware of the plaintive quality to her voice.

Snowdrop placed a hand on her back and guided her into the bathroom, sitting her down on the rickety wicker chair Beau had tucked into the corner and turning on the taps full blast. Asami didn't sit long. She hobbled to the sink and started scrubbing at her hands and face as the tub filled. Snowdrop examined the assortment of accoutrements sitting in a nearby basket, sniffing some of them approvingly and dabbing a little of the perfume on her wrists.

"This place is starting to shape up a bit since you came along."

"It wasn't me," Asami said, brushing off layers of dirt into the basin. "Beau does all the cleaning."

"Sure. *Now.*" She smiled at her, but Asami didn't quite have the energy to smile back. "So, thanks for helping get me out of there. I get the feeling that daring escape heists aren't exactly your comfort zone."

Asami snorted awkwardly. "Understatement."

"It's all right. They weren't mine once, either."

Forgetting her earlier resolve not to pry, or perhaps seeing this as an invitation, Asami asked, "why did you join the Rebellion?"

"Well, that is a *really* long, complicated, difficult story, but safe to say, I didn't feel like I had much of a choice."

Asami paused, wondering if she had a story like Clover's, where she felt death would come for her or her loved ones if she didn't. But Snowdrop hadn't mentioned any relatives, and there was something about her interactions with the others that made Asami think that *they* were her family, or as close as she had to one. She had the suspicion there was no one else.

And she could not pry.

"Why do you think Beau *didn't* join?" she asked instead. "I mean, not officially. He's clearly an ally."

"He's one of us in all but name," Snowdrop said, sloshing soap around the bath. "But if you're asking why he hasn't left the city to join us in the Outlands, I don't know. We've offered, and he's given us a range of excuses over the years. My guess is he's either utterly hopeless, or perhaps he still had hope after all."

"Hope for what?"

She looked down. "Something better."

"Don't you have that?"

"Some days," she admitted. "Not all. Not so many, any more. The longer all this goes on, the longer I think we're fighting a losing battle, or if we're ever going to win, I won't live to see it."

"But you're..." Asami glanced at Snow's face, trying to pin the years behind the dirt-streaked face. Younger than her, older than Clover.

"Twenty-two," she said. "Young to be so morbid, I know."

She swallowed, looking down at the bath. It was almost full. With very little discussion, she helped Asami peel out of her clothes and assisted her into the water, Asami far too exhausted to feel awkward or embarrassed. The hot water embraced her, thick and glossy. She almost wanted to drown in it.

She wasn't sure she'd ever been naked in front of another woman before, save her family, and only briefly. She'd had friends at school, but never close ones. Work had taken over everything. Work didn't tease or bully or let you down. And she couldn't let work down, either. She'd never forget its birthday, or what it liked to do. She could give and get and not be hurt.

Snowdrop announced her intention of fetching her some fresh clothes.

"They're in the carriage next to Beau's," Asami told her.

"Not sharing one yet, then?"

Asami blushed. "It isn't like that."

"But you want it to be?"

Asami said nothing.

"He likes you, you know. Any fool can see it. But if I'd had something like that happen to me, and then spent three years more or less on my own, I'd be hesitant too."

"I'm hardly scary."

"Love is always scary," she said, and turned towards the door. She stopped suddenly. "If you and Beast run into trouble, if you need to get out of the city, come to us. We'll help you. But don't join us if you can avoid it."

"Why not? Don't you need his help?"

"Oh, he's helpful, don't get me wrong, but I like him. I like *you*. I wouldn't pick our lifestyle for anyone I liked."

She left the room, leaving Asami to scrub herself in silence, pondering on Snow's words.

Love is always scary.

Love.

She knew she liked Beau. She knew he liked her. But love? It was true people threw that word around flippantly. When she was sixteen years old, her first boyfriend had told her he loved her. Asami had panicked and ran out of the park, because even then, she knew that love was a real, big thing, that it meant something.

Of course, he'd just been tossing out the word, saying what he thought he ought to, and apologised for scaring her off. They stayed together for a little while longer, but the romance never truly blossomed.

But with Beau...

Snowdrop returned in a few minutes with the shirt Asami had modified as a nightdress, whispering something about how she wished she'd learned to sew.

"What's it like?" Asami asked, wanting to speak about anything other than Beau and her feelings and the trembling in her chest. "The Outlands?"

At this, Snowdrop smiled. "Not quite the wasteland people think. Parts are very beautiful. Others harsh."

This matched with what Beau had told her. "Are there truly monsters out there like the rumours say?"

"There are... things, out there, that's for sure." She shuddered. "But that's neither here nor there. Let me help you with your hair. Tell me of Toulouse. I went there a few times as a girl. Beautiful place."

Tickets between the cities being as expensive as they were, Asami wondered again at Snowdrop's origins, but something else prickled to her mind.

"How did you know I was Toulousian?" She could understand the assumption that she was Yunasian—she largely bore her mother's features, she had a Yunasian first name—but very few ever pegged her for Toulousian.

"Your manners," she said. "And your voice. You don't quite have the accent, but there's a soft lilt. It's pretty. I've always liked it."

For some reason, the mention of her voice gave her a sudden pang of homesickness, one she'd all but forgotten. She thought of Papa and Sakura, and their gentle voices, and even the sharpness of her mother's seemed sweetened by loss and time.

It had been a long, long time since she'd heard them.

"Did I say something wrong?" said Snowdrop suddenly. "I didn't mean to—"

"No. It's fine," she assured her. "I just… I miss Toulouse. I miss my family. They're alive, but they're not here."

"I miss my parents, too," said Snowdrop quietly. "I have Hunter, and the others, and I'm grateful for them, truly, but it isn't the same. Sometimes I'm surprised I can love them at all, that that part of me didn't dry up when my parents died." She bit her lip. "Maybe it's like that for Beau. Losing his mother and his entire squad. Maybe he feels like he hasn't got it in him, or maybe he does, and that terrifies him more."

"Love is scary," Asami repeated, and found she suddenly agreed all too well.

20

CONFESSIONS IN THE CART

The group ate something in the lab, too exhausted to move to the table, slumped against the bedrolls and pillows Beau had sourced for them. Finally, blissfully, Asami and Beau slid off to bed.

He escorted her into her car, like a gentleman leading a lady to her door. He half looked like he wanted to kiss her hand, so when he turned to leave, she grabbed his wrist and tugged him back.

"You gave me a look, earlier," she said. "What did it mean?"

Beau stared at her, and at the hand she held in hers. "You're going to have to be more specific."

"After I gave you the waistcoat," Asami clarified, keeping her voice low. "And asked you to make breakfast."

"Ah," said Beau, looking about the room, "that was—"

"Beau." She pulled him down beside her, and caught his face in her hands, both cheeks cupped inside her palms. "*Please.*"

His throat bobbed, but his fingers moved to sweep a strand of hair behind her ear. "That was my *for you, anything,* face."

A smile tingled on her lips, spreading to the rest of her. "I wish you would have said that."

"I didn't want to frighten you."

Her fingers glided down the tangled flesh of his cheek to the knotted muscle of his shoulder. "Nothing about you scares me, Beau," she whispered. "Nothing, I promise you."

"I think that's good," he replied, his breath hitching. "But I am terrified by you."

Love is always scary.

But there were other scary things, too, like this entire day, like the memories of it all wobbling inside her, like the crushing feeling of the tunnel pressing against her, like the throbbing wound in her arm which could have been somewhere else.

She could have died. *He* could have died. And even though they were fine, and she knew that they were safe, for now, she didn't quite feel it. She needed more reassurance. She needed *him.*

"Can you get into bed with me?" she asked. "Just… just for a little while. Until I fall asleep."

Beau's eyes widened. "What?"

"Please," she said. "I'm a bit overwhelmed with everything that's happened. I'm glad we saved Snowdrop. Of course I am. But I keep thinking of those other guards."

"We minimised the use of lethal force," he said hurriedly. "Tried to shoot to wound where we could—"

Apart from the guard who'd tried to shoot her. He'd thrown a steel door at him. It was unlikely he survived that.

"I know," she said, swallowing the memory. "I'm sure. I just... What makes her life worth more than theirs? Or anyone's?"

"Snowdrop can probably do a lot more good in the world. At least, that's my hope."

"I wish we could measure lives like we can do everything else."

"What?"

"I wish there was a system for measuring a person's worth. There's probably a good reason not to, but I still wish there was. I know, I know, that's supervillain talk, and I should think that all lives are equal, but I don't believe they are. I believe in numbers, and I believe that some people *are* worth more... I'm just very glad I don't have to be the person to decide."

Beau swallowed. "What would weigh against a person, do you think?"

"You're worried the system wouldn't find you worthy, aren't you?"

He kept his gaze steady on her. "I'm worried *you* wouldn't."

"Ever killed civilians?"

He flinched. "Not to my knowledge."

Asami ignored the vagueness of that remark. "Ever killed anyone who wouldn't have tried to kill you, given the opportunity?"

"No."

"Then I think you're safe."

Beau's expression did not waver. "There was a time I would have," he said quietly. "A time when I willingly subjected myself to experimental treatment, in the name of greater good. When I killed for them. When I would have done worse for them. *Anything* for them. For him. My father, that is. I don't... I don't think I deserve less admonishment for not doing worse, when all I lacked was the order."

Asami cast her eyes downwards. "I don't know what to say to help you make peace with that," she said. "Only that if there were words to do so, I would utter them. If pain plus Asami's words equaled release, I would do so gladly. But life isn't as simple as a sum. All I suppose I can tell you is that this person you used to be, that you nearly were? I don't see him. I like the one that's in front of me. I think he's deserved very little of the bad he's received in life."

Beau said nothing to this, said nothing at all for a very long time. "I'll stay with you," he said eventually. "Just until you fall asleep."

Asami beamed, and, not giving him a moment for second thoughts, grabbed him and dragged him back against the cushions, burying herself in his neck.

"I'm on the wrong side," said Beau.

"You don't have a wrong side."

A deep, hard sigh loosed from inside his chest. "You can't mean that."

"When will you understand that I am utterly unperturbed by the way you look?"

"When I am, too."

Something hard coiled inside her. She lifted her head from underneath his chin, their faces as close as they had ever been, and touched his cheek. He shuddered slightly beneath the gentle press of her fingertips, as if she'd touched another, far more intimate part of him.

"It's not that I don't see it," she said. "I'm not blind. Of course I see it. I see your scars and lumps and bumps and bruises. I see them, and I see everything else, too. I see the strands of sunshine in your chestnut hair and the swirling colours of cerulean blue in your eyes. I see the slope of your cheek and the crooked twitch in your smile. I see your kindness and intelligence and warmth and loveliness. I see you, Beau, and I could meet everyone else in the entire world and not find anyone else I like half as much as you."

For a long time, Beau was silent.

"Don't tell me I don't mean it," she said. "Say something, please."

"I don't understand."

"Oh, Beau, please—"

"I don't understand how you stumbled into my life, and how you weren't snapped up by someone else before—"

"I was waiting for you," Asami whispered, even though it was silly and ridiculous and false but *true,* the truest thing she had ever said.

She lifted her lips to his, less than an inch, a centimetre apart. His mouth twitched, only slightly, just as gently, and for a second his breath was twinned with hers.

Beau jerked back, his eyes wide. "I'm sorry," he said, and scrambled out of bed. "I can't."

Asami watched him leave, flinging back the curtains between their quarters, watching as the fabric shifted still. She could hear Beau pacing behind it, his steps thunderous. A pain crackled in her chest, new, bitter, and of everything that had happened that day, it was this that hurt the most of all.

21
APOLOGIES AND PROMISES

Beau stumbled out of bed early, despite only catching a few hours sleep, and paused briefly at Asami's door. He could hear her slow, fluttering breath behind the curtain. Asleep. Good.

I'm sorry, he thought desperately, thinking of the night before, the closeness of his lips against hers. Desire had swelled inside him, so swift he felt sick with it, and he'd had to pull away before it could overtake him, before he went too far and he ruined it between them for good.

You don't really want me, said an insidious voice deep inside him. *Whoever could?*

And then another voice, deeper, harder. *Take her. Have her. Hurt her before she hurts you.*

Both were hard to ignore.

He shook the thoughts from him, and stumbled towards the kitchen. He could make out the sounds of snoring from the lab, the rebels shuffling in their sleep.

Someone was banging about the kitchen, making no attempt to be quiet. He'd be annoyed at the volume if he wasn't grateful for the warning. The first few days with the silent-footed Asami had been torture, but the moment he'd explained it to her, she'd made every effort to announce her presence.

She's a nice person. She'd do that for everyone. It means nothing.

And yet he wanted it to mean something, just as much as he was afraid of the exact same thing.

He wasn't surprised to find Snowdrop raiding his cupboards, her curls unbound and tumbling all around her face. She looked oddly bright for someone who'd been up most of the night and spent several hours imprisoned and in fear for her life.

"Morning," she said breezily, "I'm eating your food."

"Gears, Snow, don't you *ever* sleep?"

She shrugged. "I'll sleep when I'm dead," she declared, and shovelled a fistful of oat clusters into her mouth.

"Which will be a lot sooner if you keep eating like that. You'll choke to death."

"You're hardly Mr Manners..." She swallowed her mouthful. "I trust you'll save me from choking like you saved me last night. Thanks for that. I appreciate it."

"Any time. Only please not ever again."

She snorted. "You like me really."

"You're tolerable."

Snowdrop grinned, handing him the packet of cereal she was eating out of. Beau dug in, thinking of how Asami would hate this.

"So, Beaumont—"

Beau groaned. "I'm regretting telling you my real name."

"You don't mind when Asami does it."

"She's different."

"Let me guess," said Snowdrop, rolling her eyes, "*everything's* different with her."

Beau narrowed his eyes. "Doesn't make it any less true when you say it like that…"

"Beast, Beau, *dear*, I know, I *know* you have reservations, but you really, really need to get over them."

He sighed, looking down at his hands. "It's not that simple."

"Can you still… you know?" She glanced downwards.

Beau's cheeks went red-hot. "Gears, Snow, could you *be* any more personal?"

"Sorry," she said, not sounding remotely apologetic. "But can you, though?"

"Not that it's any of your business, but yes. We're usually fine in that department."

"Usually?"

"Snowdrop!"

"Sorry, sorry!" She held up her hands. "Just… curious. Figure it must be something serious to hold you back."

"Because this—" he gestured to his face— "isn't serious at all."

Snowdrop shrugged. "Clearly not to her."

"Well, it's serious for *me*."

"Ugh!" she flung a dishrag in his face. "See, *this* is why I was never attracted to you. You're strong and you're capable, intelligent and kind… but that whole self-deprecating thing?

Not for me. I like my lovers suave and confident…" Her eyes glazed over, lost in some vivid daydream.

Beau stared at her.

"What?"

"Nothing, just thinking of introducing you to someone."

"No, thank you." She shook her head. "You don't have to explain your traumas to me. I don't much fancy sharing mine with you, either. But I think you should share them with Asami."

Beau glanced down. "I don't want to frighten her away."

"Oh, boy…" she sighed, shaking her head. "Beast, she just crawled through a drain for *me*, a relative stranger. She is not as flighty as you think. Have courage." She slapped him on the arm. "Next time I see you, I want you two together, or dead."

"Are those… our only alternatives?"

She beamed. "Yup."

"You're… odd."

"All the best people are." She hopped off the counter. "Don't let me down, Beaumont."

"I rarely do," he replied. "And stop calling me that!"

The rebels departed after midday. Shortly before leaving, Snowdrop wrapped Asami in a quick, firm hug, and pressed a roll of parchment into her hand.

"If you're ever in trouble, here's how to find us."

Asami glanced at it briefly: a map of the Outlands. Her heart skipped a beat.

"It's not our location, obviously," Snowdrop explained. "It's just a safehouse. You need to find us, wait there. Someone will come for you."

"Thank you," Asami whispered, privately hoping that they never needed to, that there would never be any more danger. That they were safe, safe and...

Beau had not met her eyes since last night, had barely uttered a single word to her. Snowdrop had frowned at his silence a couple of times, and glanced at Asami as if hoping for an explanation, but she didn't have one. She couldn't *think* of one. Could think of very little but the crackle against her chest, the icy feeling where warmth once resided.

Hunter glared at the map in Asami's hand, and muttered something disapproving under his breath. Dandelion shook his head. "She crawled through a filthy vent to rescue Snow. This is the *least* we can do."

"If they tell anyone—"

"We shall be down one sordid shack. What a loss."

Clover laughed, clapping Beau on the back by way of goodbye and waving to Asami. "I like you. Take care."

Asami smiled, but it dropped the second the door thudded shut, and they were alone once more. Pilot creaked, sliding to the floor, the noise of his presence only amplifying the silence.

Beau turned wordlessly, and vanished into the store cupboard. Cleaning. His go-to for any stressor beyond his control, a way of vanquishing thought.

Asami marched in after him.

"I suppose you don't owe me an explanation," she said. "If it's a no, I should just accept that and move on. But… I should like an explanation, if you can give it, for I'm not sure I shall move on without one." *Or at all.*

"That's just the thing," he said, back still turned to her. "You ought to move on. You should. You will."

"You don't get to decide what I feel!"

"But you shouldn't feel *anything* for me!"

"Is this about the way you look?"

"Yes," he said, "no. It's about… Gears." He reached out to steady himself on a nearby shelf, and crunched the plank in two, sending splinters and sponges clattering to the floor. Asami jumped. "I can think of a dozen reasons for not doing this, and only one for," he said, voice hoarse. "I may not be a monster, but I'm not right. I'm too strong. I could hurt you—"

"But I don't think you will," she said swiftly. "You've had years to control it. You *do.* I've never seen you break anything—" She paused, remembering the door to the prison, the metal ripped from the wall. "At least, not by accident. Not without cause."

"I can't risk it with you. I can't risk *anything* with you—"

"What are you talking about?"

"It's not just that. It's not just what I've done before. It's not just about you being *good* and me being… something else. It's that after this is over, you'll realise you don't care for me like you think you do. I'm just your little science project, your problem to fix—"

A heat rose inside Asami, different from the one he usu-

KATHERINE MACDONALD

ally elicited in her. Anger.

She seized a sponge from the floor and hurled it at him. "Don't be an asshole. It doesn't suit you."

Beau blinked, staring at the foamy projectile in his hands. "Did you just throw a sponge at me? No one has ever thrown a sponge at me before…"

Asami glared at him. "Don't ever accuse me of not caring about you. And stop being so self-deprecating. It makes me like you less. I'm not here to make you feel better about yourself. Only you can do that."

He stared at her, a silence stretching between the two of them. Pilot creaked behind them, shifting his weight from foot to foot. "You do make me feel a *little* better about myself," he said eventually.

Asami felt her anger receding. She dropped down on her knees and started to tidy up the mess, Beau assisting. "I can't tell you what or how to feel," she said softly, "but don't patronise me about telling me what *I* feel. I understand your apprehension. I understand your fear as well as I am able, but please understand me when I tell you that I like you. For you. And not in a fleeting, erasable way. In a fierce, slightly scary way. In a, you-could-hurt-me-just-as-much-as-I-could-hurt-you way. In a I-trust-you-not-to way." She stopped, not meeting his face, not sure if she wanted to know his thoughts, not yet. "I'm going to get back to work," she said after a pause. "You can join me whenever you're ready."

For two hours, Beau cleaned and scrubbed, although exactly what, Asami had no idea. The base was as clean as it could be. She buried herself in her work, barely noticing when he slunk in a few hours later.

Barely noticing, but still noticing. He was impossible to ignore.

The flow of conversation between the two of them eased back by evening, and over the next few days. He sent something to his contact at the palace for her missing ingredients, and went above for supplies, including a couple of funny porcelain mugs with animal faces on the side. The bottoms were painted to resemble snouts, making him look hilarious whenever he drank.

"These are adorable," she remarked. *You're* adorable.

"Shut up. They were the only ones I could find."

"You look good with a snout."

He laughed. "You too."

The ease of the moment, the casualness between them, prompted Asami to ask a question which had been plaguing her for some time.

"Why don't you join the Rebellion?" she asked. "Go to the Outlands? Is it because you're afraid that they'll look at you differently?"

"A little," he admitted. "I was down here for a while before we crossed paths. I was used to it. It's hard to leave what you're used to. But I also hoped I could do more good here, be more helpful to them. And…"

"And?"

He looked down into the dregs of his mug. "I was waiting for you."

Whatever Asami had expected, it hadn't been that. "You mean… for someone to find Mortimer's notes?"

"Maybe," he said. "But I think… I think I was just waiting for *you*." He looked up at her, and met her eyes like he had done in that moment before she almost kissed him, like gazes were malleable things that could be tied together. "I think I've been waiting for you my entire life."

Asami opened her mouth, trying to reply, or move, but something froze her in place.

The door at the top of the tunnel pounded.

Beau jumped. "Stay here," he commanded.

It was a difficult instruction to follow. Difficult not to try and get a peek at his visitor, or overhear a snatch of conversation. She busied herself in tidying up the kitchen instead, waiting until he returned. He was smiling when he did so, placing a basket in front of her.

"Your list, milady," he announced. "And some medical records. I doubt they'll have anything there that we can use to implicate the palace, but it's worth a shot."

Asami grabbed the basket, her fingers brushing over his, and tore into them eagerly.

"Shall I start collecting rats for you?"

She cast a cursory glance over the rest of the ingredients.

"Yes," she said quickly, and returned to the notes. A sudden thought occurred to her. "You must have known where

Mortimer's research was, right? Even if you didn't know the code, you could have tried all the combinations by now."

"I knew."

"Then why leave it?"

Beau paused. "After Mortimer was killed, I kept watch at the warehouse for days. I hoped someone would come, someone I could blame for what had happened. I was going to kill them. I was going to take out all my rage and pain and, I think, hope they took me too. Only no one ever came. I slowly began to hope for something different, that whoever came wouldn't be one of Malcolm's lackeys. That they'd be… well, I didn't dare hope for anything like you, but something."

"What does that mean?"

"You know what that means."

Asami swallowed, trembling under the weight of his words, retreating to the safety of work. "How much evidence do you think we'd need to go public with our knowledge?"

"A lot," said Beau. "If we go in with what little we have, people will just think that our evidence of foul play is faked. We need lots and slowly, not something huge at once. And the Rebellion to gain more traction. Support from my palace contact, maybe, although that could be very dangerous. But if we have the evidence…"

"What about your father?"

"What?"

"If he knows that you're alive, what was done to you—"

"He *does* know what was done."

"What?"

"He knows. He was there. And he still works for them."

"Beau, that's… I'm sorry."

He shrugged. "It's—"

"Don't tell me that it's fine. It isn't."

"I just don't want you to worry. Or…"

"We don't need to talk about it," she said. "But you need to know you *can*."

Beau half-sighed, half-laughed. "I thought you weren't here to help me feel better about myself?"

"I'm here to make you feel better," she said, "in whatever way I can." She placed her hand over his. "But it's mutual, see? I feel better when you're around too, even though you cast the rest of my life up to this point into a rather miserable, lonely shadow."

Their gazes caught again, and Asami felt herself unravelling as he squared up to her, like her mind was sliding into poetry, into confusion and disarray.

Closer, closer.

Kiss me, kiss me.

Beau's hand went to her cheek, his broken flesh warm against the smoothness of her skin. She loved the feel of him. All of him. Every part.

"Give me two days," he said.

"What?"

"I want two days before…"

"Before?"

"I have something to show you."

"Oh, oh no. I don't like surprises."

"Fine," he said. "There's a concert playing at the park in two days' time. I want to take you. Sort of. It won't be so romantic now—"

"You want to take me on a date?"

Beau's throat trembled. "Yes," he said. "I want to take you on a date."

A smile snuck along her lips. "Then I accept," she said. "Two days' time it is."

22
ROSES AND RAINDROPS

The next two days passed as slowly as two days ever had. Beau was absent for large parts of them, spending several hours catching rats for Asami to begin her experiments, and the second day out of the base entirely. Both nights, she didn't hear him come to bed. What by the Dome was he doing?

When the day in question arose, Asami found it impossible to concentrate on her work, an impressive feat in itself. She felt jittery and nervous. That, she was used to, but it had been a long time since she'd applied those feelings to a date. It had been a long time since she'd dated anyone, and even longer since she'd cared about anyone as much as she'd cared about Beau. Every other relationship seemed fleeting and flimsy in comparison, little more than school-girl crushes.

She'd found some red fabric among the scraps in the supply closet, and had been busying herself pulling them together in some semblance of a dress. The fabric was cheap, her boots, no matter how hard she scrubbed them, weren't fit for a concert at the park, and the best she could do in terms of headgear was a battered top hat which she fixed up with her goggles and roses formed of fabric. There was no way of curling her hair, either, no pins to make it fancy, no makeup to wear. All she could do was scrub herself clean and wear it out and long, free of its usual braid or bun.

Beau rapped on the side of her carriage when it was time to depart, and she stepped out sheepishly, wishing her sleeves were long enough to pull at. He was wearing a slick outfit of black and green, a boned corset-jacket with a fetching, if faded pattern of stags and thorns, fingerless gloves and his polished pocket watch. Aware though she was of every perfect muscle of him, it was his wide eyes she noticed first.

"I know," she said, pulling at her frayed lace gloves, "I look silly, don't I? I didn't have much to work with—"

"You look astounding."

Asami blushed as crimson as her dress. No one had ever used the word *astounding* to describe her before. Cute, adorable, sweet, nice, lovely. Once or twice beautiful, on spectacular occasions. Never anything like this, with so little to work with.

Beau held out his hand. His left. He'd never offered that side of him before. She took it willingly, curling herself against the crook of his arm.

"Would you believe me if I told you you looked very handsome tonight?"

"I wouldn't argue," he said, and his smile radiated warmth.

She half didn't want to go at all. She wanted to pull him back into her carriage and tug on that smile with one of her own, to see how far this facade of confidence took him, to see what else he was willing to show her, give her.

But she didn't want the moment lost or tainted or twisted. She wanted the music, the night with him.

"It's a bit of a walk to the middle ring," said Beau, drawing her out of the base, "so I thought we might take a lift…"

He gestured to a handcar sitting on the rails, furnished with pillows and strung with lanterns. Asami beamed, stepping up onto it and sitting herself down.

"On hold tight," said Beau, and started to pump.

The handcar kicked up a speed, moving surprisingly fast. A warm, sticky breeze swept along the tracks. Asami kept her eyes fixed forwards, trying not to stare at the muscles pulsing in Beau's arms, trying to imagine the breeze as something else, more pleasant.

There was little to fixate on as they pushed along the tracks. She remembered coming to Petragrad on the train, spending hours down in the dark underground tunnel, racing by nothing. She'd read her books and chatted to the other passengers, anything to fragment the sickening nerves, the voice that kept asking her what she was doing, screeching under the monumental weight of her decision.

This journey was not so long, but a similar feeling plagued her, of bridges not yet crossed, decisions not yet made, and an unknown far more terrifying than leaving her whole life behind.

Finally, Beau stopped pumping and let the car slow to a stop. He jumped off and helped her alight, and the two set off down one of the tunnels, guided by a lamp in his hand.

"I take it we're not going above?" Asami asked.

Beau shook his head. "Much as I would love to walk through the park with you, it's probably best to avoid showing our faces at the moment."

"Yes, I am a fan of not being shot at."

Beau chuckled, but his fingers twitched at his side. Asami reached forward to grab them, feeling young and giddy and older than ever.

"You don't need to be nervous," she told him. "I already like you."

"I know you like me. I want to impress you."

"Maybe we should go back to the handcar and I can watch you pump for a bit more."

Beau snorted, harder than before, and squeezed her fingers back.

The sound of music squirmed overhead, breezy and distant. Asami's heart quickened as they moved, the music strumming against her chest, closer and lighter. A chorus of strings drifted through the hot air, and something glimmered in the darkness like fireflies.

Lanterns, dozens of them, seated around a picnic blanket arranged for two. Their rough goblets were there, together with a small hamper, and a blue glass vase filled with metal flowers. Roses. Red.

"I couldn't get real ones," Beau said, as Asami stooped to admire them.

"You made these?"

"Yes."

"They're... it's... you're..." Her eyes skipped about the soft oasis of colour. "This is *beautiful,* Beau."

He scratched the back of his neck, saying nothing as he sat beside her to uncork the wine. The music sailed overhead, and Asami realised they were sitting beneath a grate. She could make out the black, inky swirl of the night sky and the carpet of beautiful, false stars on the domed ceiling high above. Amber light danced from the stage, and she could picture it almost perfectly. She'd been to concerts before. They were the sort of thing one could enjoy alone, but with Beau, it was beyond enjoyment.

She leant against his shoulder as he filled the glasses. "Thank you."

"Thank *you.*"

"I haven't done anything."

"You've done *everything.*"

He turned to face her, closer than he'd perhaps anticipated, their mouths merely inches apart. But a trumpet blared above, startling them both, Beau's hand going to hers.

"Both as skittish as a couple of cats!" Asami laughed.

Beau squeezed her hand. "Indeed."

She leant against his shoulder and closed her eyes as the trumpet tittered away, and *listened.* A thousand different thoughts and memories twirled unending inside her. This was a song of triumph after failure, victory after battle. Sadness and grief and hope for tomorrow.

The next piece was a tragedy, of love and death and loss, no snatch of hope to clutch at. It made her chest ache, made her think of Toulouse and her father's fingers on his strings, and other pains not yet fully known to her.

She squeezed Beau's hand tighter.

For what could have been hours they sat in silence together, listening, waiting. The strings and keys played song after song, stories of ancient times, of giants and monsters, tales of ravens and doves, of sparrows in snow and wolves in winter. Asami had never thought herself creative, but when music played, she found herself transported, transformed from flesh and blood into a phantom, a spirit, a creature of air and wonder.

Her father would have smiled to hear her thoughts, and her mother would have laughed. Her father would have accused her mother of being unfeeling, and danced with her to prove her otherwise.

"Dance with me," Asami asked Beau, as the music folded into something soft and wondrous.

Beau did not argue. He pulled her gently to her feet and slid an arm around her waist, and twirled her around the space. He was a fine dancer, even if he felt out of practise.

A steady patter permeated the music, jittering on the concrete above. A drop of rain slid down her cheek, coming thick and fast through the grate.

Asami smiled. Rain was controlled in Petragrad. Either there was a fault in the system, or someone in the concert had seriously pissed off one of the environmental monitors. Or perhaps someone had bribed them to make it rain, finding it as romantic as she did.

Beau tried to pull her out of its path, but she stopped him, pulling him back beside her. The water glistened against his skin in the faint light, gold and silver, like beads of glass.

Asami leant up to brush the raindrops from his cheek, but her fingers stopped at his lips. *Everything* stopped at his lips, like all thought and reason and the world itself hung there on the narrow point at the heart of his perfect, ruined mouth.

"You're too tall," she whispered, her voice feather-soft, as graspable as dandelions in the breeze.

He raised an eyebrow. "Too tall for what?"

Asami's throat tightened, mouth dry. "You know what."

"Let's pretend I don't," he said coyly, his fingers still gracing her back.

That touch sent ripples through her, lashes of ice and fire that tingled at every pore, forcing her closer, further against the tightness of his body. "I'd very much like to kiss you right now," she whispered.

Beau bent towards her. "I'd very much like to be kissed."

It was impossible to tell who moved first, who slid towards the other, who closed the fragile gap between them and sealed their lips together for the first time. Impossible to tell who deepened the kiss, whose mouth pressed, whose mouth yielded, and if Beau's couldn't quite move as well as other's, it was not a thing Asami noticed. She noticed nothing but him, his hands on her waist, his mouth on hers, the taste of his breath inside her. She was drowning inside his kiss, drowning inside Beau, as the rain trickled down their bodies in the low amber light like a trembling sea of stars.

Eventually, of course, they parted. Beau's eyes were wide and bright, and bluer than she'd ever seen them. "Was that... was it all right? I know my mouth doesn't quite move like..."

Asami placed her hand against the stiff, knotted muscle of

his cheek. "It's still your mouth."

"I know, but—"

She cut him off with another long, lingering kiss, the kind that turned sensation to putty.

"You're wonderful, Beau, but you can still be a bit of an idiot at times." She pushed him out of the rain, against the wall, crushing her mouth back to his. His hands travelled from her neck down to her back, her waist, her thighs, and he brought her up towards him with one swift, hard motion, flipping her against the blackened brick of the tunnel.

Asami let out a gasp.

"I didn't hurt you, did I?"

She slipped her arms around his neck and gathered him against her. "Stars, no. I just... you're really strong."

"I can be more gentle—"

Asami raked her fingers down his back. "I don't *want* gentle. I want you."

Beau grinned against her mouth, and his kisses trailed along her neck, to the start of her dress. The music crashed like thunder overhead, and her insides turned to hot, liquid putty. She murmured words of encouragement, her hands sliding over his shirt for an opening, any opening. Her fingers stumbled against the hooks of his corset jacket, grappling at the buttons underneath, sliding over his tense, taut muscles, the fine line of soft, downy fuzz, the angry flesh at his side—

Beau stopped, dropping away from her.

She slid back to the floor.

"I'm sorry—"

"It's fine," he said shortly.

"Clearly, it is *not* fine—"

"I mean, don't worry about it."

"Beau—" she grabbed his arm— "don't do this. Don't push me away."

Beau's jaw clenched, and something shimmered in his eyes. "I don't know how to pull you forward."

"Like this," she said, stepping closer, grabbing both arms now, "it's just like this."

Beau shucked off her grasp, tearing his eyes away from her. "I can't," he said quietly. "I just... I can't. It's one thing kissing you, it's another..."

"I saw you almost naked before, it doesn't bother me, not at all—"

"It bothers *me*," he said, and turned away from her.

Elsewhere, music was playing, but it did not quite reach her. Nothing did, except a shift in the air, like it had transformed into a solid.

"I'm sorry," Beau.

"Me too," she said shortly.

She turned back to the picnic. The rain had spoiled most of the food, sloshing against the goblets. Droplets clinked against the steel petals of the roses.

"We should pack up," she said. "We can barely hear the music over the rain, anyway."

23

SCARS AND MURMURS

She wanted to cry herself to sleep with fury and disappointment, only she didn't dare, with Beau resting just a few feet away in the next carriage, the curtain barely a barrier between them. She couldn't let him hear.

He's been through worse, she told herself. *He tried not to let you hear him scream. You can hold in a few tears.*

But *she* was not the cause of his pain. She had never hurt him. Maybe he deserved her tears.

Nevertheless, she held them in, her sadness circling inwardly, endlessly, sleep evading her.

She tried to be patient, and kind, and considerate. She tried to think what it might be like to be trapped in a body not fully your own, how vulnerable you might feel in it. And as much as she didn't care… he did. Someone saying you shouldn't feel a certain way didn't magically take away the feeling.

Which was why she couldn't reason with her own, either, why she felt hurt, betrayed, lost… and then ridiculous for feeling any of those things. She knew she was not a strong sort of person, physically or in any other way, but she usually prided herself in her ability to place logic over an emotion. This silliness was beneath her.

And yet when morning came around, when he tried to make nice over breakfast without acknowledging the night before at all, she could not hold it in.

She put her mug down sharply.

"Last night was amazing," she said. "And then it wasn't. Really wasn't. And I want to say it's fine and be patient and sweep it under the rug, but I can't. I want you. You want me. And it's hard understanding why even when you've tried so hard to explain it. And *I'm* sorry. I'm sorry that I'm so frustrated but I have to speak it. I can't pretend it didn't happen and I don't want to."

Beau's eyes did not meet hers, and for a moment, she wondered if he planned to speak at all.

"I'm sorry," he said eventually. "Truly. I tried so hard to make last night spectacular—"

"You did, it was," she assured him, "all the parts you planned were perfect."

"And then I ruined it."

"Not… not all of it."

There was no smile, nothing. "I want you," he whispered hoarsely, "I want you more than I've ever wanted anyone, but there's still a part of me that refuses to rectify myself to the idea that you won't be disgusted, that you won't change your mind after, and that… that would be the worst thing. The most unendurable."

Asami's throat ached. "Is there anything I can do to assure

you that that won't happen?"

He shook his head. "There's a difference between knowing a thing and feeling it," he explained. "This is just something I need to work out on my own."

Asami nodded. "Boundaries, then."

"What?"

"Boundaries. We need to establish them, in case I get carried away. I'm just… I'm *very* attracted to you, regardless of what you look like, and it's been a long time for me. But that's my problem, not yours. I should have been more patient and considerate, and I will be in the future. We can take this as slow as you like."

"And what if I'm never ready?"

Asami glanced downwards. "I think I'll want you for just about forever, and I'd rather have you in my life in the smallest of ways than not have you in it at all."

"This isn't the life I would have chosen for you."

"But you don't get to decide that, Beau. I do. And I chose you. You in any way. What do *you* choose?"

"You," he said. "Always you."

She smiled, getting off her seat and sidling over towards him. "Can I sit on your lap?" she asked.

Beau smiled too. "Yes."

"And can I kiss you?"

"Readily."

Asami did both, long and slow, Beau's hand drifting to her back and waist.

Asami pulled back. "So kissing is allowed, then?"

Beau's cheeks flushed. "Encouraged."

"Hand holding?" She linked her fingers into his.

"Yes," he said. "With my right. Unless I touch you first."

"Noted. And touching—"

"Over the clothes, I think, for now."

"So snuggling is in?"

"Absolutely."

"And… bed sharing?"

Beau gulped. "The once was torture."

"We'll work up to that." She slipped her legs either side of him. "Can we just make out for a bit, now?"

"Happily," he said, and even though half his face was twisted, Asami found it to be the most beautiful smile she had ever seen.

The next few days were exquisite torture, days that began and ended in kisses but were packed with work. She supposed this was what it was like normally, when two people met and wooed in the old-fashioned way, and the relationship didn't begin with moving in together. It was the usual affair to see each other little, only spending a few hours together in the evening, but it still felt the wrong way round for *them,* that retiring to separate quarters was the very opposite of what they should be doing.

She tried to busy herself with the task of transforming the rats into "beast rodents" as Beau called them, trying to lighten the mood, as if he wasn't disturbed by the slow twisting of their bodies. Several did not survive the process, but in the end she ended up with three stable rats using the serum Mortimer had developed. The next task was to try them on the experimental drugs that Mortimer had been developing before his death. This part was horrible, agonising guesswork, as she waited to see how the first subject reacted.

This was the part of science she hated, when the experiment was in motion, when there was nothing to do but sit back and observe. She had made all the notes she could. She had planned for contingencies, drawn graphs and tables ready to be plotted. And now there was nothing. Nothing except Beau's loud, growing presence in the room.

She didn't know when watching someone work had become so tantalising, but whenever she looked up and saw Beau searching his screens, or making careful notes, his fingers poised thoughtfully under his chin, she wanted nothing more than to go over to him, slide across his notes, and ask him to undress her with his teeth.

She had never asked anyone to do something like that to her before, and suddenly it was all she could think about.

"You have been staring at me for some time now, are you quite all right?" asked Beau, not looking up.

"How—how did you know I was watching?"

"You have your skills, and I have mine. Is there something I can help you with?"

"That depends."

"On what?"

"On if you're willing to come over here and kiss me until I lose all sensation in my face."

Beau smiled, his grin turning wicked. He leapt across the

room, kicking his chair behind him, and lifted her up. He placed her against the desk. Asami gasped, legs wrapping around him as his lips went immediately to her neck.

"Hot as this is..." she murmured, "if you mess up my notes..."

Beau laughed loudly in her ear, grabbing her thighs and lifting her up again, slamming her back into her chair and ramming his lips against hers, his kiss burning. His breath merged with hers, breaking into one another, a wave, a tide, falling to the shore. A heat gathered at her centre, slashing against her, and she dragged her hands along his back to stop herself from peeling off his shirt. Her skin ached for his, a desire that thickened with every kiss, every touch.

Beau, Beau, I want you.

Her loins felt breakable, like she could shatter at the middle. His fingers spread like wildfire.

Maybe she shouldn't have asked him to kiss her, she wondered dimly, sensation dissolving into liquid. She knew it was technically impossible for humans to explode, but she was a firework in a box. This ecstasy was agony.

She shoved him off her.

He blinked at her. "Did I... did I do something wrong?"

"No," she muttered, her mouth gummy, "you did a lot of things very, very right. And now I need to go take a bath."

"A bath?"

"That's what I said."

She shifted upright without another word, heading to the bathroom and slamming on the taps full blast, wrenching off her boots and socks and sodden underwear.

She leant against the side of the tub, raw, panting.

A knock sounded at the door. "Asami?"

She tingled at the sound of his voice, at the intimacy of his presence.

"Yes?" her voice squeaked.

"Can I come in?"

Her throat bobbed. "It's not locked."

He slipped into the room, squeezing his shoulders through the door, and kneeled in front of her. A huge hand reached around and turned off the water, his gaze tight on her the entire time.

"I might not have worked up the courage to let you see me naked," he said, "but there are... other things, still, that we can do. That *I* can do."

Asami's mouth went dry. "Such as?" she asked tremulously.

He smirked, his fingers drifting to the hem of her skirt, grazing the flesh beneath. He glanced upwards, seeking permission, and she summoned the tiniest of nods, her skin prickling into goosebumps.

His hands roamed up her calves, along her thighs, kisses following, long, soft, slow. His grip slid to her hips and his mouth sought deeper, and she heard his laugh as he discovered that naked, unclothed part of her.

In a single, fluid motion, he jerked her from the side of the tub and splayed her back against the floor, cushioning her descent with his hands before diving back beneath her skirts and pressing his lips to the apex of her thighs, his breath singing against her, driving her to a narrow, white point, a folded, empty, shapeless space.

She uttered every expletive under the sun as his tongue worked inside her, pausing only briefly in her tirade to bark instructions, her voice sandpaper-hoarse.

She'd never truly, really enjoyed this before. She'd tried to, but something about the intimacy of the action had always unnerved her, made it impossible to fully embrace, release. She'd felt like something on display, a creature to be ogled, but nothing like that reached her now. Thought and reason turned to clay, logic to liquid. She trembled and ached and writhed beneath him, physics twisting into the impossible, reducing her to a single point, an iota of consciousness hanging on the tip of his tongue.

"I had no idea you had such a dirty mouth," he grinned, his breath dancing along her thigh, sending further tiny snowflakes of sensation glittering through her.

Asami breathed long and hard, forcing her thoughts back together, a jigsaw of unravelled bliss. "Oh, there's plenty you don't know about what my mouth can do."

Beau raised a quizzical eyebrow, but before he could retort, she amassed enough of herself to sit up straight, and now pinned him against the floor.

His eyes widened.

"I don't have to undress you," she said, "but if you like…" She grazed her hands down to the hard section at his centre.

He swallowed. "Oh, I like. I would very much like, actually."

Asami grinned, unbuckling his belt and sliding her hand under his flies to reveal the beast beneath. Her first immediate thought was that it might have trouble fitting in her, and she let out another expletive.

Beau raised his head from the floor. "Are you swearing at my penis?"

"It's very... proportionate."

"Proportionate?"

"To your height. You have an excellent height-to-penis ratio."

He chuckled, long and hard. "If you wanted to take measurements—"

"Much as I love numbers, I can think of a few more things I'd like to do," she whispered, leaning against his ear as she stroked a finger swiftly down the length of him, making him buckle beneath her, hissing under his breath. She slid herself down him, tongue moving in tight, tiny spirals, making him croon and gasp and beg until she reached the tip of him, and took him fully in her mouth.

She teased and nipped and licked, drawing him in and out of ecstasy, working him to the same narrow point he'd driven her too and then drawing back, allowing him to release, groaning and panting against the hard tile floor.

She lay down beside him as his consciousness gathered again, watching the pulse of his throat, the heave of his chest. His eyes flickered with energy.

"What are you thinking of?" she asked, head against his shoulder.

"That I'm really glad I cleaned this floor yesterday."

Asami spluttered with laughter, rolling on top of him and grinding against his waist until they were almost clicked together. Beau let out a sound between a groan and snarl, hips jerking beneath her. "Stars," he said, "you're divine."

"Is *that* what you were thinking?"

"I was thinking," he said, fingers caressing her hips, "that I must have done something good at some point in my life just to deserve the utter pleasure of knowing you."

"And my tongue."

"*Garters,* Asami! I had no idea you were so filthy."

"Do you not like it?"

He raised a hand to stroke a loose strand of hair from her face. "There is precious little in you that I don't absolutely adore," he whispered, "but I was trying to be sincere."

Asami leaned down to peck him on the lips. "You're a sensitive soul, my dear Beaumont."

"I am. Don't tell my father."

"Wouldn't dream of it." She lay down on his chest. "I adore you, too," she said, quiet as a falling feather. "In a silly way. In a way that makes me almost glad that I uncovered government secrets and ended up being hunted and having to go into hiding."

Beau chuckled. She raised her head against his shoulder.

"Beau?"

"Yes?"

"I *am* glad I met you."

He smiled crookedly, and their lips slotted together. They kissed for a little while longer, and then Asami kicked him out to take her much-needed bath.

When she went back to the lab, freshly dressed, damp hair cascading down her shoulders, she was greeted with the discovery that one of the rats had died.

Beau tried not to look disappointed. She tried not to feel it, tried not to give weight to the crushing devastation inside her.

It was just the first attempt, just the first. She had not failed, she'd just ruled out one option. It was fine, fine. Expected.

Nothing to worry about.

Onto test subject two.

24

THE HEIST OF THE
IMPERIAL PALACE

By the end of the week, the second rat, which held out longer than its predecessor, perished and died in a few short hours. It made horrible sounds as its condition deteriorated, like it was being squeezed apart.

Asami had to leave the room.

"Should I catch some more?" Beau asked, much later.

Asami shook her head. "We'd have to steal more supplies to remake the original serum—"

"So we just need to wait for the next medical train, or I'll speak to my contact at the palace—"

"I want to try with Novacane."

Beau blinked at her. "You know I have no idea what that is, right?"

"That doesn't surprise me. It's extremely rare. I've only handled it myself a couple of times. Supplies are extremely limited. Only Malcolm has access to it. I'm not sure your friend…"

"He's no spy," Beau admitted. "Not even really much of a thief. Is it really important?"

"Mortimer seemed to think so. He hadn't had time to try it himself, but he'd prepared the formula. It's incomplete, but I think I've finished it. I hope I have. Regardless, it's our best shot. I don't think adjusting the composition that we have so far is going to change anything."

"You want to sneak into the palace."

"I *want* it to magically fall out of the sky, but if that can't happen, then yes. Can we do it?"

"Nothing is technically impossible, if you stay alive long enough to work it out."

"And how long will it take for *you* to work it out?"

Beau thought for a moment, thumbing his chin, his eyes screwed up in concentration. "A couple of days, maybe? I'll need to speak to my contact. I don't think he can pull it off alone, but he might be able to help. Do you still have your access card?"

"Yes, but they'll have rescinded it."

"Give it to me. I may be able to un-rescind it."

Asami grinned.

"What?"

"You're very attractive when you're intelligent."

A smile ruptured across his cheek, and he pulled her into his lap. Asami balled her fingers into fists to stop her hands from wandering, and wondered if tonight would be another night of finishing herself off under the covers or if she could convince Beau to lend her a willing hand.

Beau inched back. "Wait, no, you're distracting me."

"*I'm* distracting *you?*"

"Asami, I don't mean to be self-deprecating, but you are a

lot nicer to look at than I am."

Asami twirled her fingers innocently through the end of her braid.

"Stop doing that."

"Doing what?"

"You *know* what."

"What, this?" She played with the tips of her hair, biting her lips.

Beau stood up abruptly, leaving her behind on the chair. He went to the nearest filing cabinet. "No," he said, "I'm working."

"Hmm, suit yourself," she said, as coy as she could, and rose back to her own desk, trying to ignore the throbbing between her legs. She wasn't used to having this power over someone, her previous attempts at flirting falling largely on the clumsy side, and she wasn't used to someone else having this much power over her, either. "You distract me too," she whispered, and forced herself back to work.

Beau lapsed into a strange, quiet mood for the rest of the day. Asami knew he was hoping to find an easier solution, or a way his friend could do this without their assistance. She watched him staring at blueprints, moving figures around maps, tinkering with gadgets and at one point taking out a series of locks he kept in a cupboard and trying to bend them with his hands. She didn't think it was for stress release.

In the evening, he gave up and left the base, uttering a few words to her about being back late.

She heard him return late into the night, but dozed off before he came to bed.

The next morning, she found him in the lab, welding something.

"Have you been here all night?"

"Ah, most of it? Not sure. What's the time?"

"Seven-thirty."

"Right. Hmm. I may need to rest." Despite his words, he showed no signs of stopping.

"Beau?" Asami prompted.

He looked up, turning off the blowtorch. "Yes?"

She leaned forward and lifted the goggles from his face. "What are you doing, dearest?"

He smiled at her term of endearment, and set his tools down. "Working on my disguise."

"Your disguise?"

"Well, I can't exactly waltz through the palace doors and I'm a little large for creeping around the air vents, so I need something that will hide my face but give me access."

"Right..." Asami frowned.

Beau smiled at her confusion, and lifted up the creation he'd been welding.

It was a long, hook-nosed mask.

A dread doctor uniform.

Asami recoiled.

"Looks authentic, right? There's no filter in it, of course, it's purely aesthetic. But I think it'll do the job."

"Won't... won't they still want to check your identification?"

"You ever seen a dread doctor carry one?"

"I—no."

"Me neither. The uniform is the identifier. They might wear ID in the palace when they've changed into their guard uniforms, but not when they're on the streets."

"I wonder why no one's thought of this before."

Beau shrugged. "Most people who would want to cause harm to the palace don't have the resources to pull this off, and those that have the resources don't want to harm."

"Hmm. Funny that." She looked down at the rest of the equipment, the hooded robes and thick gloves, the holsters for various weaponry.

"How am *I* getting in?"

Beau cringed. "My least favourite part of this plan," he said. "But you are going in… as yourself."

Asami's mind reeled. "You want to act like you've arrested me."

He nodded. "Believe me, I thought about a dozen other ways of doing this. But I think this is our best shot. I've intercepted the orders; anyone that apprehends you is to take you directly to the palace. I'm just going to get you up there, and then we'll steal you a white coat, and hopefully sneak about hiding in plain sight, once my contact has caused a distraction." He sighed. "We don't have to do this."

"I *want* to do it. For you and the whole city."

His face portrayed no hint of a smile. "I have a plan to get us out if it goes south. You won't like it, but it's fairly safe."

"Hmm, maybe don't tell me until it comes to that, then."

"All right," he said, with the ghost of a smile. "Shall I tell you the rest?"

When the day in question rolled around, it was hard to tell which of them was more nervous. Asami knew she was showing it more; she could barely keep still, her fingers were constantly pulling on the ends of her hair or her cuffs, and she felt like she was going to be sick at any minute. Beau was still and silent, but his jaw was taut with tension impossible to ignore. She thought about apologising for her lack of skills in espionage, doubtless the true source of his worries, until she remembered that the reason they were doing this in the first place was because she had the ability to engineer a serum. Her skills in that department were more than enough to make up for the lack of others.

They made their way through the tunnels almost silently.

"You can do this," she told herself, as she purposefully dishevelled her hair, trying not to cringe as she ran dirt through it. She had to look like she'd been on the run for weeks. *You can do this.*

She quickened her gait, hurrying up to Beau and stuffing her hand into his. He jumped, as if he'd quite forgotten she was there.

"I'll let go when we're up top," she said. "But for now, when no one's looking..." She lay her head against his arm.

Beau squeezed her fingers between his thick gloves, and said nothing until they reached the final door.

"We don't have to do this," he said hoarsely, for what must have been the dozenth time.

"I know."

Beau paused, hand on the door. "If something happens to you—"

"I know," she said. "But if we don't do this, at some point, something will happen to *you,* and I'll have to watch, and I'm not sure I can do that again." She raised her fingers to his cheeks. "You can think of us risking it for your former colleagues, if you prefer, for the chance to find something that will condemn the people that killed them, but you should know... I'd do it for just you. I'd do it for just you in a heartbeat."

She kissed him, softly, briefly, his eyes wide, and then pressed out into the alleyway before he could reply. By the time he joined her, he'd pulled the mask down, looking as terrifying as she had ever seen him. He fastened a pair of manacles around her wrists, not locked, although they looked the part.

"Ready?" he asked, his voice tinny beneath the metal beak.

"As I'll ever be."

He nodded, grabbing her arm as roughly as he dared, and steered her through the gathering crowd towards the station. Asami hung her head, trying to look too exhausted to struggle, hoping to ignore the prying stares, the hushed whispers.

Would anyone recognise her?

They weren't far from her old building, the streets lined with tall, graceful houses of white and iron. Some of these people might have been her neighbours.

Beau dragged her through the street, to the guards' post beside the station. A woman on guard looked up, brows furrowed.

"What we got here then?"

Beau pushed her forward and whipped up Asami's hair. It was not hard to tremble, to look terrified.

At first, the guard's face remained furrowed in confusion, but she turned to the posters behind her desk. Asami noticed a few inaccurate depictions of Snow, Hunter, Dandelion and Clover, plastered over her own. It took the guard a while to locate her.

"My my, our little runaway scientist," she said, grinning. "I'm sure you'll be very well received at the palace."

"Please," said Asami softly, "please, just—"

The guard turned her back. "Get her on the lift. Straight to the holding facility."

Beau nodded, yanking her away. The guard communicated with someone manning the lifts, clearing the way for them. Beau pushed her inside, the door slamming behind them. The lift whirred and started to shift.

Step one complete.

"Are you hurt?" Beau whispered, as if afraid the cogs had ears. "I don't want to be rough—"

"I'm fine," she replied. "It's weird that they didn't ask you anything."

"Yes, very weird."

"Trap?"

"I don't think so."

They rose for a few more moments in sharp silence. Asami waited for the beauty of the candyfloss clouds to reach her, but they seemed more pasted and artificial than ever. "You're very attractive when you're nervous," she said, largely to dispel her own darkening nerves.

Beau sighed. "Asami, I love you, but I'm incredibly nervous, and I need to keep my head in the game. Please save all flirting for later."

"All right," she said, and then her heart juddered. "Wait, did you just say you loved me?"

Beau stiffened. "We're here," he said. "Brace yourself."

The lift shuddered to a halt, Beau opening the doors. He pushed Asami out ahead of him, keeping up the appearances for the few people still milling about. There were a few guards stationed on duty, but no one seemed to bat an eye, other than to remind Beau to take the obvious prisoner directly to the holding cells.

"I don't like this," whispered Beau, when he seemed certain they were alone. "It's too easy."

Asami *liked* things being easy, but she understood what he meant. She was trembling under every gaze, certain that at any moment someone would wrench her from Beau's grasp and haul her off before he could think of a way to stop it. But so far no one had even talked to them other than to bark orders. She supposed she didn't look like much of a threat, and most of them might not recognise her as a "public enemy no. 1" even though her status had likely dropped after the chaos of freeing Snowdrop. Doubtless most eyes were searching for them, now.

They reached an empty corridor, and stopped beside a locker room. Beau waited outside, keeping guard. "Change quickly," he instructed.

Asami couldn't steady herself enough to utter a witty retort. She slipped inside, shed her jacket, and pulled on a spare white cloak she found hanging on a peg. It was too long in the wrists, but so was everything else. She wound her hair into a quick bun, brushed the mud from her face, and brought out the lab goggles she'd stowed in her pocket. This disguise at least, she was comfortable in. It shouldn't be too hard for her to act like she belonged in a place she once had.

Once had. Once. This place had been almost like a home.

And never again.

Because even if she cured Beau, even if she found the evidence that ruined Malcolm and toppled down the government, she couldn't come back, even if there was something to come back to.

She wanted to say that it was all worth it, that she didn't have any regrets, that she wouldn't have it any other way, but even if all those things were true, she couldn't feel them beneath the frantic beating in her chest.

Beau said he loved me, she thought, somewhat giddily. It was a better thought than all the others swirling in her brain. Still fear, or a brush of it, but a warm and tingly kind.

Beau rapped on the door. Two raps. The signal for *stay where you are.*

She froze, listening for the footsteps, waiting for them to disperse. They didn't. The handle moved.

Panic hammered inside her. She couldn't rely on her uniform, couldn't rely on Beau to sweep in and save her. The room was too small, too close. If they came face-to-face, if it was an old colleague—

She opened one of the empty lockers and rammed herself inside, squeezing the door shut.

She held her breath.

Anya walked into the room, tutting under her breath, her white coat stained with a brownish substance.

Anya would definitely have recognised her.

Would she have reported her?

What if Asami could speak to her, explain to her—

Was it worth the risk?

She held her fingers up to the slats, weaving a dialogue for discovery, a rushed explanation, a plea.

Don't find me, don't find me…

Find me, find me…

Listen to me, listen to me…

She wanted to make someone believe her. Maybe Anya could even get a message to her parents, could let her know if they knew, or let them know she was all right.

But she could not risk it, and she no longer trusted anyone.

Well, except Beau. She trusted him with everything. *Everything.* And when they got home, she was going to make sure he understood that.

Anya changed her coat, stuffed the soiled one in the laundry, and sauntered back outside.

Asami released a long, careful breath, and stepped out of the locker. Beau was waiting for her in the corridor.

"Everything all right?"

"Fine," she said, not entirely sure everything was but not wanting to go into it now.

Beau checked his pocket watch. "Come on," he said. "The distraction should be any minute now. We need to be in position."

"All right."

She kept her head down, walking behind him, only semi-confident that no one would notice her next to the great hulking mass of Beau.

No one did.

It did not stop her fear.

They arrived at the labs a few minutes later. Asami took out her keycard and placed it up to the scanner, hardly daring to breathe as it opened up. They stepped over the threshold. A few eyes went up at Beau's dread doctor presence, but they quickly dropped again. Dread doctors might not have been a common sight in the research wing, but no one liked staring at them for long.

Step two complete.

An alarm went off in the distance, the sound ricocheting closer. Asami tensed.

"That's our cue," Beau whispered. "Sit tight."

The fire alarm went off in earnest, and at the end of the corridor, smoke billowed out of one of the rooms. Scientists started to evacuate, moving quickly as guards pooled into the building. The smoke thickened. Only one person stopped to speak to them; a guard ushering them outside.

He didn't check to see if they listened. He carried on running.

"What is the meaning of this?" A hard voice sounded through the smoke.

Malcolm.

Asami hadn't seen him since that day, the day when he'd tried to kill her, and his voice cut into her as easily as any bullet.

Beau must have been able to sense her unease. He put out his hand as if intended to shield her.

"What's going on?" Malcolm demanded.

"There appears to be a small fire in laboratory six," one of the guards reported.

"Well, put it out!"

"We're working on it, Doctor. In the meantime, if you could just wait outside—"

Malcolm muttered something dark and had to be reminded that it was protocol, before one of the other guards pressed his back.

"All right, all right!" He slammed his key into his office door, locking it, and stormed off down the corridor. Asami shrank into the shadows, hoping to disappear into them, and screwed her gaze to the floor.

"Quickly," Beau said, "come on."

The guards dealing with the fire, the two of them moved swiftly to Malcolm's door.

"The key," Asami rushed, "they took it with them—"

Beau grabbed the handle, shoved the lock forward, and broke the entire mechanism. He shoved the loose handle in his pocket. "After you," he said, opening the door, his voice lined with grinning.

Asami raced into the room. The medicine cabinet which stored the novacane was locked as well, but Beau made short work of it. She tore through the vials, locating the right ones, and stuffed them into a nearby briefcase along with anything else she thought might be useful.

Then her eyes fell to his computer.

"Don't—" said Beau.

"It might have evidence on it—"

"*Gears,*" he hissed. "Right." He wrenched open the back of the unit, yanked out a few wires, and brought out a studded piece of metal about the size of her hand. "Hard drive," he explained.

"Won't he notice that's missing?"

"We're not exactly being discreet."

"Good point."

Beau lashed the briefcase to her back, securing it in place. They turned to leave the room, Beau pocketing the drive, the corridor still filling with smoke.

"Keep moving," Beau issued, "don't look back."

Asami ran, even though she felt like she'd swallowed her heart, like all of her organs had come loose and were sloshing inside her.

Not possible, but that didn't seem to matter.

Breaking in shouldn't have been possible, either, but they'd done it. They just needed to get out to the lifts before anyone realised what had—

Two hulking masses crossed their path, heavy boots thudding along the floor. A pair of shiny black shoes stepped between them. Beau halted, Asami behind him, and raised her head.

Two dread doctors blocked the way, and between them... between them stood Dr Malcolm.

He was looking straight at her.

"My, my, my," he said, his features twisting into a grin. "Dr Thorne. How good of you to drop in."

25

ESCAPE FROM THE PALACE

Asami's mouth seized up, words crumbling away from her. She could see Beau's hands flexing, inching for his concealed weapons, trying to work out how fast he could shoot, and who.

"And what's this you've brought with you?" Malcolm said, his gaze turning to Beau. "A creation of yours? Or a friend in disguise?"

Before Asami could respond, Malcolm's hands plunged inside his coat, whipping out a pistol. Beau leapt in front of her, letting out a hard cry.

Asami screamed.

Beau grunted, clutching his shoulder. He stumbled, but didn't fall. Asami inched towards him, forgetting about the pistol in Malcolm's grip, forgetting everything except that Beau was hurt—

"Hmm, human," said Malcolm, with little more than a shrug. "Over to you, boys."

The two dread doctors lunged, Malcolm readying his pistol again. Something gleamed in Beau's pocket, brassy and heavy. Without thinking, Asami yanked it out and hurled it in Malcolm's direction, striking him keenly on the head.

The handle they'd taken from his office.

The gun clattered to the floor as he clutched at the wound in his temple. Beau seized the nearest dread doctor and flung him into the other, grasping briefly at the dark stain on his shoulder. Asami tried not to think, not to watch.

The gun shone against the whiteness of the floor, a few feet from Malcolm's grip.

She dived towards it, holding it shakily in his direction, cocking it.

She'd never held a gun before.

Malcolm seemed to register this. "You won't shoot me," he laughed.

Asami fired, half praying she'd miss. She struck him in the thigh, and he let out a horrid scream, the kind that clawed against your eardrums.

She cringed, swallowed.

And recocked the gun.

Malcolm seethed, hands clutching at his thigh. He looked behind her. "I'd save a few of those bullets to help your friend."

She wheeled around. Beau was pinned against the floor. She screamed his name, firing into the back of one of his opponents.

They didn't even flinch. Were they wearing armour?

"Beau!"

Beau seized the arms of one of his assailants and pulled

it, pulled it until it was twisted at an unnatural angle, until Asami was waiting for the sound of snapping bone, ripping muscle. The sleeve began to tear. Still Beau pulled, and something did snap, or twist. But not flesh. Not bone.

Metal.

The arm fell away from the shoulder, a mass of wires and gears.

Another pistol cracked through the air.

"What's going on here?" asked a deep voice.

Colonel Bestiel.

Beau froze.

"Rebel scum!" hissed Malcolm, now pushed against the wall, a trail of blood stemming from his leg. "Traitors! Stop them, Colonel!"

"No, wait!" cried Asami.

Beau didn't. He kicked the legs out from the torn *thing* and sent it spiralling into Bestiel's path, scrambling upright. He raced towards Asami and flung her over his good shoulder, hurtling towards the exit.

There was no question of going for the lifts. They'd never get there in time, or would be apprehended at the base. Asami was sure Malcolm would order the lines cut rather than risk them slipping through his fingers.

They turned a corner, and something cracked down hard on Beau's back. Asami screamed as she catapulted out of his arms, another dread doctor towering over them. Beau spun round, kicking its knees and forcing it to the floor. He grabbed its mask and pulled.

Asami waited for the spill of gears, the shriek of wires. But all that came was a horrible, low, frothing gurgle.

Beneath the mask was a pale, contorted face, covered in contusions and stitched together with metal. One of its ears had been replaced with clockwork, most of its nose was missing, and the mask… the mask appeared to have been welded into its flesh, some sort of external breathing apparatus.

Beau recoiled, his hands trembling. When he spoke, his voice shook. "Matteo?" he whispered.

Asami's stomach plummeted. She had heard that name before.

It was one of his former comrade's.

She inched forward on her hands and knees, pressing a palm to the shuddering chest. Pale eyes glazed over, and something other than a heartbeat thumped beneath his ribcage. Something cold and loud and mechanical.

Was this body even alive? Or was it merely material to be forged and manipulated?

Footsteps sounded down the corridor, and Bestiel and the remaining, whole dread doctor burst onto the scene. Beau was on his feet in an instant, roaring, grabbing the dread doctor and crunching its mask in his fist, throwing it to the floor where it lay in a spasming pile.

He seized the colonel by the throat and smashed him against the wall.

"Did you know?" he howled.

"What are you talking about?" Bestiel croaked.

"Did you know what your government did to them?" He smacked him further into the wall, and Bestiel stared over his shoulder at the ruined mess of the former soldier, his eyes widening.

"That's... that's..."

"His name was Matteo," Beau shuddered. "Matteo Ignatius."

Bestiel froze, eyes widening in something more than horror. "I know your voice."

"You don't know me."

Another alarm sounded now, louder and different from the fire alarm. Asami touched his shoulder. "We need to go."

Beau's muscles tensed beneath her.

"*Please*, Beau!"

Bestiel's eyes widened further. "Beau," he whispered, as if he'd never heard the word before.

Beau dropped him to the floor in an instant, smacking the back of his head with his hand. He seized Asami's wrist and jerked her away.

There was no question of making it to the lifts. The place was rumbling with guards. Beau snatched a pistol from a fallen adversary and cleared the path with bullets, his left side slumping.

He was hurt. He couldn't keep moving like this.

And yet there was nothing, nothing she could do. Hitting Malcolm earlier had been a fluke. She was underskilled and unprepared and unable to help him.

Or herself.

If they couldn't get out, they were going to die.

It would all have been for nothing.

A shot narrowly missed her ear. Beau grabbed her, shoving them round a corner and pushing her to the floor. He seized a nearby guard—half dead—and snatched the bullets from his belt. Asami stared at the man as his chest heaved, trying to work out if he would live.

She still wanted to help him, despite everything.

Beau loaded his pistol and fired around the corner, drawing back every shot. More people were coming. Too many. Their bullets were spent. In a few minutes—

"Beau," she whispered, "Beau, I love you."

Beside her, Beau tensed. "You certainly picked your moment."

"So did you."

He shook his head. "You may not, after what happens next," he said, and charged out into the open.

Asami didn't watch. She didn't dare. There was a hail of bullets, the awful sound of screaming, of ripping flesh, of pain made vocal, and somewhere beneath the feeling of utter horror was relief; it wasn't Beau's scream.

She wanted to vomit.

She waited for it to grow quiet. It didn't. The firing stopped. The screaming didn't.

Beau came back for her, his robes slick with blood. "Try not to look," he said, and lifted her over his good shoulder.

She tried not to, but flashes stung her eyes, of a corridor bathed in blood, of limbs bent and missing, of flesh dangling, pumping from new places, of faces twisted in a kind of pain never to be fully erased.

Nothing could fix these men. She prayed they died before Malcolm got his hands on them, and turned them into those *things*.

It was Malcolm's doing. She knew it was.

Beau flung them into a room and wrenched off the lock, depositing her on the floor. He went over to a chute in the corner and heaved open the lid.

"Waste disposal," he said. "The next part is going to be rather unpleasant."

"Because it's been *such a joy* so far!"

Without waiting for further instruction, she pulled herself into the mouth of the chute and held herself there, braced against the side. She took a long, shuddering breath.

Something hammered on the door. She tucked her hands under her armpits, shut her eyes, and dropped.

Her stomach plummeted. Cold, hard metal stung every inch of her, her nose on fire under the vicious assault of a thousand foul odours; copper, ammonia, rot. She tried to shut her nose, but bits kept smacking against her face, her mouth, causing her to gag and splutter.

She fell forever before landing abruptly on a pile both soggy and crunchy. The blackness was impossible.

She could hear Beau racing down the chute beside her, and waded forward in the mess, doing her best not to identify any of the garbage and failing miserably. She prayed for nothing sharp.

Beau hit the pile after her, groaning and gagging.

"Beau—"

"I'm fine," he said. "Stay where you are."

He trudged through the mess towards what she assumed was the wall, his fingers tapping along the metal sides. There came a rustle of something, a clicking of whirring gears, a short, pulsing beep.

"Stand back," he said.

Asami could barely tell up from down, but she scrambled away from the sound. A second later, a bang trembled against the side of the unit, followed by a gush. Her feet wrenched from underneath her, dragging her out of the metal belly into a dim, dark light.

A warehouse.

"Waste disposal plant," Beau explained. "Beneath the palace. Don't stop. They'll soon work out where we went."

She crawled out of the mess, Beau assisting, trying not to look as she shed her coat and shook gunk from the rest of her clothes. A nearby door opened. Beau grabbed her arm and dragged her under a walkway as a guard—not one from the palace—came forward to inspect the damage.

They shot out while his back was turned, through metal corridors, past security, into the outside.

They still couldn't stop. The streets were swarming with people, and they were in no condition to blend in. The best that could be said for their current attire was that at least the crowds parted easily; no one wanted to be anywhere near them.

The bad news was that they were a walking beacon.

Beau steered them towards the back routes, the darker alleys, into the doorways of abandoned shops, shaking anyone on their tail. Several times discovery was imminent.

"We're too big a target," he said at one point, panting hard against her neck. "Maybe we should—"

"If you say 'split up', I'm leaving you," she said. "No. Absolutely not. If you get caught now, it was all for nothing."

"It's not nothing if you're safe."

"I'll be the judge of what my own personal 'nothing' is, thank you," she sniped. "And let's not pretend me going underground alone for the rest of my life is any kind of victory. We're together, Beau. Get us out of here."

He nodded, mask askew, and grabbed her hand again.

They ran until their sides burned, until their lungs felt like they were splitting. Skies, buildings, roads, crowds, all blurred together. Asami knew she was breathing, knew she was alive, and yet she felt like her consciousness was fractured, separated from her body, like she couldn't even begin to piece herself together until Beau turned a corner, opened up a door into the dark, and yanked them back into the hard, brutal silence of the underground.

HOME AGAIN

"Beau," Asami whispered in the blackness, heart racing still.

Beau propped himself against a wall, breaths shuddering. "Don't pause for long," he said. "I think we shook them, and we should be safe down here, but if you sit down now, you won't want to get up again."

Asami nodded, throat dry. "I feel that," she said, and somehow summoned the energy to drag herself upright and continue onwards down the tunnel, following Beau's shrinking form.

"You're hurt," she said.

Beau shrugged. "I'll deal with it when we're safe."

"*I'll* deal with it," she insisted, and wished he'd take his mask off so she could see his face, to gauge his reaction.

Finally, they reached the base. Never had the thud of a door sounded so pleasant and so awful. Safe, yes, but also absolute. Trapped with the unbreakable knowledge of all they'd just learnt.

And whatever Malcolm's hard drive gave them.

"Sit yourself down in the lab," Asami told him, wriggling the briefcase off her back and handing it to him. "I'm just going to wash up and collect my things."

Beau shuffled off. She set the kettle on and went to the bathroom to scrub her face and hands, stripping to her underthings. She wanted to sink into the tub and rub herself raw, but she wasn't going to do that until she had seen to Beau. Stalling the shakiness in her fingers, she poured the kettle, fetched her basket, and went to his side. He sat in his chair, face in his hands, mask discarded.

Asami pulled up his face, and kissed the cheeks beneath, the nose, the lips. Her fingers went to the front of his robes, and he stiffened beneath her.

"Let me help you," she said softly. "I *need* to help you."

He nodded, his own fingers moving to help her peel back the fabric, wincing as the sleeve rolled away from his shoulder. His torso was mottled with scratches and bruises, although the bullet wound in his shoulder was her biggest concern. She couldn't believe how he'd fought despite it, ran, held her, saved them...

The bullet was wedged inside his flesh. It had missed anything important, but a few inches...

She swallowed. No use dwelling on that. He was safe now, they were out. They had the Novacanc. The mission was a success. It was.

So why did it feel like a failure?

"I need to get the bullet out," she told him.

"Do it then."

"You'll want to brace yourself."

"I won't feel it."

He clamped his hands against the chair regardless, but barely winced as she wiggled her tweezers into his flesh until she felt them graze against the bullet, and pulled it free. It pinged into the bowl beside her. The wound bled, but not profusely.

"I'm going to need you to lie down," she instructed. It would be easy to clean and stitch that way.

Beau nodded, grunting, and repositioned himself. Her fingers went briefly to his damp locks, matted by the time spent under the thick hood.

"Beau—"

"How do you think they did it?" he asked. "Brought them back? Because they were dead. They were dead, I remember —"

"I think they're still dead," Asami said. "They didn't have *hearts*, Beau. Something else resided there. They didn't know you, or seem to feel any pain... I don't pretend to know the secrets of the grave, but your friends weren't inside those suits of flesh and metal, Beau. They died three years ago."

A tear slid down Beau's cheek. "But how can you be sure?"

Asami's throat tightened, because the truth was, she wasn't. She wasn't sure at all. She could run tests if she had one of them, examine their brain activity. But the rest was educated guesswork.

"Beau—" she started, but she found she had no words. She dropped her hands away from his shoulder and took his face in her hands, plunging her mouth against his as if a kiss could burn out pain. "I'm sorry," she breathed against him.

"I'm so, so sorry."

Beau barely kissed her back, as if he lacked the strength to. There was nothing else she could say. She applied herself to his wounds, to the broken parts of him that were visible, fixable. The damage he'd taken was immense, and although he didn't complain, she piled him with painkillers nonetheless.

"I think you have broken ribs," she told him. "Possibly just bruised. Not an actual doctor, here."

"Yes, you are," he insisted.

"I've done all I can. Let's get you cleaned up in the bath."

Beau tensed. Asami shook her head.

"It's all right, Beau. You can clean yourself, if you really want, I won't do anything you don't want me to do, or see anything you don't want me to... but I need you to know, nothing can 'put me off' or whatever you're worried might happen. I love every part of you. Every part." Her fingers grazed his cheek, and she pressed a ghost of a kiss on his chapped lips.

The slightest of smiles whispered there when she pulled away. "I thought I might have imagined you saying that," he said. "Or that you just said it because you thought we were going to die."

"I mean, I might have moved up the confession a bit earlier based on the circumstances, but the feelings are real." She thumbed his face, swallowing tightly. "I have been in love before," she said. "But not like this. Nothing has ever been like this before."

Beau took her face in his hands. "I have loved you almost since the moment I met you," he told her. "And more, every day after. I never dreamed that you would feel the same. I thought your sweetness born of pity. I had forgotten that good things could happen, had almost forgotten goodness altogether. Sweet, wonderful, beautiful Asami. However shall I let you go?"

"Don't let me go," she whispered, her voice like glass. "Don't ever let me go."

She wanted to kiss him more, harder, faster, but was conscious of the putrid dampness clinging to her skin, of hurting him, disgusting him.

"Bath," she said, inching back. "Come on."

Despite his initial hesitation, he let her undress him and help him into the bath. For one brief, glorious moment, she saw every coloured inch of him, every lump and bump and scar, before he disappeared beneath the soapy water.

She left him to his own devices and scrubbed herself off in the sink, removing the final few thin layers and dumping them in a bucket to soak. A few months ago, when she could afford almost everything she wanted, she would have burned them. Now she didn't have a choice but to clean them, even though they'd likely be stained forever.

Beau glanced upwards and sucked in a breath when he realised she was naked, and Asami tried not to buckle under the weight of his gaze.

Tried. And failed.

"I had to take them off," she said. "They were filthy, horrible—"

"I'm not complaining," Beau returned, and then paused. "Get in with me."

"What?"

"It'll be easier. You'll be less exposed and—" He faltered, throat bobbing. "Please."

Asami nodded, sliding into the tub, suddenly conscious of a thousand things, of hair and bruises, of dirt and grit, of her tiny breasts and thin hips.

She knew he probably didn't care, that he wasn't worth her affection if he did, and found herself keenly aware of how much worse it must be for him, and how no words from her could alter the feeling stitched inside.

She leaned forward and took the sponge from his hand, drifting it over his chest, over scars and muscle and remnants of filth. He took a jug from the side and pooled the water over her shoulders, careful fingers gliding over the white-blue marble of her skin and bruises, the scar on her arm.

"You're hurt too."

"Not as badly as you."

"I'll heal."

"So will I." She looked down. "We got the Novacane, Beau. I know it doesn't feel like a victory, but it was. Who knows what can happen next—"

"But we know what *did* happen," he cut across her. "We know what happened to my comrades."

She could not meet his gaze. "I don't think I can fix them."

"I know," he said softly. "I know you can't. I know they're dead or as good as, but..."

"It could have been you, right?"

He nodded.

"And we don't know what really happened to them."

Another nod.

"And now you have more questions, and more pain."

Another slow, awful nod.

Asami inched forward in the water, her legs sliding against his, knees against knees, chests brushing together. "I can't imagine what that's like," she told him. "I don't want to. But I will never be anything other than grateful that you of all of them survived. I don't believe in fate, or a higher power, or luck, or anything that cannot be felt or explained. Anything but how I feel about you." She cupped his face in her hands, thumbing away steam and tears. "You're akin to a miracle, Beau. I'd believe in the impossible for you."

His arms slid around her waist, his mouth to hers, and he kissed her like it was the first and last time, trepidation and passion intermingling, desperation and nerves.

"I love you," he whispered against her.

"I love you, too."

They stayed together that night. There was little discussion about it. After they were clean and dry, and had eaten what little food they could stomach, they crawled together into his bed, tangled up amidst the blankets, Pilot on the floor beside them breathing loud, shuddery breaths.

"My mother keeps a little dog," Asami said, mostly just to say something. "A miniature poodle. George."

"A real one?"

"Yes."

"Fancy."

They traded tiny facts throughout the night, tidbits of information, snippets of lives before. They shared no slivers of dreams, no whispers of hopes for things to come. They dared not grasp at those. They shared the little things—birthdays, favourite colours, foods and firsts—and the bigger ones, fears and hurts buried by years.

Beau told her that his first childhood pet was a clockwork mouse that had stopped working shortly after his mother died. He didn't want to tell his father it was broken, certain he'd ridicule him for still finding joy in the plaything, so he'd tried to fix it himself. He couldn't make it work, but later when he joined the military, he requested he be taught engineering in the hopes that someday he could fix it in the future.

"Where is it now?"

Beau shrugged. "Probably in a scrap heap. I left it in a box in my old rooms at my father's house. I doubt he held onto it."

Asami told him about her favourite gift; a beautiful mechanical nightingale her father had given her on her ninth birthday, that played music almost as sweet as his own. It was an object of sheer beauty, silver and studded with glass gems of blue and green, but it had been too large to bring with her to Petragrad. She'd taken nothing but a single trunk and a well-worn carpet bag she was attached to.

"I suppose that's just as well. I daresay the authorities searched my apartment and got rid of everything. The nightingale is still waiting for me in Toulouse."

She swallowed hard, the nightingale and everything else

she'd left there suddenly seeming very far away.

Beau hugged her tightly, his arms a circle around her. She was glad he made no promises of getting her home, and in that moment, she didn't need them. Pressed against his chest, tucked under his chin, she was dispelled from hopelessness, held above heartbreak. For a few moments, it was easy to believe his arms were home enough, that she would never need anything other than him.

How swiftly and irreversibly she'd fallen for him. How impossible it would be to reverse this chemical reaction. Humans were made of oxygen, carbon, hydrogen, nitrogen, calcium, phosphorus and trace amounts of six other elements. But something else immeasurable was added to that formula to make them tick. A spark of life. A soul, if you believed in such a thing. Whatever that other element was had fused itself to Beau, and if she wasn't so frightened by the rest of the world, she might be scared of the permanence of that, of how little of her would be left if she was forced to face any part of her life without him.

She snuggled down further into his chest, and wished that words were sums, to be ordered and organised and worked out. To be readable, expressible.

"Tell me something good," she told him. "Some happy memory."

Beau told her a story from when he was about twelve, of being invited up to the palace with his parents for a formal event. He'd hated the stiff clothes he was forced to wear and the pinchy shoes and the silly food, and had crept off to the kitchens and smooth-talked the chefs into giving him something sweet in return for helping them with the dishes. Another young guest had found him eating misshapen macaroons and bartered with him for a share.

"I left the party feeling like I had made a friend," Beau explained. "You don't often remember the moment you became friends with someone, but I did with him."

"Who was he?" Asami asked carefully, hoping he hadn't also enrolled in the military academy and wasn't one of the bodies stuffed into the dread doctor suits.

"Oh, one of the sons of the nobles. We kept in touch by letter when he went home, and whenever he visited he'd sneak out of the palace to come and see me."

"Sounds like a good friend."

"The best."

She told him a little more of home, of old friends and older memories, of tiny things loved and lost, filed as "unimportant" until the moment she told him.

Slowly, finally, sleep came.

She remembered a warmth in her bones, a presence unfelt until that moment. Sleeping beside him was like sleeping in a tangible bath, hot waters and steam made solid. It was a place she never wanted to be pried from, not even when he jerked in his sleep, sometimes whispering, sometimes half screaming. This time, she was there for him. This time, he reached for her.

In the middle of the night, he woke fully. Shaking, and then wincing as he pulled at his shoulder.

"Are you all right?" she asked.

He ran a hand through his matted curls. "Mostly," he

slurred. "But a bit too awake. I'm going to get something warm to drink. Go back to sleep."

"I can get it for you—"

He shook his head, almost smiling, and leaned a hand across to brush her hair from her shoulder. "You've done enough today," he said softly. "Go back to sleep."

"If you're sure—"

He kissed her, his lips warm and gentle. "I am. Anything you want from the kitchen?"

"Hmm, no," she said, sleepiness pulling against her. *You, you, you. I just want you.*

His warmth shuffled away from her, and she sunk once more into sleep.

A little while later, she woke again, startled by the coldness of the bed. Beau hadn't returned. Worried that he'd had another attack and passed out somewhere, she scrambled out of bed, nearly stumbling into Pilot.

"Gosh, you're still when you're in rest mode!"

The dog's gears groaned as he raised a weary head, and promptly lowered it again, unperturbed. Asami hurried along to the kitchen, stopping short when she heard voices. Beau's, and someone else's. The stranger from before, if she wasn't mistaken.

"Sorry it took me so long to get here," said the voice. "Security is a nightmare right now."

"I'm sure it is."

"So... did you get it?"

"We did."

"Right." The stranger went quiet, no doubt wondering

why Beau didn't seem more elated. "You look awful," he said eventually.

"I always look awful."

"I meant… are you hurt?"

"Few scrapes. Nothing major."

"And Asami?"

Asami liked the fact he used her name. He must have known it from the wanted posters, but there was a sliver of intimacy at the sound of it which made her feel he knew it because *Beau* had told him. Because he spoke about her.

"She's all right, too?" the stranger continued.

"I wouldn't be if she wasn't."

There was something of a smile in the stranger's voice. "I've never known you to be this sweet on a girl before."

"That's because I hadn't met *her* before."

Asami's heart skipped.

"It's serious, then?" came Beau's companion's voice again.

"Yes."

"Reciprocated?"

"Yes. I don't expect you to understand—"

"You'd be surprised what I know about love," said the stranger, somewhat wistfully. "But enough of that. If you're together, and she's fine, and you got what you needed, what's the matter?"

Beau's voice went low, and he explained to his friend all that had happened regarding the true identity of the dread doctors.

His companion went quiet for a moment, and then swore under his breath.

"Stars above, I had no idea. That's... there aren't words."

"Malcolm needs to pay for what he did."

Another, stronger pause. "You won't hear any disagreements from me," he said. "Do you... did the Colonel know?"

Beau went quiet. "I don't think so. He seemed as horrified as I was."

"Well, good. He should be." The stranger cleared his throat. "Mira must have known. She would have ordered it. Even when they're dead she still forces her soldiers to serve. If there's an end to her depravity, I've yet to see it."

"I've a feeling we haven't seen the last of it."

"I was afraid of that." There was a shuffling in the room, a moving of chairs. "Shall we have a drink?"

"I need to get back to Asami."

"Ha! I'll try not to be too put out."

Sensing that the conversation was drawing to a close, Asami slunk away back to her room. A few minutes later, Beau slunk into bed, the springs groaning beneath him.

"Sorry," he said, when she turned towards him. "I didn't mean to wake you."

"You didn't," she returned. "I heard you speaking to your friend again." There was no question in her voice, no probing. She just wanted him to know she had overheard them.

"Thank you."

"For... not pestering you about his identity?"

"That, yes, but also for just being you. I quite like that part of you."

"You mean all of me?"

"Yes, that. All of you is my favourite part."

Asami wriggled further into his arms, basking in the glow of him, the warmth that only he could emit. "You're silly and soppy and I should hate it but I like it when it's from you."

"Good," he said, and kissed the top of her head.

"I like all of you, too."

Their mouths found each other in the dark, and they kissed until Asami felt she might break, sponge inside a fragile shell that could fall apart at the slightest pressure.

Beau groaned, his body taut with pain.

"Sorry!" she rushed, rolling off him. "I forgot about your ribs—"

"You're a terrible doctor."

She pressed her nose to his. "I'm an excellent doctor," she said, refusing to be taunted. "And tomorrow, you'll see why."

27
THE CURE AND THE CAGE

Over the next few days, Asami carefully worked on the serum she hoped would offer them a cure, carefully utilising their ingredients. That part wasn't too tricky. The worst part was applying it to their test subject, and waiting.

Beau, who had already spent the last few days pacing around like an expectant father, tapping nervously on any surface unlucky enough to fall beneath his fingers, became unbearable at that point.

"Get out," Asami said at one point.

"What?"

"Get out. Go for a walk. Go steal something. Take some spare supplies to the outer ring. I don't care. Just get out of this lab. You're making me unbearably nervous."

"I'm making *you* nervous?"

"Yes. Far more than I can deal with. Please leave."

She was as short as she had ever been with him, and he elected to go through some of the supplies he'd pilfered earlier in the week and donate them to the poor, perhaps believing that such an action would evoke a karmic reaction.

Asami's nerves settled slightly in his absence, but her heart continued to hammer madly in her chest. She kept glancing at the rat, trying not to think about drawing further blood samples, trying not to check every minute for improvement.

She built another serum of the one Mortimer had created to stabilise Beau in the first place out of the leftover supplies, just as a back-up option, although she wasn't sure she'd risk wasting that on the rat.

She reorganised her lab while she waited, and sat down to look through Malcolm's hard drive, searching for something incriminating. There was a lot on the original experiments, including what had been done to the soldiers after they'd died. Records of the horrible infusions of science and engineering.

At least she knew they'd been dead the whole time, their bodies no more than re-animated flesh.

But he did not mention the crown, the queen, or who organised the experiments. It was all medical, confidential.

Come on, Malcolm. Give me something.

By the time Beau returned, there had been no change to the rat. They ate a meal together in uneasy silence, and slunk off to their own beds at different times, exhausted and struggling to sleep. She heard Beau wake several times in the night, coughing with nerves, and she felt hardly any better herself.

Eventually, she slunk to his side.

"You keep coughing like that, you're going to hurt yourself." She placed a hand against his ribs, lightly, softly, pleased he didn't immediately recoil.

"Just as well I have you to help me then," he said, and closed his fingers over hers.

"You'll always have me."

For a second, Beau froze, and she wondered if her words had alarmed him, but a second later he squeezed her hand and tugged her into bed with him.

Somehow, they grabbed a few more hours of sleep.

Beau was gone by the time Asami woke, the bed cold. The clock on the dresser showed it was still early morning, but she was stung by the sensation of oversleeping, of being in the wrong place.

She bolted from her bed, flinging a shawl around her shoulders, and sprinted to the lab. Beau was there, his massive form staring over the cage that housed their single, solitary rat.

His eyes brimmed with tears.

"Beau?" she whispered desperately. *Not the rat, please. It's our last hope...*

Not quite the last, because she was never giving up, but the last idea she had. Their last shot with their available resources.

Please, please, please.

"Asami," Beau raised his head. "Look. Look at it."

He moved away to give her a clear view. The fat rodent, which yesterday had been a ball of fur and boils, was now almost completely normal.

Asami stared, certain her eyes were playing tricks on her. It still had patches of baldness, a few lumps and contusions, but in every other respect...

"You did it," Beau said, his voice breaking. "You actually did it."

Asami shook her head, refusing to believe it. She fetched a syringe and took a blood sample from their subject, placing it under a microscope, not daring to believe, to let herself hope, until she was sure.

A strange numbness crept over her when she saw the sample under the lens, and she stepped away from it.

"Well?" said Beau.

"It's... it's working," she muttered dumbly. "The cells are repairing themselves."

Their eyes met, and Asami wasn't sure quite what to feel, or why relief was being held so far above her.

Beau's beautiful, wounded face broke into a grin of pure starlight. He wrapped her in his arms and lifted her off her feet, twirling her around the room.

"Beau! Your ribs!"

"Don't care!" he said, barely wincing. "You did it. You did it, you beautiful, perfect goddess!"

"I'm not perfect," she said quickly. "And gods don't exist."

"Maybe not ones in the heavens," he agreed. "But I see one before me, clear as day, and although she is clumsy and easily flustered and cannot clean, she is the most wonderful, most perfect person I have ever known, or ever will." He caught her face in his hands. "Asami," he said, his voice a ghost. "Asami."

Suddenly his mouth was on hers and he was kissing her, fiercely and breathlessly. Her back pressed against the desk as he towered over her, his body a cage over hers. Her heart raced, her body tingling beneath the touch of his. She murmured words or sounds or something in between, words of nearness and wonder and desire. A need to have him. His fingers clung to her face, her limbs, her hair, and her own hands traced the shape of his back and lifted the shirt at his waist.

"Not yet," he said, parting. "Give me the cure, first. Let me have you as myself."

She touched his cheek. "You've always been yourself."

He shook his head. "You know what I mean," he said. "Please, Asami, don't make me beg. Not for this."

She wriggled beneath him, pulling herself into a sitting position. "I can't give it to you yet," she told him, and before he could protest, continued. "It's too dangerous. We need to monitor the rat for a bit longer, assess for any possible side-effects—"

"I'll put up with *anything,* I assure you—"

"You know you could die, right?"

"Don't care."

"*I* care."

Beau shifted off the desk. "What if I don't want to wait? You don't have any idea—"

"Give me *some* credit, Beau. You don't think I want you 'fixed' almost as much as you do?"

"Don't say 'fixed' like that."

"Like what?"

"Like you refuse to believe I'm broken."

"You can call yourself whatever you like, but how can you be broken when you're still here, and alive, and a person so utterly magnificent that you've made me fall in love with you?" She paused, aware of the hardness in her voice. "I won't pretend to know exactly what you've been through, but you don't get to decide what I see, or what I want. And you definitely don't get to override me on matters of science. I'm not giving you anything that could hurt you. Ever."

Beau shuddered, his eyes falling away from her. For a long, desperate moment, silence filled the room. "Except yourself," he said quietly.

"What was that?"

"*You* could hurt me," he said. "You could destroy me. In a way no secret government experiment has ever done."

"But I won't," she said, her voice just as light. "You know that, right?"

He leant his forehead against hers. "Yes," he whispered. "I know that."

"You trust me."

"Of course I do."

"Then trust me on this."

"Always," he replied. "On anything."

She wrapped her hands around his neck. "I trust you too."

The rat improved. Beau's patience did not, becoming more and more restless as the days went by, a jittery, spasming mess of nerves. He could barely sit still even when Asami was dealing with his stitches, the wound healing over within a matter of days. His ribs were fine within a week.

"I will ban you from the lab," Asami barked at him one afternoon.

"It's my lab too!"

"When I'm running life-changing experiments in it and you're distracting me, it's mine."

"That is... fair," he agreed, and slunk off to find something else to do.

He was back within the hour.

Asami gave up, let him watch the creature, and went over to his computers where she struggled through the rest of Malcolm's research. There were a few pieces, whilst not incriminating anyone higher up the chain, that were dark enough to cause a stir, and some horrible, horrible images.

If the Rebellion utilised them, they might be able to cause something of a disturbance, uniting others to their cause, if nothing else.

There were also the falsified death certificates of the soldiers, reporting that they were killed in action. Coupled with the details of the experiments and the gruesome images of their bodies, it certainly painted a grisly picture. They'd make excellent propaganda with the right resources, although every time she thought about smearing their images across posters or pamphlets, she thought of their families seeing them, of learning how loved ones died...

Many of the soldiers came from well-to-do families. It might be a good way of gaining allies.

Or enemies.

When did she become the sort of person who thought this way? Making plans to spread chaos and pain?

When you realised those things were already there, and all you are doing is shining a light on it.

Asami clenched her jaw. Beau's certificate was in the file too. She'd counted ten, but hadn't sought it out. She couldn't bear to see his name printed there.

She glanced across at Beau, now hoping for a distraction herself. "Haven't you ever heard the expression, 'a watched kettle never boils'?"

"As long as it's interchangeable with, 'a watched rat never dies,' I'm all right with it."

Asami sighed, shifting off her seat, and came over to drape her arms around Beau's back. "Anything I can do?"

"Have you developed a serum for speeding up time?"

"You wouldn't do that using a serum," she said pointedly. "A machine, maybe, although the mechanics of such a thing —"

"Asami."

"Right." She slid off him. "I'm going to make some tea, and you're going to join me, and if you come back to watch this rat again, I'm pouring it down the pretty side of your face."

Beau sighed, shaking his head, and slid out of the room after her.

Although he left the rat's side, Asami could tell his thoughts stayed with it. He was still jittery, nervous, his eyes never quite reaching her, his plate full, his stomach empty.

"You're going to make yourself sick with nerves."

"Can't help it."

"Beau," she said, putting her hand over his twitching thigh, "I'm nervous too."

"It's not… I know you are," he responded. "But it's been so long. I never even hoped before now, before you… not really, not truly. It's unbearable. You don't know what it's like to be trapped in a body that's not your own—"

"This *is* your own body, Beau, and I love it—"

"But that doesn't matter, see, because I don't, and unless it's you, unless it's happened to you, you don't get it." A hard sigh shuddered out of him. "You were right, before."

"I'm usually right," Asami snipped, frustration and sadness twisted into impatience. "Please clarify."

"When you said you weren't here to make me feel better about myself. That only I could do that." His jaw tensed. "Only I'm not sure I can. If this doesn't work—"

"Then we find another way," she said, just as fiercely. "I'm not giving up on you, Beau. So don't you dare give up either."

He nodded, swallowing. "Yes, Doc."

"Good." She got up to make another pot of tea. "If you can't eat anything, you should at least drink. I won't have you wasting away to nothing."

He went on a long walk afterwards, which Asami wondered if he was doing mostly for her benefit, just so she didn't have to watch him struggle. She completed a few more observations on the rat, went through another of Malcolm's files, and tidied up the lab. She thought about cleaning something but Beau would doubtless tell her she had done it all wrong and she didn't want to risk his ire. Organising she could do. Cleaning she could not.

It was late when Beau returned.

"Want me to run you a bath?" she asked, twirling a finger around a lock of damp hair. "I've already had mine."

Beau consented, utterly silent, and once more she wondered if he was just doing this for her sake.

"I'll be late to bed tonight," he said after emerging from the bathroom, his loose shirt clinging to his skin. "Please don't wait up."

Beau stared at the serum in Asami's desk as a man might stare at an oasis in the desert.

Except no human could survive three years without water, and suddenly, that's exactly how Beau felt.

He was beyond parched, beyond dehydration. He'd died long ago, and this serum was the miracle cure needed to bring him back to life.

I am a ghost, and this is my chance at having a body again. My chance to exist, to experience, to touch…

To be with Asami, without fear of hurting her, without the fear that she might hurt *him*, be disgusted when everything was laid bare.

Because even though she insisted it didn't matter, he wasn't sure that was the case. He knew how lonely she'd been above, and he couldn't shake the feeling that if they returned, if they exposed the Crown's sordid truth, everyone would finally see how amazing she was.

He had no competition down here.

A perfect cure might not exist, but he was certain that one day they'd have enough evidence to go back.

"You'll always have me," she'd said.

But would he? He had so little to offer her. No home, half a face, a dysfunctional body...

He could give her more.

Don't do this, said another voice, one of sense and reason. *The last time you took experimental drugs? Didn't end well for you.*

But how much worse could it be?

Besides, the original serum was rushed, ill-thought out, created by scientists who saw them as fodder. He had far more faith in Asami.

Just wait a little longer...

But it might not be a little longer. It could be weeks, months. And if the rat started showing even the slightest of side effects... she'd never let him take it.

And he wanted her more than he feared *this.* Wanted her with a thick, guttural ache that grew worse with each passing day.

He wasn't afraid of death. He was used to pain.

The only thing he was afraid of was not being with her.

He picked up the serum, and filled the syringe.

Don't do it, don't it, don't it—

Beau hissed the voices into silence. Just for once, he was making his own decisions.

He plunged the needle into his arm.

For a moment, there was nothing. He should have expected that. The original serum had taken hours to start affecting them, days until it reached its max—

Oh gears, what if Asami realised the serum was missing before it was clear whether or not it worked? She'd kill him herself—

He stood up, whether or not with the intention of running to her and begging for her forgiveness, or to bolt away and hide, he wasn't sure.

He got nowhere. His legs turned to jelly, falling out from underneath him. Ice crawled through his veins. His left arm jerked and twisted, spasms raking through his body.

He hit the floor, eyes rolling in their sockets. He searched for the sound of a ticking clock, for the reminder that everything passed eventually. *Everything passes.*

But not the worst kinds of pain.

Asami, Asami. I'm sorry.

When Ash came to deliver the news to Beau that Mortimer was dead, Beau remembered that as being the worst of all the losses, somehow. Worse than his mother, his squad, his old life. Maybe that was just because he *could* remember it; it was one of the few awful moments not blurred by pain. Or maybe it was because of what that death triggered; the blistering, blinding hopelessness. The end of every positive thought.

It had been a good day. Ash's exercises were paying off. His left arm worked as an arm now, even if the hand didn't move as well as he wanted it. He'd just managed to beat his personal weight-lifting record, and he'd fixed Pilot's motor so he wasn't leaking oil everywhere.

It was a good day.

Then the door clicked open.

Beau almost smiled, recognising the sound of Ash's footsteps, and went out to greet him.

Unlike when he saw his father outside the bank, Beau couldn't tell from Ash's face that something awful had transpired. He looked solemn, but Beau had seen him wear that exact same expression when Jon accidentally spilt ale on his favourite suit.

"You look glum," he said, half-laughing. "Step in muck on your way down?"

Ash shook his head. "It's Mortimer," he said.

"Mortimer stepped in something?"

"He's dead."

Beau waited for the rest of the sentence, the words that erased them, that turned them into something else. *Dead bored, dead tired, dead sick of this.* Maybe Ash hadn't even said 'dead'. Maybe he'd said 'done', maybe—

Mortimer could not be dead. It was too much. Not after his mother, and his team, and his life...

Mortimer couldn't be dead, because if he was, there was no getting any of it back. If Mortimer was gone...

Beau might as well be dead too.

"No," he said, shaking his head. "No, no. That's not right. He can't be dead. He can't—"

"There was an accident at the palace," Ash continued, voice shaking. "His lab caught fire—at least that's what they're saying."

"No, no! They're wrong—"

"I saw the body, Beau," he said. "I made sure."

Something exploded inside Beau, something shattered and crumbled. He punched the wall, fury live in his fist. The brick cracked. Bone did, too.

He did not feel it.

Ash came towards him, trying to tug Beau into his arms like he had when his mother had died, but Beau pushed away from him. His mouth tasted like poison.

"You should have let me die," Beau hissed. "You should never have saved me."

Ash shoved him, hard. Fury blazed in his eyes. "Fuck off."

"What?"

"I said, fuck off. No, I shouldn't."

Beau sunk to the floor, staring at his ruined hand. "I don't want to live like this for the rest of my life."

Ash sank down with him. Somewhere, dimly, Beau remembered sitting with him the first day they met, a plate of macaroons between them. A long time ago now. "You're my best friend, Beau. I've already lost…" He shook his head, dislodging some painful memory only half shared. He swallowed, and when he breathed again, there was a hard quality to his breath. "You're my team."

"What?"

"You lost your team. You know how awful that was. Well, you're mine. The thing in my life that makes the most sense. The person I can't lose. Won't."

"I'm only one person."

"Not to me." Ash glanced downwards. "Did I ever tell you about my great-uncle, Antiono De Ferone, the Duke of Veronia?"

"Shockingly, no."

"Lost both of his legs during the War of the Nations. I never knew how much it affected him at the time, because I'd always known him as he was: tough, uncompromising, and hilarious. Then after *a lot* of drinks one evening, he got oddly serious and told me he was really glad he hadn't ended his life after the incident, he was having such a blast now."

Beau paused. "How... how did he... you know... *adapt?*"

"Wheelchair, at first. Then a couple of rather badass mechanical legs."

Beau shook his head, scowling. "I don't think I can get a clockwork *face.*"

"Well, of course not, you don't need one." Ash flicked his forehead. "One day someone might tell you you're perfect, but I won't. I will say that you're functional, though. How can you be broken when you're still breathing?"

"You're making an alarming degree of sense right now and I don't like it."

Ash snorted. "I'll only be the sensible one when you can't be. And honestly, I don't really like it, so if you could go back to being that so I can return to being a devilish fool, I'd appreciate it."

Beau smiled, half of his cheek unable to follow through with the action, but it was a smile nonetheless. The first in months. The first since he'd taken the serum.

Perhaps Ash was right. It would be the first time. But then he'd just smiled after thinking he would never do so again.

If he could smile today, maybe he could laugh tomorrow.

Or next week.

On the floor of the lab, Asami's cure burning through his veins, Beau felt the cool metal of Ash's watch in his waistcoat pocket, remembered the feel of it being pressed into his hands the first time he'd had an episode. He'd been certain he wouldn't survive that, but he had.

Time is passing, Beau. And so will this.

Maybe one day someone might tell you you're perfect.

Maybe.

One day.

It was how he would live for the next two and half years.

But not one moment longer.

28

A RELEASE OF SOULS

Asami settled down for the night in her own carriage, a place becoming colder and colder with disuse. She shared with Beau most nights, but sometimes after a particularly bad night's sleep it was prudent to spend the next one apart to catch up, or if she didn't want to risk being woken when he finally came to bed. She wished they could share all the time, but she also knew the benefits of getting uninterrupted sleep once in a while, and Beau's fidgetiness and nightmares didn't make things easy.

She knew he hated waking her up, too.

She hated there were things she couldn't fix.

There was no serum for that, no cure but time.

Sleep did not come easily, and when it did, she dreamed of being late to school, only to find out she was supposed to teach a class, but she didn't have any of the right resources. Suddenly, her ancestors popped out of the ground, grey and rotting, and spoke words of disappointment and displeasure.

Her parents sighed.

"Now look what you've done," they said, as her great-grandmother's jaw fell off. "Couldn't even get to school on time. How do *you* hope to save anyone?"

Sakura materialised on one of the desks, playing a violin. "You should have been a musician. At least then you would have put some beauty into the world, instead of all this ugliness."

The students in the room morphed into dread doctors, emitting horrible, clawing voices, growls made of nails and slate.

Screams, they were screaming. Screaming as mechanical limbs fell from their bodies, only they transformed into flesh and blood when they hit the floor. Wires and gears hissed amongst pulping muscles.

And through it all was Malcolm's face, laughing.

Asami woke sobbing, clutching the sheets to her chest. She expected Beau to race in, but he didn't come.

She shuffled upright in search of him, drifting into his car. He wasn't there either.

She rubbed her eyes, scanning the clock.

It was almost morning. He hadn't come to bed.

"Beau," she called out, her voice turning to panic in a second. The fear of the dream flew away, replaced by fear for him. He'd had another episode. He was alone, and hurt—

She flew into the lab.

Beau was lying on the floor beneath the rat cage, the rodent scuffling madly at the bars.

"Beau!" she screamed.

He started to shift at the sound of her voice, rolling onto his elbows. The relief didn't quite reach her, the little voice that ought to have told her he couldn't move so easily if he was hurt refusing to speak.

"Asami," he murmured. "What—"

His face met hers, and she stopped shortly. His lumps and scars had all but vanished, his left cheek as smooth as his right. When he held out a hand towards her, it was no longer twisted and gnarled. Only a few blemishes remained.

Beau stilled, staring at his hands.

Beside him, on the floor, was an empty syringe.

The serum. He'd taken it.

"Beau," she said, her voice sharp and fragile as glass, "what did you do?"

For the longest moment, Beau did not reply. He stared numbly at his fingers, rubbing them together, touching his face, his chest, too shocked to look anything like amazed. "It... it worked."

Asami swallowed. "You took the serum."

"I did."

"Do you have any idea what—"

"I'm sorry," he said. "I couldn't wait any longer."

"You couldn't..." Anger wrestled inside her. "This could kill you. You understand that, right?"

"I have faith that it won't."

"You have *faith?*" Her words were laced with fury. "That's

been known to work fabulously in the laboratory. Why bother using science at all?"

"Don't be angry," he said, reaching towards her.

"You don't get to decide how I feel!" She shied away from his outstretched hands. "I don't understand why you'd risk it. I just... I don't."

"Asami," he said, "it's been three years. Three years since I've felt like myself. And I couldn't... I just couldn't bear it any longer. I couldn't bear having you and not *having you.*"

Asami's voice shrunk in her mouth. "You could have had me any time."

"You don't get to decide how I feel," he echoed, without a note of anger. "I can't explain it to you. I know that. Anyone who could have understood is dead. And if you need time, I understand that, and I'll give it to you, but I'd ask you please... could you just look at me?"

"I *am* looking at you," she hissed.

He tugged a hand from her side, and placed it against his cheek. "Look deeper. Look *more.*"

Asami swallowed, her throat raw. "I always have," she said, trying not to shake. "Always have. Always will." She caught his eyes, beautiful, perfect, unspoilt, but she remembered a time when she hadn't always seen them that way, brief as it had been. She remembered struggling to find him beautiful.

Not now. Not now and never again.

She wanted to whisper his name, but found she didn't have the words. Her panic and anger tempered to something less than amazement, less than relief, but good and whole and warm.

He was alive. He was whole.

She'd done it.

For a moment, if only a moment, she let herself believe that, let herself stop worrying about the side effects, the lack of testing, the hundred-and-three worst case scenarios her mind was calculating.

Later, later, later. Just… just let me have a moment. Just one.

She lay a hand over his heart, against the hard panel that held his chest. There was not a whisper of distorted flesh beneath, and unlike before, he did not flinch or pull away. He sighed beneath her fingers, soft and sure, and a second later he grabbed her waist and yanked her to him.

His kisses fractured and splintered against her, fragmenting thought. Her skin blurred with contact, the lines between the two of them faint and fuzzy, indistinct. Each kiss, each caress, every hazy touch sent her reeling in sensation, lost to the giddy dark. Hotness pulsed inwardly, drawing up from between her legs, curling her toes, spreading to every trembling inch of her.

"Beau, Beau, Beau," she murmured, mouth dry. "I love you, I love you *so much.*"

"Asami," he said, his words a soft snarl. He stared at her, eyes glassy, and whispered her name again like people once must have uttered prayers, like there was no other word sweeter, more divine. She tugged his mouth to hers, claiming it, exploring every perfect new part, gently teasing on his lips, not wanting them anywhere else, not right now. There was a desperate, pressing urge to have him fold into her.

She grappled for the openings on his shirt, wishing she had the strength to rip it from him, as he hauled her own clothes over her head until she stood perfectly naked before him. He stopped for a second, taking her in, before his head fell to her bare chest and his mouth made its way down her small, pert breasts, murmuring against her skin.

His touch reminded her of champagne, of something decadent and glistening. She was reminded of other things, too, summer rain, hot coals, the smell of dust and heat. And yet his scent slashed through her, cutting her to the core, whispering to her of something far more ancient than flimsy memories of a former life; something older than her body, older than earth, something written into her DNA from the start.

It was nonsensical, irrational, unscientific. Her mind was splintering into fragmented poetry, lines of lust and ardor. Every rule she'd held irrefutable transmuted itself into insubstantial rumour, the rest of her following. She knew she still had a body because it was falling to crumbs in his hands, but the world was spinning around her at a speed akin to madness, and direction and gravity were lost to her.

He lay her back against the floor, his kisses descending. "I love you," he whispered hoarsely.

"I am—distinctly—lovable," she hissed out, barking beneath his exquisite lips. "Gears, stars, garters and domes, you're good at that."

He grinned against her middle, arms roped around her legs.

She grabbed his cheeks. "Get back up here."

"But I thought—"

"Not right now," she said. "Right now I want you up here with me. Your face on mine. You *in* me."

"Are you sure?"

She tugged on his face. "Yes. Your face, please."

He rose from her waist until his nose brushed against hers, eyes wide and luminous. They kissed without closing them, without daring to look away, her hands cupping his flawless, pristine cheeks.

She tugged his chin, the rough, sandpaper line of stubble. "You're going to rub me raw."

"We could stop—"

"I'd rather not."

She raked her hands down his back, revelling in the delightful hisses she elicited, and whipped the length of him into a frenzy. His fingers found the softness between her thighs, circling around the apex, and she lifted her hips towards him.

"Now, please," she instructed.

Beau's hands squeezed hers, and he slid into her with a hard, ragged gasp, twinning with her own as he drove into her, soft and heavy, and she felt like she was splitting apart at the centre with wonderful, delicious joy. She tilted herself against him, wrapping her legs around his back and clinging to him for dear life as he rocked inside her, drawing her further and further and further into exquisite delight, rolling and endless as the skies.

Or what she knew about them anyway.

Skies are practically theoretical, her mind reasoned

numbly. *But this is not.*

Slowly, her fractured thoughts drew together, just in time for Beau to release, long and hard. She held him in her arms as he emptied, clinging to him as he started to pull away.

"No," she said, "not yet. Just… stay there. Lie on me. Don't move out just yet."

He grinned, lowering his damp face to her breast, and hugged her middle, seeming smaller and bigger than ever.

He was still inside her.

"We didn't use protection," she said. "Sorry to spoil the moment."

While a great deal of technology had been lost or limited during the old wars, one that Petragrad and the other mechanical kingdoms had clung onto was contraception, made freely available even the outer rings. Over-population was always a concern.

Beau shook his head. "All military personnel have an implant. Mine will need replacing in the next year or so, but it's still effective. I wouldn't do that to you."

"And you're clean?"

"This post coital talk of yours needs work, but yes. Military very big on testing. You?"

"Spotless."

"Hardly a surprise."

Asami grinned. "Very unlike me to not discuss these things beforehand!" She brushed a hand through his hair. "You make me a bit reckless, you know."

"Sorry," he said, and kissed her chest. "Genuinely. For I don't like putting you in harm's way."

"You're worth it, Beau," she said softly, and she tugged his face to hers, drawing him out of her. "You're worth everything."

They kissed again, raw, slow, sweet, and drew out a blanket from one of the drawers, utterly entangling themselves inside it. Asami pressed her ear to his chest and bathed in the glorious rhythm of it, thinking of beautiful, silly, impossible things.

"I think I must believe in souls, after all," she whispered against him, "because I can see yours, and it is beautiful."

29

THE BONES IN THE ASHES

For the better part of the day, they existed inside one another, only breaking to eat, and bathe, and even those two activities didn't get far without interruption.

"Are you still mad?" Beau asked as she slid onto his lap in the middle of lunch.

"Tomorrow," she said, nibbling at his ear. "I'll be mad tomorrow."

Beau made love to her like he could stall time if he kept at it long enough, as if tomorrow could be kept at bay by keeping her up all night, as if kisses could dissolve anger.

Asami bit his lip. He growled into her.

"You were a good kisser before," she said. "You're excellent now."

Beau grinned wickedly, and kissed her into silence.

Sleep came eventually, black and blissful. When morning rolled around, Asami felt like the carriage was teeming with sunlight. Her limbs and centre felt sore, but in a good, tingling, deeply satisfied way. Beau was sleeping next to her, still apart from the slow rise and fall of his chest, a soft smile spread across his face, his left cheek dimpled. She had never seen him look so calm, or tranquil, or happy.

I did that.

But then the niggling fear set in, the doubts she'd kept back, although her fury seemed oddly sated. All the lovemaking had clearly worked, damn him.

She raised her fingers to his wrist and counted, measuring his pulse. Steady. Normal. Fine.

Beau's eyes flickered open. They ought to have been unchanged, and yet somehow they seemed even more luminous than before. Brighter.

"Good morning," he said.

"Good morning."

"You're staring at me."

"That is because you are beautiful."

"So superficial."

"You've always been beautiful to me, Beau."

She stroked his features, and slid on top of him. He let out a quiet groan, hands landing on her hips. "Stars, you're exquisite," he said, his thumbs caressing the bones of her hips. "You don't know what agony it's been, living beside you all these weeks, not being able to touch you…"

"Oh, don't I, now?" she said, tracing a finger down the hollows of his chest, grinding against him. He buckled beneath her, swearing under his breath, and grabbed her waist, flipping her back underneath and yanking her to him. He was inside her in an instant, and she rolled under his touch, splitting apart at the centre, hot and dizzy and delirious as his fingers worked at the apex of her, drawing her in and out of perfect, blissful ecstasy. Undone, unmade, destroyed and utterly and perfectly moulded.

After, they lay beside each other on the damp sheets.

"I was worried it might fizzle out, afterwards," Asami admitted. "That sometimes happens with me. I like someone, I bed them, *poof.*"

Beau rolled over, staring at her incredulously. "Why didn't you tell me that?"

"Because I didn't want to scare you? You were already dealing with so much, I didn't want you dealing with that fear, too."

"Is… is it? Do you…"

"No. Not at all. It's worse than before."

"Worse?" he grinned.

"Better. It's better with you. *Everything's* better with you. And by that I mean I'd like to go again, please."

"Say that again."

"I'd like to go again."

"Just the last part."

"Please," she murmured. "Please, *please,* Beau. I want you. Just you. No one else but you."

Days drew by like this, lost to each other. Asami's own bed lay abandoned, the second train car more an extension of the first, a private dressing room. She made new curtains for the main one, Beau strung lanterns across the bed. He let her bring in a mirror. For a week they barely talked of work at all, as if the rest of the world outside the underground had stalled to a stop.

Eventually, of course, they remembered.

"The next time the Rebellion passes by, we should tell them what we've found out," Asami announced one morning. "Let them decide what to do with it."

He nodded. "I agree."

"How often do they tend to come?"

He shrugged. "It's erratic. They don't always drop in here unless they need something, so it can be months between visits."

Asami squirmed uncomfortably in her seat.

"What is it?"

"I don't know. I just... I don't like doing nothing." *I've been doing nothing for a week.*

"Doing... nothing?" He grinned, letting a hand fall to her thigh. "We don't have to do *nothing...*"

"Beau," she whispered, her mouth suddenly dry, "please, I'm working."

"I'm working too..." His lips brushed her skin.

She shoved him away. "Later," she hissed. "I'll never get anything done at this rate..."

"Fine," he said, pouting but in good humour. "I'm going to take a cold bath and then clean something."

He'd barely filled half the bath before Asami gave up and joined him, turning off the tap and hauling her shirt over her head.

Beau stared at her, eyes wide. "What do you want?"

"I want you to kiss me until my face is numb and then I want you to kiss everything else."

Beau grinned wickedly. "Work, work, work."

She took the memory of his smile into her even as her vision sunk into delicious darkness, lost to the perilous pressure of his mouth.

The break actually helped resettle her thoughts, and after she was clean and dry, her mind seemed more in the mood for going through Malcolm's research. Two days ago, she'd discovered a series of journals from a recent project. Like most journals, it made more sense if you knew what they were working on, but Asami had yet to discern it. Malcolm was careful in his record keeping.

She opened the journal at the point she left off at, and frowned at his final entry.

Running low on fuel and test subjects. Will have to speak to the authorities about adjusting the filters again.

It was a small, throwaway line, the sort of thing easily dismissed if you weren't paying attention, laced with carelessness.

Low on fuel and test subjects.

It would not have surprised her in the least to discover that Malcolm was using anyone as a test subject. What unnerved her was the mention of "adjusting" the filters. What did that have to do with running out of test subjects?

No, she thought, a coldness gripping her, *not even Malcolm would do something like that.*

Except it wouldn't be Malcolm's doing. Orders like that would have to have come from much, much higher up.

"Beau…"

He looked up from his own desk. "Yes?"

"Look at this."

He hopped over towards her, eyes darting over the entry. Once, twice, three times. Then he looked to Asami, face white.

"I'm not jumping to conclusions, am I?" she asked.

Beau shook his head. "Where this government is concerned? No."

"What should we do?"

He thumbed his chin. "I think we should follow one of the dread doctor vans and work out what they're really doing with the people they're taking."

Asami grimaced. "I was afraid you were going to say something like that."

Beau smiled weakly, squeezing her shoulder. "It's not as risky as breaking into the palace *or* a prison. I promise."

"My, my, Beaumont, it's almost like you *enjoy* putting me in dangerous or uncomfortable situations."

"You know that's not true." He sighed, running a hand through his hair. "I can probably do this alone, you know."

"Be safer with two, though, wouldn't it?"

He looked down. "Yes."

"Where you go, I go, right?"

He smiled, long and soft. "Hardly seems fair that you follow me into danger and I follow you into a nice, safe lab."

"One day I'll make you follow me somewhere harder."

"And I'll follow," he said, bending down to kiss her. "Promise."

Beau formulated a plan for following the vans quickly, although it took a few days to execute. It involved the rather depressing step of combing the streets, searching for any victims. Luckily for the people, but unluckily for the two of them, there didn't seem to be any cases of late.

Eventually, they settled on waiting outside the hospital, finding an abandoned building with a decent view nearby. Although the guards seemed unaware of it, when a patient grew too ill, when they feared the pain more than the end, they were helped out into the open, and the guards alerted by a third party.

Asami watched as a middle-aged lady, around the same age as her mother, was brought into the street by a younger man with the same crow-black hair. Her son, she thought. One of the volunteers went to fetch the dread doctors, while the woman lay in her son's lap, still but not still enough.

Beau tensed when the dread doctors arrived, the clunk of their boots shuddering through the night. Asami knew he was probably wondering which of his former comrades was behind the mask, but he said nothing, instead taking a tiny clockwork bee out of his pocket. The bee hovered on his palm, buzzing faintly, before descending out of the broken window, down into the waiting van.

The patient was loaded up, the doors closed, and the vehicle drove away.

The son was left alone on the street, a dark figure on the cobbles beneath a dim, amber light.

Asami's eyes stayed on him, with him, even as Beau whipped out a beaten old scanner, tracking the van. "Odd," he said, after a few minutes.

"What is?"

"It's not heading towards the hospital."

"Did we expect it to?"

Beau stilled. "No, I suppose not." He touched her shoulder. "We need to move. We don't want it to get too far ahead."

She nodded, pulling up her hood, and followed him into the darkened streets. She hugged his arm and buried her face in his side, partly for concealment, but partly for comfort. She tried to convince herself they were an ordinary couple, out for a moonlit stroll. Maybe when all this was over—

But like most positive thoughts, it did not stick.

"Asami," Beau said, drawing to a stop, "look."

Asami did. They were in front of the coal manufacturing plant, a huge black building of chimneys and funnels, wreathed in smog. The van had parked behind the fence, the driver conversing with a guard on duty.

"Why would they bring the patient here?"

In answer to her question, a white-coated scientist stepped out of the shadows. Not a medical doctor, someone

Asami knew from the lab. Dr Harrison, perhaps? A colleague of Malcolm's.

What was he doing here?

"You don't have to come in with me," said Beau. "What we see…"

"Will be just as unpleasant coming from your lips. No, I'm coming with you."

In truth, she did not want to go, would never get used to the feeling of throwing herself headlong into danger. But greater than any fear for herself was the fear of something happening to him, and whatever harsh truths lay inside that place, she would not have him unearth them alone.

Beau didn't argue, only nodded. He climbed up the side of a nearby building and leapt over the fence, rolling silently to the ground and shooting into the shadows. He waited until the patient had been removed from the van, until the driver returned to his seat, until the gates opened and the van passed through them.

Then he snuck up behind the solitary guard and wrestled him into unconsciousness with surprising efficiency.

Asami snuck in through the open gate, staring at him as he maneuvered the guard into the recovery position at the bottom of his booth.

"What?" Beau asked.

"I'm very anxious right now, but also a little aroused by that show of agility and strength."

Beau snorted. "Keep it in your pants, darling. We have a job to do." He snatched the keycard from the guard's belt. "Let's see how far this takes us."

He wrestled into the guard's jacket and cap, and Asami kept close to him as they slunk in through the back entrance, stopping only briefly at a locker room to suit her up in a white coat and protective gear that did an excellent job of hiding her face. The place was almost silent, devoid of all but a few people. Security was light, of course it was. Nobody wanted to sneak in here, where the filters were probably rusty and broken, and no one was processing coal at this hour.

So what were they processing?

They walked carefully and briskly down the corridors and walkways, through the hot, stifling air. The place was lit with a strange, green light, glinting off the steam and metal . Asami didn't know where they were going, but she trusted Beau did, that he'd come here before as a soldier, or memorised the blueprints.

Beau stopped abruptly, Asami shortly behind him. Dr Harrison had emerged from one of the rooms, talking to another doctor, a grey-haired, scowling man with a bronze cane.

Malcolm.

"Here." Beau grabbed her wrist and pulled her into a nearby room.

The patient from the van, unconscious but still breathing, was strapped to a table in the centre.

Asami's lungs shrivelled. Footsteps sounded in the corridor.

"Shit," Beau hissed, scanning around the room. He picked up Asami and squeezed her behind a screen in the corner.

"Beau—"

There was no space for him. Barely anything in the room

came close to covering his size.

The footsteps were getting closer.

He dived under the table, the patient above him. She gave a hard wheeze, making Asami stiffen. Was she still awake?

The door opened.

Asami shrunk to the bottom of the floor, only able to spy a sliver of what was happening through a gap between the folded panels. She tried to control her breathing, her thoughts spiralling. She was certain, even though she knew it was impossible, that her heart was beating loud enough to be heard by human ears.

"Latest subject, Dr Malcolm," said Dr Harrison. "Just brought in a few minutes ago. I'm not sure if she meets your requirements—"

"Hmm." Malcolm moved across the table, taking a stethoscope off the table and pressing it to the patient's chest. He carried out other tests Asami couldn't quite make out. "No, sadly. Too far gone to be usable. Too old for parts."

Usable?

"Shall I recycle her, then?"

Malcolm nodded. "Yes. Take her down for stripping."

"Very well, sir."

Usable. Recycle. Stripping. Parts.

Asami's stomach knotted more and more with every word, but hurtled into her throat when Dr Harrison went to grab the gurney.

Beau was underneath it.

"What's the matter?" barked Malcolm.

"It's stuck…" Harrison pulled at the handles. "It won't

budge."

"Just put your back into it—"

Malcolm let out a sharp cry as his cane was wrenched from his grip. A dark blur shot around the room. A crack sounded; Harrison slumped to the floor. Malcolm started to scream, but Beau whipped out a pistol and held it under his throat.

"Don't," he warned.

Asami skittered out from behind the screen, Malcolm's eyes glowering as they fixed on her.

"You."

Asami bit back the fear his glare elicited in her, and instead said briskly, "nice cane."

"And you..." Malcolm's eyes turned back to Beau. "I know you."

"I looked a little worse for the wear the last time you saw my face," Beau said, the muzzle still trained on him. He gestured to his cheek.

Malcolm's face was white. "You're one of them, the soldiers we..." His eyes went back to Asami. "You fixed him."

Asami could only nod.

"I wasn't sure that could be done. Interesting."

"Enough of that," said Beau. "Talk. Tell us what's going on here. What do you need the patients for?"

"Research," replied the doctor, as if this much was obvious. "No progress without sacrifice."

"Harrison said he would take her to *recycling*," Asami started, only half-wanting him to answer the question. "What did that mean?"

Malcolm snorted.

"Laugh at her at your own peril, Malcolm," said Beau, nudging him with the pistol.

"So Miss Curiosity doesn't know everything after all…" He grinned. "The bodies that aren't suitable for testing, we recycle. In the compression chambers."

"The… the compression chambers."

Beau cast a look at her, both slowly, silently realising.

"The coal," said Asami. "The artificial coal. You make it using… *people*?"

Malcolm's mouth grew crooked. "Well, animals work too, but we have precious few of those any more, and little space to breed them." His eyes glinted at the horror in her face. "Waste not, want not, girl."

Asami fought the urge to be sick. "How can you smile at that?"

"I had my reservations too, when I first learned about it, but it's a necessary evil. The cities take power to run, more than—"

"More than you can produce naturally," Beau concluded. "Even if *natural* means using the bodies of those that died naturally."

Asami's insides iced. "Beau?"

"The filters aren't broken, are they?" Beau continued.

Malcolm glanced downwards, as if even he regretted this truth. "They were, once. Almost a century ago, now, or so the records show. The city had been using the bones of the dead for some time, but it had never had to… outsource, before. But the Dome was struggling to function. Power loss. Disrepair. The Crown didn't know what to do.

"Then there was an accident in the lower ring, and the filters were damaged. No one noticed until the people started dying. Hundreds in the space of a few weeks. A tragedy, to be sure. But a necessary one. It saved the city."

"And every time there's been a power shortage since, you've tampered with them again." Beau's voice was low. "You've been literally grinding the bones of the poor to power it."

"The needs of the many, boy—"

"What about *their* needs?" Beau bellowed. "*Hers?*" He pointed to the body on the gurney.

"There was no other way—"

"There's always another way," Asami said hoarsely. "You just haven't tried to find it." She looked down at him. "And you haven't tried, have you? I've been through your research. There's nothing about alternative power, just genetic modifications. Making the strong stronger."

Malcolm's eyes narrowed. "You don't know what we're up against. The war with Sparta—"

"I know what we're up against," Beau growled. "And nothing, nothing they have ever done comes to the atrocities you've committed here."

Malcolm's gaze darkened. "You won't say that when the Dome is crumbling down around us, boy—"

"You're right," said Beau, and cocked the pistol, "and neither will you."

An alarm blared into life.

It distracted Beau just long enough for Malcolm to seize

his cane and strike Beau in the stomach with it. Winded, he dropped the pistol. Asami raced towards it, but Malcolm scrambled upright, bolting into the corridor and locking the door behind him.

"*No*," hissed Asami, banging on the glass as Malcolm backed away with a wide grin, vanishing down the corridor. She threw her weight into it, but it didn't budge. "Beau—"

"It's all right," he said, "stand back."

He pulled himself to his feet, still wheezing, and brought a thick copper disk out of one of his pockets. He pressed it against the lock and clicked something into place, covering Asami as it fizzed and heated.

The lock fell off.

Beau kicked down the door, stepping onto the walkway. He glanced behind him, waiting for Asami.

Her eyes were rooted on the patient. She could not move.

"We can't help her," Beau said.

He was right, of course. Even if they could get her out, she had only a few days to live at most, unconscious if she was lucky, in pain if she wasn't. Her heart was still beating, but she was already dead.

Would she still be alive when they 'recycled' her?

"Asami?" Beau touched her elbow. "We have to go."

Asami nodded, and lifted the pistol. "I'm sorry," she whispered to someone; the woman, herself, the son she left. Some higher power she'd never believed in.

She closed her eyes and pulled the trigger.

Beau yanked her out of the room before she could look, before she could commit the sight to memory, but she knew she'd always remember the jerk of the grip in her hand, the sound of that particular bang, the crack of bone and blood.

She did not have time to be sorry.

Beau took the weapon from her hand and flung her behind him, racing down the narrow walkways, firing into pipes and cylinders, filling the space with steam. The cries of guards raked through the air, the clang of bullets against metal.

At the bottom of the stairs, a dread doctor rose out of the greenish gloom.

Beau stilled. He fired a bullet into the shoulder, but it made no difference. The figure advanced, raising a hand towards them.

Beau slid the pistol back into its holster and drew out a knife. He met the outstretched hand with his fist, jerking the arm backwards in a move that should have broken it.

Only the sound of gears grinding permeated the air.

Beau slammed the dagger into its back, against where the heart would be. The body jerked and stilled. "I'm sorry," he whispered.

A bullet narrowly passed Asami's shoulder. She shrieked. Beau grabbed her hand and flew down the stairs, trading knife for pistol. Two guards raced up to greet them, but Beau dispatched both in seconds, one with a swift kick over the railing and another with a bullet to the leg.

The guard screamed in pain, and Asami fought against the instinct to stop and help her, to fix some of this mess.

Or maybe that instinct wasn't there any more, only a faint memory of what the person she used to be would have done.

Another bullet cracked through the air. A cylinder exploded in front of them. Water and glass shattered across the floor.

"Stop!" bellowed a deep, gravelly voice.

Beau stilled. So did Asami, but there was something different in the way his body tensed, something far more fearful than before.

"Drop the weapon," the voice commanded. "I won't ask again."

Beau complied.

"Put your hands up."

Beau did, Asami following. She glanced at him imploringly, waiting for some signal, some clue as to what to do, some bright idea.

But he did nothing. His body was as rigid as stone.

"Turn around," the man commanded.

Asami complied, shaking, and found herself facing Colonel Bestiel. She waited for Beau to do the same.

"Turn!" the colonel commanded.

Beau did. Colonel Bestiel's eyes widened, the gun in his hands trembling. He gripped onto it harder, as if the feel of the metal could steady him. "Beaumont," he said, "it... it is you, isn't it?"

Beau's jaw couldn't have been any harder if it was forged of rock. "Forgotten my face already?"

"I don't understand," Bestiel continued, his voice shakier than Asami had ever heard it, the hardness crumbling. "They said you'd died—"

"I might as well have. All the others did."

"Beau—"

"You knew, didn't you? You knew that the serum was untested, and you still let us take it. *Encouraged* us to, for the good of the kingdom—"

"It was a calculated risk—"

"Is that what you told their families?"

Bestiel stilled. "I'm sorry—"

"You know that doesn't fix a damn thing, don't you?"

Far off, something rumbled. Reinforcements.

"Beau," Asami whispered, "we have to go."

The colonel stared at them. Beau stared back. "Are you going to shoot me?"

The older man's jaw tightened, and something glazed in his eyes, as if he was ashamed Beau could ask such a thing in the first place.

"No," he said. "Of course I won't."

Voices sounded overhead, and Bestiel raised his weapon again, as if having second thoughts. Beau sighed, shaking his head. "Ever the loyal soldier."

"Loyalty is not a trait to be ashamed of."

"Depends on who you're loyal to."

Bestiel's jaw clenched. "Come back with us. I don't know what you're trying to accomplish here, but I can make it all go away—"

"Make it go away?" Beau hissed incredulously. "Like you poison the outer ring, and make them go away?"

Bestiel said nothing, his face frozen. "It's for the many. The ends justify the means—"

"Once upon a time, I'm sure that was true," Beau said

coolly. "But not in this city."

The shouts grew closer. Asami tugged at his elbow. Beau turned, the colonel's eyes still on him until they vanished into the steam.

Beau held her wrist, sprinting down the walkways, towards a back exit. They ducked and dived out of range as they hurtled across the yard, towards a narrow point at the end of the fence.

"Get up," said Beau, gesturing to his back.

Asami didn't hesitate. She leapt up, flinging her arms around his neck, wrapping her legs around his middle, and only squeaked once as he launched himself onto the fence and shot up the side.

Her bones jolted as they hit the ground. Beau grunted, but didn't stop. He hooked his arms under her knees and belted down the streets. The whine of the military vans followed them, but he flew into a back alley too narrow for them to give chase, counting under his breath, measuring how far away they were before racing into the next street.

The whining of the vans trickled away, and Beau slid Asami to her feet a few streets before the entrance to the underground tunnels. They hurried inside, breathless, hearts racing.

For a long time, they stood in the dark, steadying themselves, not speaking.

"Are you all right?" Beau asked, still panting.

"Physically, yes," she replied. "You?"

"Shockingly, yes. Emotionally..." His voice muted. A hard, cold pause stretched between them.

"Beau," Asami started, "What's your surname?"

Beau looked down. "I think you already know."

Asami cast her eyes down. In Malcolm's notes, Beau had been assigned a number. She'd come across the records of the test subjects with their death certificates, but she'd never sought Beau's out. She couldn't bear to look at it.

She'd never asked him, but she knew.

"Colonel Bestiel's your father, isn't he? That's where your nickname came from. Bestiel. Beast."

Beau hung his head further. "I didn't know how to explain —"

"You don't owe me an explanation," she assured him.

The pause grew longer, sharper. "We should keep moving," Beau suggested. "Get… home."

"Right." Drenched with sweat, she took off her coat, folding it under her arm. Beau did the same with his, and she cast a cursory glance over his form, checking for cuts. He was unscathed.

"I'm sorry," she said as they walked.

Beau sighed. He didn't need to ask what she was sorry about. "I thought he knew," he said. "I thought he knew everything that had happened to me, and didn't care."

"He thought you were dead."

Beau's jaw tensed. "It doesn't matter, really," he said, "because he knew about the coal. He knew everything that was going on here."

"He's still your father."

"Maybe. But I'm not his son."

"It's all right to be conflicted," Asami told him. "It's all right to feel *anything*."

"What would *you* feel?" Beau asked roughly.

Asami stilled. "Ashamed," she said. "If one of my parents knew something like that, had been part of it, I'd be ashamed. I wouldn't want to have anything to do with them. And yet I'd still feel awful turning my back, and I don't think I'd ever stop wanting to reconcile, to find some middle ground."

Beau sighed, quiet as a whisper, and said little else until they were safely back inside the base. He locked the door thoroughly behind him, all three locks. He frequently didn't bother. Who was going to find them all the way down here?

Pilot came forward to greet them. They patted his scrappy ears and pushed into the lab, discarding extra clothes. Asami helped Beau remove his shirt.

"What arc you doing?" he asked.

"Checking for injuries."

"I'm fine."

"Are you?" She took his face in her hands, and clasped them, his face drifting towards hers, mouth bruising against her lips. Soft, at first, and then harder, desperate. Kissing was easier than talking. And sometimes… sometimes there were no words. She savoured the taste of him, the feel of his body as it caged over hers, savoured the warmth and the silence of the underground—

The silence.

She pulled back.

"What?" he asked. "What is it?"

"Beau," she said slowly, "is it too quiet in here?"

"What do you mean?"

"There's something…" She held up her hand, asking for quiet. The low hum of the city overhead ran as usual. A constantly flickering light continued to flicker. Beau's computers whirred. Something else was missing.

Asami's heart plummeted.

The rat.

There was no scuffling, no squeaking. No clatter of its wheel.

It was night time. It shouldn't have been sleeping—

Asami wanted to cry out, but her voice had vanished. Instead she ran, ran towards the cage.

The rat was lying in the middle of its hay, legs up. At least, she thought its legs were up; it was hard to tell. Its entire body was covered in tumours, so riddled that she could tell the bottom of it only by its tail.

She stared at it, willing it to disappear.

I've slid into a nightmare, she told herself, *I'm just exhausted. This is just the stress of everything else twisting my vision.*

She tore away from the rodent to look at Beau, willing him to correct her.

Instead Beau's eyes—his entire beautiful, perfect face— widened into something horrific. He let out a sound somewhere between a cry and a gasp, the very sound she felt inside herself, and she barely had time to hold out her arms before he came crashing down to the floor.

30

THE CONSEQUENCES

"Just one more test, just one more—"

"Asami—"

"It will only take a minute—"

"You've run everything you can think of. Stop. Please."

Asami bit her lip, steadying her breath. "I'm sorry," she said. "I'm just… I need to be sure."

"I know," he said. "But I'm tired. Run more tomorrow. Let's just go to bed. We'll figure everything else out in the morning."

But what if there isn't a morning? Her mind prompted dangerously. *What if this happens to you in the night, and you don't live to see another dawn?*

His blood didn't look any different under her microscope. There were days between the rat's apparent recovery and Beau taking the serum. If this was going to happen to him, they should have more time.

Should. Hardly an absolute.

How could he think of sleeping like this?

"How are you not terrified?" she asked him, unable to hide the tremor in her voice.

"Of course I'm terrified," he replied, curling his fingers around hers, "and of so much more than before, but I rather thought one of us should be the calm one."

"Right," she said, and dabbed furiously at her eyes, "calm..."

"Asami—"

"No," she said, shaking her heading furiously, "no, you're right, I need to be calm and rational and—"

He jerked her roughly into his chest as her thoughts and face fractured. She sobbed erratically, endlessly, her tears choking. Beau remained still the whole time. She thought about apologising—it was *his* life on the line, after all—but the idea made her furious at him, because *he'd* done this to himself, done it to her.

She did not want to be angry, so she let herself be sad.

Somehow, they slept. Somehow, they got up the next day, and Asami began dissecting the rat, trying to work out what went wrong, and how quickly.

She was building a roadmap of what would happen to Beau.

It might not, said a thin sliver of hope at the back of her mind. *Maybe it will work for him. You don't know.*

At least she'd prepared another version of the serum Mortimer had used to stabilise Beau in the first place. If it did go wrong, at least that should stop him from dying.

Should.

Hopes, dreams, should, might. Nothing absolute, nothing

concrete.

She threw down her scalpel, ran to the bathroom, and vomited into the toilet, shaking. There wasn't much to bring up; she'd eaten so little for breakfast.

Beau knocked quietly at the door. "Asami?"

She swilled her mouth out with water, leaning shakily against the basin. "Would you believe me if I told you I just hate dissecting things?"

A pause. "Do you *want* me to believe that?"

She twisted her sleeves into his fists. "I don't want you to feel like you're responsible for what I feel, even when…"

"I'm sorry," Beau whispered, behind the door. "I'm so sorry. If I'd only listened to you—"

"Don't think about that now—"

"But you were right   "

I'm usually right, she thought, horribly, hopelessly. *I'm usually right and right now I hate it.* "It doesn't matter now."

"If I'd—"

"Beau," she said shakily, "please, don't."

"I'm sorry," he repeated instead. "I'm so sorry."

She crept over to the door and opened it slowly. Beau sat on the floor behind it, back to her. "Don't pull away from me," she asked him. "Promise you won't. No matter what happens, even if you think it's worse than before, don't pull away from me, please, I can't bear it, not on top of everything else—"

"I won't," he swore. "I won't, I promise. Not again." He wheeled around, catching her face in his hands. "I'm sorry. I'm so, so, so sorry…"

She leant her forehead against his. "I'm going to brush my

teeth," she said. "And then I'm going back to the lab."

For days, she worked and fretted, examining the rat for clues, testing Beau's bloodwork, testing everything. Searching for changes, preparing drugs for the worst.

Not that drugs would help if his lungs or heart gave out, like what had happened to the rest of the patients.

He survived once. He can survive again.

But she also knew how desperate he'd been the first time. There was more to life than just surviving.

She hated that she hadn't been enough for him, that there was no cure for that darkness in him, the one that told him he needed to be something else, that he wasn't right the way he was before.

She wanted to scream and yell at him, and hold onto him, and kiss him, and hurt him…

Nothing fair. Nothing easy.

"You can be angry with me, if you like," said Beau one evening, reading her silence.

"And what good would that do?"

"Might make you feel better."

"And you, worse."

Beau turned away from her. "There's something else we need to discuss."

"Something more important than your impending doom?"

Beau's face hardened. "Yes," he said.

Asami tore her eyes away from her work, raising an eyebrow quizzically, not believing him.

"We need to let the Rebellion know about the coal."

"I agree."

"I don't think we should wait for them to come to us."

Asami put down her pen. "You want to go into the Outlands?"

"Yes."

"Absolutely not! We don't know what's going to happen. We need to be here, in a nice, safe lab, waiting to monitor for any side-effects, treat whatever we can—"

"It's only a couple of days across the desert to the location Snowdrop gave you. If we left soon—"

"Two days there, two days back, almost a week if we don't leave immediately. No. No, I'm not risking it."

"People are dying, Asami."

"*You're* dying!" she snapped, and then immediately regretted her words. She turned away from him, folding her hands in her lap. "There's nothing amiss in your blood work yet," she said quietly. "But the rat seemed fine until he wasn't, too. I can't... I can't risk it, Beau. Please don't make me."

He sighed, running his fingers down his face. "I don't want to buy my time with other people's lives," he said.

"I understand that," she replied. "Truly, I do. Because if the situations were reversed, I'd be the same. I would hate it. But you wouldn't want me to do it, would you?"

"No," he said softly, "I wouldn't. I would beg you not to, because the thought of being without you..." He shook his head, releasing a long, heavy sigh. "I want you to promise me something you'll hate even more."

"Beau—"

"If I *do* die, if there's nothing you can do, I want you to go to Outlands alone if the Rebellion doesn't come back."

Asami stared at him, certain she'd misheard. "You can't possibly think—"

"Stick to the path marked on the map. I'll get some masks from somewhere, pack some supplies. Take Pilot."

"I'm not going anywhere without you."

"You may have to." He swallowed. "Please, Asami. It might be the only real good I've ever done."

"You never wanted me to go into danger and now—"

"I know," he rushed. "I know, I can't believe I'm asking, but I need to know something good will come of this, and that you won't…"

Asami swallowed, suddenly aware of what he meant. He didn't want her alone in the dark. Alone with nothing but his corpse.

She hung her head, hating his words, hating herself, hating him. "All right," she said, her voice barely a whisper, "I'll do it."

He closed his hands over hers. "Thank you."

She lifted up her chin, placing a soft, quick kiss on his lips, and tugged her hands free to pick up her pen. "But that's a worst-case scenario," she said, as brightly as she could manage. "I'm not giving up yet."

Over the next few days, Beau packed a couple of bags, made a copy of the map, and filled it with notes. She didn't read them. Reading them would make her feel like she was preparing for the worst, preparing to go without him.

She focused instead on what she could change, or what she hoped to.

I'm not giving up. I'm not.

Late one night, as she sat bent over a page of messy, complicated formulas, trying to predict another possible trajectory, Beau stood up sharply and left the room. She waited for him to come back, assuming he'd left to relieve himself.

He didn't.

Worried, she crept towards the bathroom. "Beau?" she whispered at the door.

No reply. Silence within. She turned the handle. Nothing.

"Beau?" she called down the corridor.

He wasn't in the kitchen or the gym either, or any of the storerooms, but a light emanated down the corridor from the train car.

She tiptoed trepidatiously to the door.

Beau stood over the dresser, hands braced against the side, staring at the mirror there.

"Beau?"

He still did not move.

"Beau!"

Slowly, with an agonising, awful finality, he turned to face her.

A rash was spreading down the side of his face.

Asami stilled, hand flying to her face. Words fell out of her, reduced to sounds. He came towards her, hands outstretched, but she shucked him off, scrambling for the door.

"The serum," she says, "I need to get—"

"Stop," he said, "it can wait. I had a few days before, before it got..."

The rat didn't.

Asami swallowed, her throat feeling like cut glass. Tears stung her eyes. "Does it hurt?" she asked hoarsely.

He shook his head. "No. No. Not right now."

Her hand went to his cheek and fell to his shoulder. Already she could feel something growing there, a slight distortion that made her stomach cave.

But more than any horror, more than grief, was the need to be with him, to hold him, to have him.

I can fix this, I can fix this, I can fix this.

In the tales of old, a simple kiss could have reversed this, a declaration of true love. But life was no fairy tale.

And there was no such thing as magic kisses.

But despite knowing that, she pressed her mouth against his, gently, then desperately, as if she could make this melt away with kisses. His hands gathered her into him, holding her tightly, whispering words that meant everything and nothing.

Her fingers slid under his shirt, over smooth skin and thickening lumps and the soft, velvet hair of his stomach. Beau let out a groan, and she peeled back the layer dividing them.

His left side was dotted with malformations, twisted flesh and muscle. She paused, taking in the sight of them.

"I know, I know, they're ugly—"

She slammed her lips back to his, pulling him down to the bed, arching over him, pushing down. "You're beautiful, Beau," she insisted, "you've always been beautiful to me. You always *will* be. Do you understand?"

Beau moaned into her mouth, sounding almost painful, and his hands slid to her thighs. He shucked her against him, deft fingers moving to the buttons of her blouse. "I love you," he breathed. "I love you so much, it hurts more than anything else."

Asami paused, forehead scrunched against his. "I don't want to hurt you."

"You can't," he said, hand cupping her cheek. "You won't."

She fought against her clothes, and his, wrestling through the fabric, yanking everything off until she was naked and astride him. His mouth went to her neck and she raked her fingers down his back, turning soft and careful at the last moment.

She pushed him beneath her, kissing him long, hard, slow, dragging her lips down the curve of his damaged cheek, the hollow of his neck, the slope of his chest and the hard, burning panes of his stomach. Her fingers rode down his hips to the long, hard length of him, and he buckled under her touch.

She wanted to scream. She wanted to scream at him or the world or herself, for loving him, for letting him inside her in a way that transcended physical, for leaving her soul against his to be frayed beyond all measure if he ever left this world without her.

She let herself scream, too, but only once he was inside her, only when her cries merged with something else, raw and real and fracturing.

After, when they were done, she drew his face to her damp breast, and sobbed into his hair.

"I want to hate you," she whispered. "I want to hate you so much for making me love you. But I can't. I can't, I can't, I can't…"

He silenced her with a kiss, but he could not kiss her hard enough to blot away her weeping.

31

THE OLD AGONY

In the middle of the night, Beau bolted upright.

Initially, Asami thought nothing of it. He frequently thrashed himself awake in the night. She raised up slowly, carefully, just to see if he needed her, but instead of finding him staring glassy-eyed at the pillow, as if he were surprised to be there, she found him on the edge of the bed, doubled-over and shaking.

"Beau?" She placed a hand against his back, and found it drenched in sweat.

Beau rocked beneath her touch, his body tensing. "I don't feel well..." he said, and grabbed a bowl from the floor, promptly vomiting into it.

Asami froze in place. Behind the acidic smell of the bile was something else, thick and coppery.

She turned on the lamp.

The vomit was flecked with blood.

Beau heaved again, and in the dim, watery light, Asami saw that the rash had evolved into thick, red welts running down the side of his face.

No, no, NO!

She launched out of the room, sprinting to the lab, snatching up the serum she had on standby and raced back to his side. Beau was still heaving as she rolled up his sleeve and slammed the syringe into his arm. He didn't subside afterwards. He continued to retch until there was nothing left in him, until he was a weak, shivering mess on the floor.

Slowly, carefully, Asami pried the bowl from his grip and tugged him back into bed. She pulled the covers up around him, took the bowl to rinse it out, and tried to steady herself as she gathered her equipment and supplies, and headed back to his side.

Despite his shivering, he was liquid hot. She pressed a cold compress to his head, cleaned up any mess from the contents of his stomach, took a sample of his blood for analysis, and checked the growing welts visible on his skin.

Beau's eyes flickered open as she examined the lumps on his forearm. "Is it bad?" he asked.

"I won't know until I've checked your blood."

"I wasn't talking about my blood." He raised his trembling hand, staring at the angry skin, and brought it up to his cheek. His eyes brimmed with tears as his tips grazed the welted skin.

Asami seized his hand. "Don't," she said. "Don't think about it."

"It was all for nothing, it was stupid and foolish—"

"Maybe not nothing," she said, as she rubbed cream into his blistering skin.

Beau coughed. She raised a glass of water to his lips.

"I'm sorry," he whispered hoarsely, "I'm so sorry..."

She pressed her forehead against his, lacking the strength to tell him not to worry, not to be sorry. Her anger was tempered by his present state, but it was still there.

Instead, she focused on what she could do, administering careful doses of the drugs she had available. One for nausea, one for pain, one for swelling... keeping the rest back for whatever happened next.

Whatever happened next...

Hopefully, the serum worked just how it had the last time. He wouldn't get better, but he wouldn't get any worse, either. Maybe she'd administered it soon enough that the swelling would go down, or at least stay as it was...

She took her sample back to the lab, and started to work. It was better than staying at his side, watching.

But there was little to do but wait here, too.

He didn't have much of a stomach, but cooking occupied her mind for at least a little while. He felt cooler after a few hours, no more vomiting.

"Tell me what's wrong," she told him. "I can't help you if you don't tell me."

"It's... it's all wrong." He admitted. "It's like before, when..." He stopped, his face pale, eyes glassy. "I can hear them, Asami. I can hear all the others. Sarah and Matteo and Jon, beside me, choking, loud and then quiet, so quiet..."

"Hush, hush, it's all right," she said, gripping his hand tightly. "They're gone, Beau. They went a long time ago. But you're here. You're still here. And you're absolutely forbidden from going anywhere else."

He whimpered, nodding, and curled forward into her arms. The welts were spreading along his back.

Asami stiffened. "I need to undress you," she said. "Just... just to check."

Beau nodded, shuffling into a sitting position, Asami leaning forward to undo the buttons and haul the shirt from his back.

Angry red blotches covered half of his skin, the muscle beneath them stiff and tightening. "Does this hurt?" she asked, probing them gently.

Beau shook his head. "Tender, maybe." He paused. "They're getting worse, aren't they?"

"I only administered the serum a few hours ago. It might not mean anything."

"You're still worried."

"Of *course* I'm still worried, fool. I love you. I'll probably still be worrying about you in forty, fifty years' time."

At this, Beau smiled. "That's a long time."

She kissed his cheek. "Not quite long enough."

Thankfully, the welting seemed to stabilise, if not recede over the next few hours, and by the following day, he seemed to be recovering.

The bloodwork told a different story. The worst. Asami stared at it numbly, waiting for it to change, reverse, do *something*.

But science didn't work like that.

No. *No.* She refused to let this be it. She couldn't, she wouldn't—

And this was why she could not believe in the gods of old. Nothing with consciousness, with empathy, would do this. Science was just that. Dependable and uncaring. Neither just nor cruel.

Although this... this was cruel.

Why him? she wondered. *Why him of all people? You couldn't have taken someone awful?*

No god would have brought her down here, just to witness this.

"Tell me," said Beau, reading her silence.

Asami took a deep, shuddering breath. "The serum has slowed the deterioration of your cells," she said. "It hasn't stopped it. Not this time."

"I wasn't exactly the picture of health before."

Asami knew he wanted her to smile, but she couldn't manage it.

"How long?" he said.

"I've not quite—"

"Your brain is a calculator, I know you've already figured it out. Just tell me. Please."

"Six months," she said, "give or take."

She left out her other predictions, how bad it would get, the things she'd need to keep him alive towards the end of it. Things they didn't have here. All the drugs in the world wouldn't be able to help him much in the end.

Beau sighed, turning to face his pillow. For a long while, they sat in silence, not speaking, tears trickling.

"I'm sorry," said Beau, repeating what he'd been saying for days, crying even. "I'm sorry, I'm sorry. If I could have just been happy the way I was—"

"You *should* be sorry," said Asami, unable to hide the venom in her voice. "How dare you risk my life like that—"

"*Your* life?"

"Yes, my life. My life's the one at stake, here, mine is the one that will be obliterated if I can't fix you. I'm the one who will have to live without you, and I hate you for it. I hate you, I hate you, I hate you—"

But just as much as she hated him, she loved him, and she kissed him to stop herself from saying any more. His lips tethered her back to normality, to sense and reason and logic.

His mouth was going stiff again.

"I'm going to fix you, Beau," she said, drawing back from him. "I swear it."

32

OUT OF THE DARKNESS

A few days later, Beau had seemingly recovered, but Asami was no closer to finding out a way to prevent any further deterioration. Previously, he'd been able to go months and weeks without any issues.

It was unlikely to be so kind, this time.

Fresh supplies running short, he went above. Asami tried to concentrate, but her mind kept conjuring worst-case scenarios, wondering if he'd had another episode, if he was lying hurt somewhere, if he'd died.

No one would think to tell her if he had. She'd never know.

Or maybe he'd just been caught by the guards, dragged back to the palace. Maybe he was back in Malcolm's clutches —

Would that really be so bad? His father was certain to protect him, and Malcolm had access to way better resources than she did—

The white, twisted face of the body under the mask came rushing back.

Yes, it would be bad. For Beau, it would be worse than anything else, and no matter how much she wanted to keep him alive, she could never, ever do something like that.

The door to the base opened. Beau's footsteps thudded down the corridor, and he banged into the room with a heavy bag. She gave him a quick, cursory glance, not wanting to fuss over him after the past few days.

He didn't meet her gaze, heading straight for the table and unloading his supplies.

Two dread doctor masks hit the surface.

Asami's stomach recoiled, vanishing into some faint, distant part of her. "Beau—"

"We'll need protective gear if the conditions in the Outlands are to be believed," he said. "I think I can modify these."

She stared at the masks, and the tightness in his shoulders, wondering what to say, wondering if he'd speak again.

"Jon," he said quietly. "He was under one of these masks. Or what was left of him. I didn't recognize the second one. One of the women. Probably Mariah, from the build, but there was nothing in her face..." He stopped. Asami reached out a hand, but he was already moving away. "I'm going to get started on adapting these. You know. Just in case."

She nodded, unwilling to dissuade him further. If it gave him something to do, then so be it. It was hardly any different from what she was trying to do.

They would go to the Outlands together, even if he meant risking his life.

Beau tossed something in her direction. An old radiometer. "Can you see if this still works?"

"I think so."

"Figured we'd need it in the Outlands."

"Smart."

"I notice you're not trying to dissuade me anymore."

Asami sighed, tugging the end of her braid. "I don't want to fight. I don't have the energy."

"Are you still angry with me?"

She rubbed her temples. "I think I love you too much to be angry, especially when you're paying the price. I think I'm a little bit angry at the world, and at myself."

"Yourself?"

She stared down at her notes. "I'm… I'm trying really hard here."

"I know, I know you are—"

"I hate this. I hate not being able to work faster or better or see what it is that I'm missing, and I hate that I'm exhausted and not strong enough to…"

"To…?"

"To fix this. Or to…" Her throat seized up. *Or to survive losing you.*

Beau bridged the gap between them and circled his arms around her. He offered her no words, and none would have helped her.

After her sobs subsided, Beau released her and turned back to working on the masks. She watched him deconstruct them, placing each part on the table in front of him, examining every component with careful fingers. She loved watching him work, and was a little awed by the skill, how he seemed to know instinctively the function of each piece.

Watching someone do maths was not nearly as impressive.

For hours, they worked in silence, punctuated occasionally by Beau coming over to measure the mask against Asami's face. She hated the cold feeling of the metal, knowing where it had come from, knowing what its former role had been. Breathing apparatus. The bodies still needed oxygen and blood, if only to keep them from rotting.

Asami didn't like to think of herself as a violent person, but she hated the mind that had conceived those poor creatures.

Malcolm needs to die.

Sometimes, you didn't need a way of measuring souls to know a person's worth. Sometimes, you just knew someone needed to die.

She still didn't want to be the one to do it, but if Beau died... there wouldn't be enough of her left to care.

A thud sounded from above. Beau looked up.

"Are we expecting someone?" Asami asked. A twinge of hope gritted inside her. Maybe it was the Rebellion, assistance. They could tell them everything, let them take care of it while she worked on another cure. There was no need to search for them, to risk Beau's life—

Beau shook his head, leaping from his seat. He sprung towards the dashboard.

He paled. "Shit."

"What is it?"

"It's the military."

Asami's insides iced. "What?"

"They must have followed me back when I..." He shook his

head, throwing one of the packs in her direction. "Put this on."

"We can't possibly—"

"We're getting out. Now."

"But—"

"Now!" He stuffed the half-rebuilt masks into his bag and clipped it onto his shoulders, gathering up his weapons.

A whirring started at the door.

"How long will it take them to—"

"I don't know," he said. "Five minutes, maybe, with the right equipment."

The right equipment....

Asami glanced down at her desk, scrambling up her papers. She snatched the drive from Beau's desk and stuffed it into her pockets. There was no time to work out what was valuable and what wasn't—

Beau grabbed a tin can from the side of the room, shoving her discarded papers inside it. He fumbled for a lighter, dousing the dashboard, the filing cabinets in fuel.

Three years' work. He was planning to destroy it all.

The thick, cloying scent of oil and smoke blazed through the lab.

"Come on," said Beau, not looking at it burn. "Quickly."

"How are we getting out, if they're at the door?"

"The back way," he said. "Hurry."

He sprinted down towards the train, and Asami paused briefly at the door, thinking of everything inside it, the map dress, Beau's waistcoat, the books he'd bought her. The steel roses on the dresser. Their little life together. Home.

Gone. All gone forever.

Beau let out a low whistle, and Pilot emerged, shooting onto the tracks after him as he pelted to the old entrance of the tunnel.

"It's boarded-up," Asami remarked.

"Not for long."

He traced his fingers along the brickwork, searching for a space where the plaster wore thin, and took out a slab of explosives from his pockets, setting them quickly.

Something exploded in the main corridor. The door? The lab?

Shouts through the smoke.

The soldiers had entered the building.

"Stand back!"

Beau grabbed her, stuffing her behind the train, as the explosives detonated. Black dust shrouded the air like a cloud, thick and pulsing. The cries got closer.

"Three o'clock!"

A hail of bullets rained overhead. Asami shrieked, sliding back to the safety of the train car's shadow. Beau bolted from her side, thrusting a pistol into her hands. "Fire this," he said, "but don't go into their line of fire, just keep them occupied."

"Are you crazy?"

"Do it!"

She wasted no further time asking questions, cocking the gun and firing into the dark. Beau shot behind her, to the space where the carriages connected, unbuckling them. The rusty brakes screeched. He heaved behind her, spluttering and straining, forcing the cars apart.

Slowly, the first one started to move. He gave it a painful shove, tossed a grenade onto the platform, and grabbed her as the car grinded along the tracks, offering them just enough cover to flee through the gap in the tunnel, Pilot quick at their heels.

He lobbed another grenade into the safe, fracturing the remains of the wall, but didn't look back to inspect the damage.

"Run!" he hissed.

Asami didn't question it. She pelted forward into the dark, keeping to the side of the tracks, guided only by a faint green light on Beau's belt, her feet churning in the black gravel.

Behind them, soldiers cried out. Bullets rang overhead. She didn't dare stop, even when her sides were splitting and her throat felt like it was on fire.

"This way, this way!" Beau yelled, grabbing her hand as they reached a fork in the tunnels.

An old handcar swam into view. Beau shoved her onto it, leaping on himself and driving madly at the pump. It grated along the tracks, gathering speed. Pilot ran along behind them, his gears shuddering and thudding with every bound.

"He can't keep up," Asami said.

"He'll have to!"

Something clicked and spun behind the mechanical dog, a small spot of light, shining directly in their eyes.

"Get down!" Beau covered Asami, flattening her against the base. Bullets blazed overhead, striking brick and metal.

Pilot let out a sound like a groan, and they both chanced a look up. He still bounded down the tracks towards them, but part of his shoulder was missing, and black fluid leaked onto the floor.

Beau let out a sound, not quite a cry, but something like it. He braced himself against the edge of the car, now speeding along, as if readying himself to leap out after him.

Bang!

A bullet struck his shoulder, and he smacked down to the base..

Asami screamed.

"Keep pumping," he said, gritting his teeth. "It's just a flesh wound!"

Asami nodded, seizing the handle, as Beau wrapped a scrap of fabric round his arm. He pulled out his pistol, firing over her, whispering, "Come on, come on," as Pilot hobbled after them.

Another bang shot down the tunnel, and the dog slumped to the tracks.

Beau slumped too, a movement, a sound, that echoed against her very bones.

No.

She waited for Pilot to get up, but he didn't, and a second later he was swallowed up by darkness.

For a few moments, there was silence. Doubtless their pursuers had had no choice but to stop to remove the beast from the tracks. He had bought them a few seconds.

Nothing more.

Beau placed a hand around her waist, and without uttering a world, flung them from the car. It sped off down the tunnel as he dragged her down another.

For a minute, only one, they sat in the dark, catching their breath, listening to the enemy as they sped past them.

"You're really all right?" Asami asked eventually.

"I'll live," he grunted, and climbed back to his feet.

"How far are we from... well, wherever it is?"

"Not far," he said. "I've had the way memorised for a while, just in case."

"Right."

They jogged forward in the dark, Asami keeping behind him, watching the blood seep through the rough bandage on his arm. The tunnel narrowed abruptly, reaching a wall of rock.

"The government sealed up this entrance decades ago," Beau explained. "Rebellion dug it out again." He paused, leaning against the wall.

"Beau, are you—"

He shook his head, but she wasn't sure if that meant he was fine or just not to talk about it.

"Beaumont!" called a rough voice.

Beau stilled further. "Shit," he hissed. "He can't—If they follow us out of here—"

Beau knew the tunnels, Asami realised. He knew where to go, where to hide. He was fighting on his own turf. But outside—outside could bring anything. No cover, no shelter. Nothing for miles.

And they'd know the rebel's entrance.

"I know you're here!" the colonel called again. "Please, son, come out."

"Stay quiet," Beau whispered, almost imperceptibly. "If he doesn't see us..."

He gave a low moan and slid to the floor, knees buckling underneath him.

"Beau!"

Her hands went immediately to his arm, thinking the damage worse than he'd let on, hoping to stem the bleeding—

"It's not my arm," he said. "It's, well... everything else."

The crunch of gravel sounded close by, and a harsh light shone in the tunnel. Colonel Bestiel's face appeared, eyes widening.

"Beaumont," he said, dropping to his knees. He glanced at Asami. "What's wrong with him?"

"Your government," she hissed. "Your government did this to him!"

"But, the last time I saw... he was fine, you... you fixed him."

Asami swallowed. "I tried to," she said. "But I—"

"Father," said Beau, with a plaintive quality she had never heard him use before. "Let her go, please. Don't let Malcolm get his hands on her."

"She's... she's an enemy to the state," Bestiel replied shortly. "If I don't bring her in—"

"She's the best thing in my entire world," Beau said, voice soft and hoarse, "and I think she stands a good chance of fixing it, even without me."

Asami shook her head, unable to speak. *No, no. Not without you.*

"Don't talk like that," his father barked. "You're still breathing."

"Not for much longer."

Asami looked up. Over Bestiel's shoulder, standing in the dark of the tunnel, stood Malcolm and a handful of guards.

"Well done for apprehending them, Colonel. Of course, I'd expect nothing less from an officer of your calibre."

Bestiel stood up. "I don't think they've got much fight left in them. Let's take them back to the palace." He gestured to guards to come over and cuff them, but none of them moved. "I gave you an order, soldiers."

"With… with all due respect, sir," said one, "the queen said to kill them on sight."

Bestiel's throat trembled, just a fraction. "Please," he said, "he's my son."

Malcolm's eyes narrowed. "Orders are orders, Colonel."

Asami swore she could almost see the war happening behind those sea-blue eyes of the colonel, the battle between duty and family.

Orders are orders.

He's my son.

Beau did not give him time to pick one. He seized a smoke grenade from his belt and launched it into the space, rolling over Asami as the inevitable hail of bullets began.

Someone screamed.

"Hold fire!" bellowed Bestiel. "You'll only injure yourselves!"

Beau whipped out his weapon and fired in the smoke, and then, somehow, rose to his feet with a terrific roar and vanished into it. Asami screamed, scrambling after him, keeping low as gunpowder crawled through the thickening air. Bestiel was shouting out orders, Malcolm too, but the soldiers were screaming. Things were snapping, ripping. Blood stung the shadows.

"Beau, Beau, where are you?"

Bestiel's yells cut short, and he slumped down beside her in the smoke, bruised, but alive. She rolled him onto his back.

A cane smacked against her hand.

She let out a sharp cry, struggling backwards, hitting a wall. The steel cap of the cane's tip struck the stone behind her. She tried to jerk out of the way, but hit a pile of stone.

"You," sneered Malcolm, "you have been far, far more trouble than I could ever have anticipated."

Asami didn't know what to say to that. It was a shock to her as well.

"But not anymore."

His eyes fell to a discarded pistol, but Asami, for all she wasn't used to firearms, didn't have a wounded leg. She snatched it off the ground, kicking Malcolm's bad leg as she scrambled, and cocked it.

Trembling, she climbed to her feet, knees like jelly, heart racing.

"You won't kill me," said Malcolm, spitting out soot. "You're a doctor."

"I've killed before," she replied, voice shaking.

Malcolm's eyes flickered, just a fraction. He had not been expecting that reply.

Never mind that it was mercy, it was still death, brought on someone far less deserving than Malcolm.

I killed once for kindness. I can do it again for hate.

Asami steadied her arm, aiming for the head.

He deserves to die, she told herself. *You know he does. Think what he'll do if he stays alive.*

Of course, there were others like him. Mira could appoint his successor within the hour. The cycle would go on.

But he deserves it. Far more than that poor woman did.

It turned out there was a difference between killing someone to save them, and killing someone because you hated them.

But not much.

Asami fired.

Malcolm howled, clutching the side of his face. She'd missed her mark, and she was out of bullets.

"Asami," Beau called softly, and she turned to find him next to her.

The smoke dispersed. Bodies were littered around the space, bleeding, mostly breathing. Some not.

Beau slumped, and she reached forward to steady him. He was too heavy for her, and they both spiralled towards the ground.

"We stopped them," he said, as Malcolm's howls subsided, sinking into bloody unconsciousness. Perhaps he'd bleed out after all. Perhaps she'd killed him. Right now, she wasn't sure she cared.

"You... you can get out," Beau said. "You'll be safe..."

Asami shook her head. "You can't think I'd possibly go without you."

"Not sure I'd make the journey."

She clutched his fingers, winding his hands into hers, swallowing her tears. This wasn't it. It wasn't. "I'll find a way to save you, Beau," she whispered. "I will. I promise."

A ghost of a smile flickered across his face, and his free hand reached up to brush her cheek. "You already saved me."

She shook her head, wilder, harder. "Not for long enough. Not nearly long enough. I'm not done with you yet. I'm not done with *us*. You promised to follow me, Beaumont, so get up, because I'm not going anywhere without you."

Beau stared at her, long and hard, and somehow found the strength to nod, to move, to pull himself upwards, to grip onto her and place one foot in front of the other, hobbling towards the tunnel. He instructed her on how to set the charges to collapse it behind them, and wrenched the masks from his pack to place over their faces.

And then, with the tunnel still shuddering around them, they walked forwards into the light.

EPILOGUE:
INTO THE LIGHT

He collapsed again the second they were out in the open, and Asami followed him, eyes widening inside the mask as she stared at the world opening before her, rocky plains unrolling beneath a setting sky.

She had never seen so much space. The Cold Desert stretched out for miles around her, sand and stone, harsh, bitter warmth.

Sunlight. Real sunlight.

And an impossible, deafening silence.

She could hear everything. The soft crunch of the ground beneath her, the lilt of the wind as it breezed through her hair, Beau's ragged, steady breaths.

She had never known anything to be so quiet in all her life.

Gone was the constant rumble of gears, the whirring of fans, the ticking of cogs and clocks. All that was far, far behind them, trapped beneath metal and glass.

They were exposed, cut loose, driftwood spilling away from a wreck.

They were free.

She took several deep breaths to steady herself. The air tasted funny, but it was probably just the clumsily adapted mask. She hoped it was working.

Curious, she drew out the radiometer. It was a simple thing, easy to use, to read.

The meter was green.

She shook it, wondering if it was faulty. There must have been places where the radiation was low, but here, in the open, outside the city?

She tried it again.

Still green.

She handed it to Beau, who checked it over, shrugging defeatedly.

She turned back to the open sands, the green forests far beyond, and wondered.

No. It couldn't be. The kingdoms would know, surely? There's no way that they wouldn't.

And yet...

Asami sighed. What, at this point, did she really have to lose? She pulled off her mask and breathed in deep, beautiful breaths.

There wasn't any radiation at all.

Beau's eyes widened, but she unbuckled his mask, letting him breath. "It's safe," she said. "I don't know if all of it is, but this part is."

She was almost certain that the radiation, like the origins of the coal, was a complete and utter lie. She just didn't want to think about what *that* meant, not right now.

Later, if there was one.

Beau laughed, hard, painful. "I bet it's all fine. I bet we wore those accursed marks every damn day we were out here for not a damn reason."

"But... why would they lie about that?"

"You're honestly surprised at this point?"

"I suppose not." She shook her head. "Nice of the rebels to tell us."

"They did hint at it a couple of times..." His eyes shuddered closed.

Asami turned her face up towards the blue, unbroken sky. Even from the palace, the thickness of the Dome had filtered it somehow. It was a colour that defied description, pure, vivid, endless.

"Beau," she said, "look up. Sunshine."

He kept his eyes closed, brow furrowed. "Do you mind... can we just rest a bit?"

"Of course."

He lay his head in her lap, and she knew that if someone could see them from afar, resting beneath the sun, it would cast a very different image from what was actually transpiring, if you couldn't see the fractured lines in Beau's face, the worry in her gaze, his temples twitching with pain.

She bent down and kissed him, hard as she dared. His hand circled up to hold her neck, pinning her closer, eyes still tightly shut. She held on to the image in her head a little longer.

They were free. They were safe. They were together.

"I'm going to save you, Beau," she said. "I swear it. So no dying until I say so."

He smiled weakly. "I like it when you're bossy. I always want to do whatever you say."

"Then do it."

"Yes ma'am." He paused. "Asami?"

"Yes?"

"Regardless of how long I have… a few weeks or a few decades or even a few centuries… I want to spend it with you."

She twined her fingers into his. "Forever then," she said. "Mine forever."

They held hands as the sun began to set, and let the strange path laid out ahead of them vanish into the night.

Thank you for reading *A Rose of Steel.* I do hope you enjoyed and will be looking out for the sequel, *A Slipper in the Smoke*, coming next spring!

Reviews are vital to indie authors and a book's success, so please consider leaving one on Amazon/Goodreads.

Many thanks,

Katherine Macdonald

Coming Spring 2022

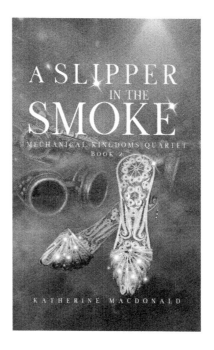

Other Books by this author:

The Phoenix Project Trilogy
Book I: Flight
Book II: Resurrection
Book III: Rebirth

In the "Fey Collection" series:
The Rose and the Thorn: A Beauty and the Beast Retelling
Kingdom of Thorns: A Sleeping Beauty Retelling
A Tale of Ice and Ash: A Snow White Retelling
A Song of Sea and Shore: A Little Mermaid Retelling
Heart of Thorns: A Beauty and the Beast Retelling
Of Snow and Scarlet: A Little Red Riding Hood Retelling

Standalones:
The Barnyard Princess: A Frog Prince Retelling

In the "Faeries of the Underworld" Duology:
Thief of Spring: A Hades and Persephone Retelling (Part One)
Queen of Night: A Hades and Persephone Retelling (Part Two)
Heart of Hades: A collection of bonus scenes (subscribers only)

The Mechanical Kingdoms Quartet:
A Rose of Steel

Coming Soon:

A Slipper in the Smoke

About The Author

Katherine Macdonald

Born and raised in Redditch, Worcestershire, to a couple of kick-ass parents, Katherine "Kate" Macdonald often bemoaned the fact that she would never be a successful author as "the key to good writing is an unhappy childhood".

Since her youth, Macdonald has always been a storyteller, inventing fantastically long and complicated tales to entertain her younger sister with on long drives. Some of these were written down, and others have been lost to the ethers of time somewhere along the A303.

With a degree in creative writing and six years of teaching English under her belt, Macdonald thinks there's a slight possibility she might actually be able to write. She may be very wrong.

She currently lives in Devon with her manic toddler in a cabin in the woods.

"Rose of Steel" is her 13th novel.

You can follow her at @KateMacAuthor, or subscribe to her website at www.katherinemacdonaldauthor.com to be notified of new releases and free review copies!

Printed in Great Britain
by Amazon